WHO *DOESN'T* LOVE AGATHA RAISIN?

"Few things in life are more satisfying than to discover a brand new Agatha Raisin mystery." —*Tampa Tribune Times*

"Beaton has a winner in the irrepressible, romance-hungry Agatha." —*Chicago Sun-Times*

"M. C. Beaton has created a new national treasure . . . Agatha Raisin is the strongest link." —Anne Robinson

"The Miss Marple–like Raisin is a refreshingly sensible, wonderfully eccentric, thoroughly likable heroine . . . A must for cozy fans." —*Booklist*

"Anyone interested in . . . intelligent, amusing reading will want to make the acquaintance of Mrs. Agatha Raisin." —*Atlanta Journal Constitution*

"The Raisin series brings the cozy tradition back to life. God bless the Queen!" —*Tulsa World*

"[Beaton's] imperfect heroine is an absolute gem!" —*Publishers Weekly*

AGATHA RAISIN AND THE FAIRIES OF FRYFAM

"Witty . . . [a] highly amusing cozy." —*Publishers Weekly*

"Agatha is as fractious and funny as ever. Don't miss this one." —*Tulsa World*

"Outwardly bossy and vain, inwardly insecure and vulnerable, Agatha grows more endearing with each installment." —*Cleveland Plain Dealer*

"More great fun from an endearing heroine." —*Library Journal*

MORE . . .

Mystery Titles by M. C. Beaton

AGATHA RAISIN

HAMISH MACBETH

WRITING AS
MARION CHESNEY

AGATHA RAISIN
AND THE
LOVE FROM
HELL

✝

M. C. BEATON

St. Martin's Paperbacks

AGATHA RAISIN AND THE LOVE FROM HELL

Copyright © 1999 by M. C. Beaton.
Excerpt from *Agatha Raisin and the Day the Floods Came* copyright © 2002 by M. C. Beaton.

Library of Congress Catalog Card Number: 2001041965

ISBN: 978-1-250-03954-5

Printed in the United States of America

St. Martin's Press hardcover edition/December 2001
St. Martin's Paperbacks edition/January 2003

St. Martin's Paperbacks are published by St. Martin's Press, 175 Fifth Avenue, New York, NY 10010.

P1

For Joan and John Dewhurst
~ With affection ~

ONE

†

IT was supposed to be the end of a dream—the perfect marriage. Here was Agatha Raisin married to the man she had longed for, had fantasized about. Her neighbour, James Lacey. And yet she was miserable.

It had all started with one incident two weeks after they had returned from their honeymoon. The honeymoon in Vienna and then Prague had been taken up with sightseeing and sex, and so no real day-to-day life together had really bothered them. Agatha had kept her own cottage next door to James's in the village of Carsely in the English Cotswolds. The idea was to make it a thoroughly modern marriage and give each other some space.

Sitting now in her own cottage cradling a cup of black coffee, Agatha remembered the day it had all begun to go wrong.

Anxious to be the perfect wife, she had bundled up all their dirty washing, ignoring the fact that James kept his dirty laundry in a separate basket and preferred to do it himself. It was a brisk spring day with great fleecy clouds being tugged across the sky like so many stately galleons by a breezy wind. Agatha sang as she piled all the dirty clothes into her large washing machine. Somewhere at the back of her mind was a little warning bell telling her that real housewives separated the colours from the whites. She put in washing powder and fabric softener, and then went out to sit in the garden and watch her two cats playing on the lawn. When she heard the washing machine roar to a finish, she rose and opened the door of the machine and tugged all the clothes out into a large laundry basket, preparatory to hanging them out in the garden. She found herself staring down at a basket of pink clothes. Not light pink but shocking pink. Dismayed, she searched through the clothes for the culprit, and at last found it, a pink sweater she had bought at a street market in Prague. All James's clothes—his shirts, his underwear—were all now bright pink.

But in the rosy glow of new marriage had she not expected to be forgiven? Had she not expected him to laugh with her?

He had been furious. He had been incandescent with rage. How dare she mess about with his clothes? She was stupid and incompetent. The pre-marriage Agatha Raisin would have told him exactly what to do with himself, but the new, demoralized Agatha humbly begged forgiveness. She forgave *him,* because she knew he had been a bachelor for a long time and used to his own ways.

The next incident had happened after she had picked up two microwaveable dinners in Marks & Spencer, two trays of lasagne. He had picked at his plateful of food and had commented acidly that as he was perfectly well able to make *proper* lasagne, perhaps in future she had better leave the cooking to him.

Then there was the matter of her clothes. Agatha felt frump-ish when not wearing high heels. James had said as they lived in the country, she might consider wearing flats and stop teetering around like a tart. Her skirts were too tight, some of her necklines were too low. And as for her make-up? Did she need to plaster it on?

Yes, there was love-making during the night, but only during the night. No impulsive hugs or kisses during the day. Bewildered, Agatha began to wander about in a fog of masculine disapproval.

And yet she did not confide in anyone about the misery of her marriage, not even to her friend, Mrs. Bloxby, the vicar's wife. Had not Mrs. Bloxby cautioned her against the marriage? Agatha could not bear to admit defeat.

She sighed and looked out of her kitchen window. Here she was in her own cottage, *hiding* like a criminal in her own cottage. The phone rang, startling her. She tentatively picked it up, wondering whether it might be James about to deliver another lecture. But it was Roy Silver. Roy had once worked for Agatha when she had owned her own public relations company in London and was now working for a big public relations firm in the City.

"How's the happily married Mrs. Lacey?" asked Roy.

"I'm still Agatha Raisin," snapped Agatha. Using her own name seemed to be the last shred of independence she had managed to hold on to. She had not quite realized that using the name of her late husband, whom she had heartily despised, was hardly a blow for freedom.

"How modern," remarked Roy.

"What's up?"

"Nothing. Haven't heard from you since the wedding. How was Vienna?"

"Not very exciting. Not much pizzazz. Prague was all right. Are you sure this is just a friendly call? Nothing up your sleeve?"

"There is one thing that might interest you."

"I thought there might be. What?"

"There's a new shoe company opening in Mircester. We're handling the account. Not a big account, but they want a public

3

relations officer to launch their new line coming out of their new factory. It's called the Cotswold Way."

"And what's that?"

"Those sort of clumpy boots the young like, not to mention those serious ramblers who plague the countryside. Short-term contract, right on your doorstep."

Agatha was about to say she was a happily married woman and didn't have time for anything else. She always told everyone in the village how happy she was. But she suddenly felt desperately in need of an identity. She was good at spin, at public relations. Failure as a housewife she might be, but she felt secure in her talents as a business woman.

"Sounds interesting," she said cautiously. "What's the company called?"

"Delly Shoes."

"Sounds as if they ought to be selling liverwurst and submarine sandwiches."

"So can I fix up an interview for you?"

"Why not? The sooner the better."

"Usually I have to spend ages into talking you back into work," said Roy. "Sure the marriage is okay?"

"Of course it is. But James is usually writing during the day and doesn't want me underfoot."

"Mmm. I called his number and he told me you were on the old number."

"I kept on my cottage. These little cottages can be claustrophobic. This way we have two of everything. Two kitchens, two bathrooms and so on."

"Okay. I'll fix an appointment and call you back."

When she had rung off, Agatha lit a cigarette, a habit James detested, and stared off into space. How would he react to her rejoining the work force? Despite a feeling of trepidation, she felt her emotional muscles hardening up. He could like it or lump it. Agatha Raisin rides again!

4

• • •

And yet she had not really thought he would object. No man, not even James, could be that old-fashioned. When Roy told her he had managed to get her an appointment for the following afternoon at three o'clock, she called to her cats and, with Hodge and Boswell following behind, made her way to James's cottage next door. Never *our* cottage, she thought sadly as she opened the door and shooed the cats inside.

James was sitting in front of his computer, scowling at it. He had managed to have one military history published and had felt sure the next one would be easy, but he seemed to spend days frowning at a screen on which nothing was written but "Chapter One." He had his hand on his forehead, as if he had a headache.

"I've got a job," said Agatha.

He actually smiled at her. His blue eyes crinkled up in his tanned face in that way that still made her heart turn over. "What is it?" he asked, switching off the computer. "I'll make us some coffee and you can tell me about it." He headed for the kitchen.

All Agatha's misery about their marriage disappeared. The old hope that all they were doing was experiencing some initial marital blips lit up her soul. He came in carrying two mugs of coffee. "This is decaf," he said. "You drink too much of the real stuff and it's not good for you. Your clothes smell of smoke. I thought you'd given up."

"I just had the one," said Agatha defensively, although she had smoked five. When would people grasp the simple fact that if you wanted people to stop smoking, then don't nag them and make them feel guilty. People are told when dealing with alcoholics not to mention their drinking or pour the stuff down the sink because it only stops them looking at their problem. But smokers were hounded and berated, causing all the rebellion of the hardened addict.

"Anyway," said James, handing her a cup of coffee and

5

sitting down opposite her, "what's the job? Who are you fund-raising for now?"

"It's not a village thing," said Agatha. "I'm taking on a contract to promote some new shoes, or boots, rather, for a firm in Mircester."

"You mean, a real job?"

"Why, yes, of course, a real job."

"We don't need the money," said James flatly.

"Money's always useful," said Agatha cheerfully. Then her smile faded as she looked at James's angry face.

"Oh, what's up now?" she asked wearily.

"You have no need to work. You should leave employment to those who need a job."

"Look, I need this job. I need an identity."

"Spare me the therapy-speak. In proper English, please."

Agatha cracked. "In proper English," she howled, "I need something to bolster my ego, which you have been doing your best to destroy. Nit-picking all day long. Yak, yak, yak. 'Don't do this, don't do that.' Well, stuff you, matey. I'm going back to work."

He rose abruptly and headed for the door. "Where are you going?" demanded Agatha. But the slamming of the door was her only answer.

The following day, Agatha put on a charcoal-grey trouser-suit, pleased that the waistline was now quite loose. There was something to be said for marital misery. James had stayed away the whole of the previous day and had not arrived back home until Agatha had fallen into an uneasy sleep. Breakfast had been a doom-laden, silent affair. She could feel herself weakening. She had prepared breakfast but everything had gone wrong. She had burnt the toast and the scrambled eggs were lumpy and hard. And she could feel the atmosphere weakening her. She longed to say,

"Forget it. You're quite right. I won't take the job." But somewhere she found a little bit of courage to help her ignore his mood.

It was another fine late spring day as she motored along the Fosse to Mircester. Following Roy's directions, she cut off before the town to an industrial estate on the outskirts. It was a new estate, the ground in front of the factories still having a raw, naked look.

She thought it a good sign that she was not kept waiting. In Agatha's experience, only unsuccessful business people massaged their egos by keeping people waiting. She was ushered into a boardroom by an efficient middle-aged secretary—another good sign, in Agatha's opinion. She was introduced to the managing director, the advertising manager, the sales director and various other executives.

In the middle of the boardroom table was a large leather boot. The managing director, Mr. Piercy, began right away. "Now, Mrs. Raisin, that boot on the table is our Cotswold Way model. We want to promote it. Mr. Hardy, our advertising manager, suggests we should get one of the rambling groups and kit them out."

"Won't do," said Agatha immediately. "Round here, people think of ramblers as hairy militant types. How much is a pair of boots?"

"Ninety-nine pounds and ninety-nine pee."

"That's quite expensive for the youth market and it's the young who go for boots like that."

"We've done our costing and we can't bring down our price."

"What about television advertising?"

"We're a small company," said Mr. Piercy. "We want a simple launch and then the boot will sell on its merits."

"In other words," said Agatha brutally, "you can't afford to pay for much hype."

"We can afford a certain amount but not nationwide coverage."

Agatha thought hard. Then she said, "There's a new group in Gloucester called Stepping Out. Heard of them?"

Heads were shaken all round.

"I saw a documentary about them on *Midlands Today*," said Agatha. "They're an up-and-coming pop group—three boys, three girls—all clean-cut, good image. They recently had a record that was number sixty-two in the charts, but they're being tipped for stardom. If we could get them fast, kit them out in the boots, get them to write a song about rambling—they write their own songs—and give a concert, you might catch them just before they become famous. Then your boots will be associated with success."

The advertising manager spoke. "How do you know about this group, Mrs. Raisin?"

"It's a hobby," said Agatha. "I automatically look out for who I think is going to be famous. I'm always right."

They thrashed her idea around, Agatha bulldozing them when they seem tempted to reject it. In the back of her mind, she wished she were working for a large company and not this hick outfit, as she privately damned it. Something to really impress James. But James was not going to be impressed by anything she did, she thought sadly.

They finally decided to accept Agatha's scheme. "Just one thing, Mrs. Raisin," said Mr. Piercy. "Your name was given to us as Mrs. Lacey."

"That's me."

"Don't you use it?"

"No, I've used the name Raisin in business for years. Easier to keep it."

"Very well, Mrs. Raisin. Would you like an office here?"

"No, I'll work from home. I'll try to set up something with the pop group and arrange to meet you tomorrow."

Agatha drove back to Carsely feeling exhilarated. But as her car wound down to the village under a green archway of trees, her mood darkened. She let herself into her own cottage where she still kept her business papers and computer. She had logged the name of the pop group and their manager into her computer, a sort of public relations reflex. She then went to a stack of telephone directories. She selected the Gloucester directory and began to look up the manager's name, Harry Best. There were several H. Bests listed. She settled down to phone them all. One of the H. Bests turned out to be the father of the manager she was looking for. He gave her Harry Best's number and she dialled that. She crisply outlined her plan for publicizing the Cotswold Way boot.

"I dunno," said Harry Best in that estuary-English accent that Agatha found so depressing. "We're hot stuff. Cost you a lot."

Agatha took a deep breath. "This needs to be discussed face to face," she said firmly. "I'm coming over to Gloucester. Give me your address."

He gave her a Churchdown address. Churchdown is actually outside Gloucester. As Agatha drove off again, past James's cottage, past the white blur of his face at the window, she reflected she would not be back in time for dinner. A good wife would phone and say she was going to be late.

"But I am no longer a good wife," said Agatha out loud, gripping the steering wheel tightly.

The traffic was heavy and there were not only road-works on the A-40 to contend with but various lethargic men driving tractors at ten miles per hour. By the time she found Harry's address, she was feeling weak and disheartened. She longed to chuck it all up and return to James, try to conciliate him, try to make the marriage from hell work somehow. But a weedy, balding man with what was left of his hair worn in a ponytail was standing outside a shabby villa waiting for her.

Agatha studied him as she approached. He had those little half-moon glasses perched on a beaky nose which drooped over a small pursed mouth. She judged him to be nearly forty and he was wearing that clinging-on-to-youth outfit of cowboy boots, jeans, and a black leather jacket.

Mr. Harry Best was as little impressed with Agatha as she was with him. He saw a stocky woman with shiny brown hair worn in a French pleat. Her round face had a good mouth and a neat nose, but her eyes were wary, brown and bearlike.

"I'm Agatha Raisin." Agatha gave one of his limp, clammy hands a firm shake. "May we go inside to discuss business?"

"Sure. Follow me."

The room into which he led her showed signs of hasty and not thorough house-cleaning. A wastepaper basket was bulging with empty Coke cans. Under a cushion on an armchair Agatha could see a pile of newspapers and magazines which had been thrust underneath to hide them.

Agatha got down to business. She outlined the promotion, the idea of writing a song to go with the new boots and then they haggled over price. He tried to drive the price up by saying if the group advertised something, people would think they were unsuccessful. Agatha pointed out that many successful pop stars had appeared on advertisements. "What about Michael Jackson?" she asked crisply.

Harry Best began to visibly weaken under her onslaught. Agatha reminded him of his grandmother, a forceful woman who had terrified his early childhood. At last, the deal was struck. The one good thing he felt he had got out of Agatha was that she agreed to hire a rehearsal hall for the group, as they were shortly to be evicted from the friend's garage they were using.

When Agatha finally left, it was dark and late and she was hungry. She stopped at a pub on the road home and had a simple meal and a glass of water. Now to deal with James.

Residents of Carsely, walking their dogs along Lilac Lane where Agatha and James had their cottages, were to describe later how they had heard Agatha shouting, and then the sound of breaking china. James had decided to put his foot down. Agatha was told in no uncertain terms that she had to give up this stupid job and start trying to behave like a married woman.

If he had been angry at that point, Agatha might, just might have capitulated. But it was the calm scorn in his voice that got to her. He looked pained, as if she were giving him another headache. She had never thought of herself before as a china-smashing woman, but the row took place in the kitchen and so Agatha swept a whole shelf of dishes to the floor and danced with rage on the shards.

"You disgust me," said James quietly. And then he had walked out, leaving Agatha red-faced, panting, and totally demoralized.

Wearily, she packed up her belongings and carried them next door to her own cottage. She went back and cleaned up the mess of broken china, boxed it up, and left it out for the garbage collection. She collected the same number of plates she had broken from the supply in her own cottage and placed them on James's kitchen shelf. Then she called to her cats who followed her next door, their raised fur only just beginning to settle after the fright they had received from their mistress's noisy scene. Once in her own house, Agatha forced herself to relax. She would apologize to James for the broken china.

Next day she was kept busy—reporting to the shoe company, hiring a rehearsal hall and meeting the pop group. Agatha had dealt with pop groups before and found Stepping Out refreshingly pleasant. The group consisted of three young men and three girls. All were in their late teens. They had a clean-cut, happy look. Agatha felt she was on a winner. She plunged into work, but always at the back of her mind was a black cloud of misery. If only she could confide in someone—but no one, *no one*, must know that Agatha Raisin's marriage was a failure.

Several times she thought about phoning James, to clear the air, to apologize. But each time she held back. How on earth could he be so old-fashioned? And yet, and yet, she thought weakly, she had made a dreadful scene, had broken his china, behaved like a fish-wife. Why did people still blame fish-wives for violence and bad language? she wondered. What fish-wives, anyway? Probably from the old days of Billingsgate fish market.

Harry Best studied her. She was quite a girl, he thought. Look at the way she had set to and helped load the equipment into the rehearsal room. Look at the way she had established a rapport with the young people. She wasn't nearly as hard-boiled as he had first imagined. In fact, he thought, there were times when she looked almost on the edge of tears. Funny woman.

Agatha was sorry when the long day was over. Two of the young men were already working on a sort of rambling pop song. "Don't be scared of being old-fashioned," Agatha had urged. "Make it sound like something cheery—something people will want to whistle as they walk along a country road."

When she drove back to Carsely, she braced herself for a confrontation with James. But when she let herself into his cottage—she never thought of it as *their* home—it was to find it dark and silent. With a beating heart, she ran up to the bedroom and checked the closet. All James's clothes were still there.

She sat down on the bed and wondered what to do. Where would James be? Probably in the pub.

Perhaps it might be an idea to follow him there. He could hardly make a scene in front of the villagers, thought Agatha, forgetting that she was the one who usually made the scenes.

She went to her own cottage and changed into a blond silk trouser-suit and wrapped a deep-bronze lamb's-wool stole about her shoulders, then walked slowly along to the pub. She would be breezy, cheerful, as if nothing had happened.

Somehow, the fact of taking some action brightened her immensely as she strode along the lane under the heavy blossom of the lilac trees which gave it its name. Agatha's great weakness was that not for one minute would she admit to herself that she was afraid of James. She would admit to being afraid of losing him, but to being actually scared of him was something that Agatha, who had laminated her soul over the years with layers of hardness, could not even begin to contemplate. Nor would she realize that love had made the unacceptable almost acceptable—the put-downs, the scorn, the silences, the lack of easy, friendly affection.

She walked into the Red Lion with a smile on her face.

Her smile faded.

James was sitting at a corner table by the log fire, laughing and smiling at a slim, blonde-haired woman whom Agatha recognized as Melissa Sheppard. As she watched, Melissa leaned forward and squeezed James's hand.

As Miss Simms, secretary of the Carsely Ladies' Society, was to describe it later, Agatha Raisin went "ape-shit." Sour jealousy rose like bile in her throat. In seconds, the misery she had endured flashed across her mind. She strode across and confronted the startled Melissa. "Leave my husband alone, you trollop."

Melissa rose and grabbed her handbag and sidled around Agatha and made for the door. Agatha leaned across the table. "You bastard," she shouted. "I'll kill you and that philandering bitch!"

James rose, his face dark with anger. He seized her wrists. "Stop making a scene," he hissed.

Agatha broke free of his grip, picked up his half tankard of beer and poured it over his head and then turned and ran out. She ran all the way to her cottage, stumbling over the cobbles. Once safely inside her own cottage, she sat down in her kitchen and cried and cried.

Then she went upstairs and carefully washed her face in cold water and put on fresh make-up. James would call to continue the row and she wanted to be armoured against him.

The doorbell rang. Agatha gave a pat to her hair, squared her shoulders and marched down the stairs.

"Now, see here . . ." she began as she opened the door. But it was not James who stood there but her old friend, Sir Charles Fraith.

"I called next door but James told me you were here," said Charles. "Can I come in?"

"Why not?" said Agatha bleakly, and walked back into the cottage, leaving him to follow her.

"What's up?" asked Charles, following her into the kitchen. "Don't tell me the marriage has broken up already."

"Don't be silly," said Agatha. "We're divinely happy. Would you like a drink?"

"Whisky, if you've got it."

Agatha was torn between telling him to leave in case James came and yet wanting him to stay in case James did not. She led the way into the sitting-room, lit the fire which she had set earlier, poured him a generous measure of malt whisky and then one for herself.

Charles sat down on the sofa and surveyed Agatha, who had slumped into an armchair opposite him.

"Been crying?"

"No. I mean, yes. I cut myself."

"Where?"

"What d'you mean, where?"

"Aggie, cut the crap. This act of being a happily married woman must be killing you."

She looked at him in silence. He sat there in her sitting-room where he had sat so many times before, neat, groomed, well-tailored, as self-contained as a cat.

Agatha gave a weary shrug. "Okay, you may as well have it. The marriage is a disaster."

"I won't say I told you so."

"Don't dare."

"I suppose the problem is that James is just being bachelor James and wants his usual lifestyle and you are getting in the way with your rotten cooking and your nasty cigarettes. Criticized your clothes yet?"

"Never stops. How did you know?"

"It is a well-known fact that stuffy men, once they are married to the object of their desire, start to criticize the very style of dressing that attracted them in the first place. I bet he told you not to wear high heels and that your make-up was too heavy."

"Am I such a fool? I should have known this. But it seemed to me we had so much in common."

Charles took a sip of his drink and eyed her sympathetically.

"People never realize that love is indeed blind. They feel like a soul mate of the loved one. No awful loneliness of spirit. Two against the world. So they marry, and what happens? After a certain time, they look across the breakfast table and find they are looking at a stranger."

"But there are happy marriages. You know there are."

"Some are lucky; most go in for compromise."

"You mean, I should dress the way James wants and live the way James wants me to?"

"If you want to stay married. Or go to one of those marriage counsellors."

"I don't see how a bachelor like you can know anything about marriage."

"Intelligent observation."

Agatha clutched her hair. "I don't know what to do. I made such a scene in the pub. James was flirting with this Melissa woman and I happen to know he once had a fling with her."

"James is not a bad sort, you know. You probably rub him up the wrong way. You're a bit of a bully."

"You haven't heard the whole story. He doesn't want me to work!"

"And are you? Working, I mean."

"I've got a short-term contract with a shoe company in Mircester. James hit the roof. He said I should leave work for those that need it."

"Maybe the pair of you should go back to separate lives and date occasionally."

"I'll make it work," said Agatha suddenly. "I love James. He must be made to see reason."

"Does he talk to anyone about his troubles?"

Agatha laughed. "James! Not on your life."

James at that moment was sitting in the vicarage parlour facing the vicar's wife, Mrs. Bloxby.

"It's not too late to call?" James was asking.

"No, not at all," said Mrs. Bloxby, amused that James had not seemed to notice that she was in her night-gown and dressing-gown.

"I really don't know what to do about Agatha," James said. "I am a very worried man."

"What is the matter? Would you like some tea or something stronger?"

"No, I feel if I don't talk to someone, I'll burst. You're a friend of Agatha."

"I hope a very good one."

"Has she said anything to you about our marriage?"

"If she had complained to me, I would not tell you. But as a matter of fact, she has not. What was the scene in the pub about? It's all round the village."

"I went along to the pub and Melissa was there, so we had a drink together. Agatha came in and threw a jealous scene."

"That is understandable. It is well know in the village that you had an ... er ... episode with Melissa before your marriage."

"Well, it's all the other things. She's a lousy housekeeper."

"She has Doris Simpson to clean for her, that is, her own cottage. Why not let Doris do yours?"

"But Agatha should do it."

"You are very old-fashioned. You cannot expect a woman who has been successful in business and who has always paid someone to do her cleaning to do yours."

James went on as if she had not spoken. "Then, she knows I hate the smell of cigarette smoke. She smells of cigarettes."

"Mrs. Raisin was smoking when you first met her and when you were married."

"But she promised to give up. She said she would. And she said she would never smoke in my cottage. But she puffs away when she thinks I'm not looking."

"You said, 'my cottage.' It's a very odd marriage. Why did you encourage Mrs. Raisin to keep her own cottage?"

"Because mine is too small."

"The pair of you have surely enough money to sell your homes and move into a bigger house."

"Perhaps. Now she's taken a job. A public relations job for some shoe company in Mircester."

"What is up with that?"

"Agatha doesn't need to work."

"I think Mrs. Raisin does need to work from time to time. Perhaps you made her feel like a failed wife. Do you complain a lot?"

"Only when she does something wrong, and she always glares at me and says something rude."

"And does she often do something wrong?"

"All the time—bad meals, sloppy housekeeping, tarty clothes . . ."

Mrs. Bloxby held up one hand. "Wait a minute. Mrs. Raisin's clothes tarty? Really, I cannot allow that. She is always smartly dressed. And it does seem as if you complain a lot and you are not prepared to compromise on anything. I know you have been a confirmed bachelor, but you are married now, and must make certain allowances. Why are you so angry and touchy?"

There was a long silence and then James gave a sigh. "There's something else. I have been having these recurring headaches, so I got a scan. It says I have a brain tumour. I have to go in soon for treatment."

"Oh, you poor man. It is operable?"

"They are going to try chemotherapy first."

"Mrs. Raisin must be distressed."

"She does not know and you are not to tell her."

"But you must tell her. That is what marriage is all about, sharing the bad times as well as the good."

"I feel if I tell her, then somehow there will be no hope for me. It will make the brain tumour very, very real. I must get through this on my own."

"But I can see the whole thing is putting you under a great deal of stress. In fact, you are ruining your marriage by not telling Mrs. Raisin."

"You must not tell her! You must promise me you will not tell her!"

"Very well. But I beg you to reconsider. Mrs. Raisin does not deserve the treatment you have been meting out to her. Tell her."

He shook his head. "It is my cross and I must bear it alone. Agatha is very independent. Why, she even still uses her old married name, as if mine isn't good enough for her. *You* even call her Mrs. Raisin."

"That's because she asked me to. You see, she might have listened to you if you had only complained about that one thing, but you do seem to have criticized her a great deal."

"It's her fault," said James stubbornly. "I'd better go."

"Please stay a moment longer. You must be terribly frightened and worried."

James, who had half risen from his chair, sank back again and buried his head in his hands.

"Mrs. Raisin would be a great help," said Mrs. Bloxby gently.

"I should never have married her," muttered James.

"I assume you were in love with her."

"Oh, yes, but she's so messy and infuriating."

"I think you are very hard on her because you are frightened and ill."

James got to his feet. "I'll think about it."

As he walked home, he thought guiltily that he had seemed to go on and on too much about Agatha's faults. All he had to do was tell her what was up with him. But when he turned into Lilac Lane, he recognized the car outside Agatha's cottage. Sir Charles Fraith. And still there! So Agatha had gone back to her old ways. Two could play at that game!

TWO

†

THE fact that Agatha and her new husband were living in separate cottages, not speaking to each other, spread round the village like wildfire. Mrs. Bloxby kept quiet about James's revelation about his brain tumour. She did not even tell her husband, the vicar, Alf Bloxby, who, on hearing the news of the breakdown of Agatha's marriage, merely remarked sourly, "Don't know how anyone could live with that woman."

James was often seen with Melissa Sheppard, Agatha with Charles.

This miserable state of affairs might have gone on forever had not James had a change of heart. He was afraid of dying. He did not want to depart the world and leave bitterness and misery behind. He wanted to be missed. He wanted to be mourned.

He bought a large bunch of red roses and presented himself

on Agatha's doorstep a week after what was known in the village as The Great Scene in the Pub.

Agatha answered the door and stood for a moment looking at him and then at the bouquet he held in his hand. "Come in," she said, and walked off to the kitchen without waiting to see whether he was following her or not.

"Sit down," she said, leaning on the kitchen counter. "Why have you come?"

The correct answer, the sensible answer would have been, "Agatha, I have a brain tumour, and I think I am going to die," but instead James remarked, "You look terrible."

Agatha had deep pouches under her eyes and her normally glossy hair was dull. She was wearing a shapeless print house-dress and flat sandals.

"I have been working hard. Coffee?"

"Yes, please."

"It's the real stuff," said Agatha, plugging in the electric percolator. "No unleaded in this house."

"Fine," said James, stretching out his long legs.

Agatha sat down opposite him. As if by silent consent, both of them waited until the coffee was ready. Agatha filled two mugs and then looked at James.

"You still seeing that tramp, Melissa?"

"I felt I needed company while you were running around with Charles Fraith."

"Charles is just a friend."

"That makes a change," said James sourly. "You had an affair with him in Cyprus."

"That was before we were married. And you had a fling with Melissa."

"We are just friends," said James stiffly. "You shouldn't be working. You don't *need* to work. You look awful."

"Well, Mr. Health and Beauty, you've been nagging me for

22

ages about wearing make-up and heels. You ought to be happy. Why did you come here? To nag me again?"

"I thought we should give the marriage another go," said James.

"Why?"

"Because I'm not a quitter and neither are you."

"Couldn't you say it was because you loved me?"

"Oh, Agatha, you know what I'm like. I never was any good at that lovey-dovey stuff."

"All right. I'll try again. But you have to stop seeing Melissa."

"She's a friend."

"I'll stop seeing Charles or any other man, if you stop seeing Melissa."

"Very well."

Agatha suddenly smiled at him. "What a pair of chumps we are," she said happily. "Wait there until I put some make-up on. It's all right for you, James. The thing I love about you is that you always seem so fit and healthy." She went out of the kitchen. I should have told her, thought James. But we'll have dinner this evening. I'll tell her then.

Happiness is a great rejuvenator. Agatha returned to work that afternoon looking fresh and businesslike. The rambling song was a jaunty whistle-along tune. Delly Shoes proclaimed themselves delighted with Agatha. She was to arrange a concert in Mircester to launch the new boot and the new song. She bought herself a dark blue dress ornamented with glass beads and pearls. It had a square neckline and a very short hemline. She then bought sheer stockings and a garter belt, the latter being an item of clothing which Agatha despised, but she planned a hot night and was prepared to sacrifice her comfort.

She carried her purchases home and proceeded to prepare herself for the evening ahead. James was to drive them into

23

Oxford for dinner at a French restaurant on Blue Boar Street.

She bathed and made up her face with care and then brushed her hair until it gained some of its lost shine. Then she put on the dress and stood in front of the mirror.

And scowled.

The sequins and beads had glittered in the electric light of the shop and had looked beguiling. In the late sunlight streaming through the bedroom window, it looked vulgar, tasteless, and middle-aged. And that same cruel sunlight fell on her face, showing Agatha Raisin that she had an incipient moustache. She tore off the dress and left it on a crumpled heap on the floor. In the bathroom, she applied depilatory to the area between her nose and her upper lip and then went to her closet to rake through her clothes to find something suitable. Five try-ons later, she realized she had forgotten all about the depilatory and was only reminded by a burning sensation on her face. She went back to the bathroom and washed it off. Above her upper lip there was now a scarlet line. "I hate being old," howled Agatha at the mirror.

She returned to the bedroom and gloomily selected a white satin blouse and a short black velvet skirt. Now to do something about her face. She had planned to wear only a little light make-up, but heavy foundation cream would be needed to cover that red mark.

When she finally got into James's car, although he glanced at her without comment, she could sense his disapproval. She should tell him what had happened, but somehow to confess that she had reached the shaving age seemed impossible.

James actually thought Agatha had put on too much make-up as an act of defiance. His cancer treatment was to start the following week. He would start to lose his hair and then he would need to tell her something. He had meant to tell her that evening, imagining a soft and sympathetic and womanly Agatha. But Agatha, he thought sourly, had never been soft or womanly.

24

So on the road to Oxford and throughout dinner, he talked about his new book, which was to be about the Normandy landings in World War II. Agatha ventured that surely enough had been written on them already and then promptly realized that, once again, she had said the wrong thing. As usual with James, she felt she was facing an unbreakable wall of resentment.

"We should be talking about what we really need to talk about," said Agatha abruptly, cutting through one of James's history lessons. "I can assure you, Charles is just a friend. Nothing has been going on. What about you and Melissa? What prompted you to take her for a drink in the first place?"

That usual look of distaste and weariness which always crossed James's face when confronted with any intimacy of conversation was back again. "I told you, I happened to meet her in the pub. Then I knew Charles was with you, and so . . . Do we really need to go through all this?"

"Yes, we do," said Agatha. "Did you sleep with her?"

"No," said James. He despised the euphemism. What he had done with Melissa could hardly be described as sleeping.

"Do I have your word on that?"

"I have to trust what you say about Charles and you have to trust what I say about Melissa, or there is no point in going on." He suddenly smiled at her. "Let's forget about the whole sordid quarrel."

Agatha melted before that smile. "About my job. The concert is next week and after that I will be a lady of leisure again."

"Good," said James. I should tell her about the cancer, he thought. Maybe tomorrow.

They made love that night. Pillow talk had never been James's forte and yet Agatha tried. "It seemed a good idea keeping our separate cottages, James, but now I don't think it very sensible. Why don't we sell our cottages and buy somewhere bigger?"

James thought of Agatha being perpetually underfoot,

Agatha with her bad cooking and her smoking. He manufactured a faint snore.

Agatha rose on one elbow and peered in the moonlight at his apparently sleeping face, and then fell back on her pillow with a little sigh. Perhaps she should settle for a James-type marriage. James, it appeared, would rather they lived separately and dated. She had this job to finish. Yes, perhaps she would try things his way.

For the next couple of days, harmony reigned. James worked at his computer and Agatha worked at her public relations. In the evenings they met up for dinner, and then retired to bed and made love. I've cracked this marriage business, thought Agatha gleefully.

But on the third day, she decided to take her washing along to her own machine and check on her garden. She had just put the first load in when the doorbell rang. If that's Charles, thought Agatha uneasily, I'll need to tell him to go away. But when she opened the door, it was to find her friend, Detective Sergeant Bill Wong, standing on the step. Bill was a young man in his twenties, with an oriental cast of face inherited from his Chinese father. Normally chubby, he was looking trim and fit, and so Agatha led him into the kitchen and said, "You've got a new romance."

"How did you know?"

"You're looking fit and you always look fit when you're in love. Who is she?"

"She's a saleswoman. Works in that Miranda boutique."

I've been in there, thought Agatha, and was served by a hard-faced redhead. "Not the one with red hair?"

"That's her. My Mary."

"She's a lot older than you, surely."

"A bit. I like mature women. So how's marriage?"

"It's okay. We had a few rocky bits but we've settled down nicely. Any juicy murders?"

"Nice and quiet. Just the usual drug busts, car thefts, and burglaries. Why have you kept on your cottage?"

"It's a modern marriage, Bill. We like our own space."

"The pair of you could afford a big house and have all the space you need."

Agatha bit her lip in vexation. She had ventured her suggestion again that they buy one big place, but James had stonewalled it by murmuring, "Maybe. I'll think about it."

"Oh, we're happy as we are."

The doorbell rang again. "I wonder who that is?" Agatha went to answer it and found herself facing Melissa Sheppard. She made to slam the door in the woman's face, but Melissa cried, "We need to talk. Poor James."

Agatha hesitated and then said curtly, "Come in." She led the way into the kitchen, introduced Melissa to Bill, and then said to the detective, "I think it's a private matter, Bill."

"All right. I'll phone you and we'll have lunch sometime."

Agatha saw him out and reluctantly returned to the kitchen.

Melissa was wearing a tight tube top which exposed her tanned midriff. Her skirt was short and her bare tanned legs ended in high-heeled sandals.

"What?" demanded Agatha.

"I had to see you. I wondered how poor James was getting on with his treatment. He won't speak to me."

Agatha sat down slowly. In that moment, she felt as if part of her had floated to the ceiling and was looking down at two women sitting at a cottage kitchen table.

"What treatment?" she asked. Her voice sounded dry and dusty to her ears.

"For his cancer, of course."

"Oh, that," said Agatha. Her heart was hammering hard and blood was drumming in her ears. "Very well."

"I'm so glad. You must have been devastated when you heard the news so soon after you got married."

"I've got used to the shock. Do you mind leaving?"

Melissa got to her feet. "We should be friends, Agatha. We have so much in common."

Agatha looked up at the hard, tanned face above her and said, "Look, sweetie, we have bugger-all in common. Just move your scrawny arse out of my kitchen and never come here again. And stay away from James!"

"If James will stay away from me," mocked Melissa. She stood for a moment, but Agatha sat, rigid and unmoving.

Melissa shrugged and walked out. Agatha heard the front door slam shut.

James. Cancer. James. Cancer. Over and over it sounded in her head. And he hadn't told her. He had told Melissa.

The doorbell went again. She rose like a robot and went to open it.

"Christ," said Sir Charles Fraith. "You're as white as a sheet."

"Something terrible has happened," said Agatha. "Come in."
"James?"

Agatha nodded dumbly.

In the kitchen, Charles pressed her down into a chair and went and fetched a goblet of brandy. "Drink that."

"I don't understand." Agatha began to cry, great gulping sobs racking her body.

Charles took one of her hands in his and waited patiently until she recovered.

"Tell me about it, Aggie."

So, in a halting voice, Agatha did, ending with a wail of "He told her. He didn't tell me."

"The main point, Aggie, is that the man has cancer. It must have been a hell of a shock to him. Shock makes people behave in strange ways. Maybe it was easier to tell someone who wasn't close. Maybe he felt that telling you would somehow confirm the horror."

"I'll kill him," said Agatha. "I'll kill the bastard."

"He might already be on his way to death. What kind of cancer?"

"I don't know! Oh my God, if it's cancer of the lung, he'll blame my smoking!"

"Aggie, this is silly. Please just walk next door. I know it must have been awful hearing the news from Melissa, but the chap's got cancer, and surely that cancels out any jealousies or resentments. Look, I'll wait here and if you're not back in an hour, I'll take myself off. But I'll wait here in case you need me. Go on."

"I'll just put some make-up on."

"It's hardly the time for make-up. Go on!"

James was in the local village store. He reached up and took down a packet of coffee. "How are you, darling?" cooed a voice beside him.

He turned and saw, facing him, Melissa. His face darkened. "Just leave me alone, Melissa. I told you, I made a mistake. I just want to get on with my marriage."

"Agatha seems very upset about your illness."

He stared at her in dismay. The packet of coffee fell to the shop floor.

"You told her!"

"You wouldn't talk to me and I was worried about you, so I went to ask Agatha how your treatment was coming along."

"You silly bitch," he roared. "I could kill you, strangle you, shut that malicious gossipy mouth of yours."

The listening, shocked silence behind them in the shop was almost tangible.

Melissa gave a nervous little laugh. "You didn't tell her. That's it, isn't it?"

James walked straight out of the shop. When he turned into

29

Lilac Lane, the first thing he saw was Charles's BMW parked outside Agatha's door.

"He wasn't home," said Agatha miserably to Charles when she returned. "And this is the day of the concert. I've got to rush to Mircester. I don't know how I'll cope."

"Let's get it over with. I'll take you. You're in no fit state to drive."

Agatha wearily went upstairs and made up her face and put on a charcoal-grey business suit and a striped cotton blouse. She did not know what to do. She had promised not to see Charles again, but the news about James's cancer had shaken her.

As Charles drove her to Mircester for the concert, he suddenly said, "You know, Aggie, James is a weird bird, but a good sort. Forget, please, about the fact that he told Melissa. Help him cope with this cancer business. If you love him, you'll do that. Aggie?"

But Agatha stared numbly at the passing scenery and did not reply.

Once they arrived at the marquee where the concert was to be held, Agatha threw herself into her work, chatting to the press, to the representatives of record companies. The group already had a recording company, which was, in Agatha's opinion, pretty small beer.

The weather had held up and it was a perfect evening. Agatha had urged Delly Shoes to charge as little as possible for the tickets. Midlands Television was setting up its cameras and Agatha wanted as large a crowd as possible.

Only once she had taken her seat in the front row and the concert had begun did a great wave of dark misery engulf her. Stepping Out ended their show with the new rambling song. It was effervescent and jaunty. "Got a winner," whispered Charles, but Agatha sat like stone.

The group played encore after encore. Then the managing

director of Delly Shoes, Mr. Piercy, took the microphone. He talked about the glories of the new boot, and then he said, "I'm glad you all enjoyed yourself. I am sure we would all like to put our hands together and thank the organizer of this evening, Mrs. Agatha Raisin. Agatha, come on up."

Charles nudged her to her feet. Like a sleep-walker, she walked up the steps at the side of the stage.

"I think you should make a short speech," hissed Mr. Piercy.

Agatha looked out over the crowd in a dazed way. Then she adjusted the microphone.

But before she could speak, a voice called from the back of the hall, "Police! Make way, there."

Agatha shielded her eyes and peered out over the audience. Police and detectives were making their way down the centre aisle.

"It's another stunt, isn't it?" asked Mr. Piercy.

Agatha felt the world had just come to an end. She was sure they had come to tell her James was dead.

Detective Inspector Wilkes of Mircester CID came up to her and took her elbow. "Come with us, Mrs. Raisin."

She let him lead her down the steps, through the now silent crowd and out into the night.

"What is this?" she asked, aware that Charles had appeared beside her.

"If you will accompany us to Carsely, Mrs. Raisin."

"Put her out of her misery," shouted Charles. "Is James dead?"

"We don't know," said Wilkes. "He's missing and there's signs of a fight."

Agatha was never to forget the journey home. She seemed to be moving through some sort of black nightmare. She prayed to a God she only half believed in, promising everything she could think of, doing deals, anything, if only James would turn out to be still alive.

• • •

They went to Agatha's cottage because the Scene of Crimes Operatives were busy at work in their white overalls behind the taped-off front of James's cottage.

"The situation is this," began Wilkes. "A certain Mrs. Melissa Sheppard was passing Mr. Lacey's cottage and saw the door open. She was going to walk past, when she saw a dark stain on the front step. She went to examine it, touched it, and found it was fresh blood. She looked inside and saw furniture overturned. She called us. Mr. Lacey's car is missing. We are searching the countryside for any trace of him. Preliminary questioning reveals that you had been heard threatening to kill him, Mrs. Raisin. I also learn that you preferred to keep your previous married name and that you and Mr. Lacey, although recently married, preferred to live in separate cottages. Mrs. Sheppard also tells us that Mr. Lacey was about to undergo treatment for a brain tumour and that he had told her but not you. Is that the case?"

"I threatened to kill him because I was jealous of what I believed to be a relationship with Mrs. Sheppard," said Agatha. "But James, who does not lie, assured me that he had not slept with her. We were reconciled."

"Mrs. Sheppard, who has been very frank, tells us that she had sexual relations with Mr. Lacey twice since his marriage to you."

"That's not true," said Agatha flatly.

"I must ask you for your movements today."

Agatha felt some other woman was answering all these questions. She described her day and Charles said he had been with her all afternoon and all evening. Agatha had been in full view of press and television all evening.

"It looks as if there was some sort of fight. We cannot establish yet whether the blood belongs to Mr. Lacey or his assailant. We will need to take your fingerprints and a blood sample, Mrs. Raisin. You too, Sir Charles. Mr. Lacey was heard threatening Mrs. Sheppard in the village shop. He was overheard saying he could strangle her."

Did I ever really know James? wondered Agatha. Could he have been in love with Melissa?

"Are you charging Mrs. Raisin with anything?" asked Charles.

"Not at present."

"Not at present," jeered Charles. "She has an excellent alibi. She was in full view of several hundred people. Can't you see she's nearly dead with shock? She's not going anywhere. Leave her alone."

But Agatha and Charles had to give blood samples and fingerprints and promise to report to police headquarters the following day before they were left alone.

"You'd better go, Charles," said Agatha.

"Sure? You're not going to do anything silly?"

Agatha shook her head. Charles would have insisted on staying had not the vicar's wife arrived.

"You poor thing," said Mrs. Bloxby.

"I can't believe it. He has cancer and he never told me."

"He talked to me about that," said Mrs. Bloxby.

"Of course he did. He probably told the whole world!"

"He said he did not want to tell you because telling you would make it real."

Agatha put her head in her hands. "What am I going to do?"

"He appears to have driven off, which means he was not badly hurt. The blood in the cottage may not even be his."

"Who would attack him? James didn't have any enemies."

"I am afraid the police are going to be concentrating on you for a bit."

"Why me?"

"You've been heard threatening him."

"What about Melissa? God, that woman says she slept with

33

James twice since we were married. How could James do such a thing?"

"I think the fright of cancer made him behave most oddly. I've brought a bag. I'll stay with you tonight."

"But I should be out there looking for him!"

"Come, now. There is nothing you can do. The police will be searching everywhere. He took his car, so he's still alive."

Agatha allowed herself to be led upstairs. Mrs. Bloxby ran her a bath and sat on the bed until Agatha emerged from the bathroom.

"Now, into bed with you," said the vicar's wife. "I'll only be next door. Call me if you need anything."

Agatha lay awake a long time, clutching the duvet, horrors racing through her mind. She began to blame herself. Somehow, if she had been a better wife, then James would have confided in her. Something told her that James had indeed lied to her, that he had slept with Melissa. Melissa had no reason to lie to the police. And James would not have gone to Melissa for comfort if she, Agatha, had treated him better. Just when she thought she would never sleep again, she plunged down into a nightmare where she was searching the lanes and woods for James, dressed in her nightgown.

The next thing Agatha knew, Mrs. Bloxby was shaking her by the shoulder and saying, "The police are here again, Agatha. They insist on seeing you. James's car has been found."

Agatha struggled out of bed, tore her night-gown off and began to scramble into clothes. "And James? Have they found him?" she asked.

"No sign of him, yet."

Agatha went downstairs. Wilkes was there with Bill Wong and a woman police constable.

"You've found his car," said Agatha. "Where?"

"Up in the woods, just before you reach the A-44," said Bill.

"Was there any clue in the car?"

"Only more blood-stains," said Wilkes, and Agatha groaned. "It does look as if he was injured."

"May I see the car?"

"No, it's been taken away for examination. Do you know of anyone with any reason to attack him?"

"None whatsoever," said Agatha. "I've thought and thought."

"You had better come with us to Mircester and make a full statement."

"I'll just phone my husband," said Mrs. Bloxby. "I'm coming with her."

As Agatha was driven past James's cottage, she could see men in white overalls dusting for prints and searching everywhere. A numbness had settled on her. Once at police headquarters, she answered all questions like a dutiful child while Mrs. Bloxby sat beside her and held her hand.

The vicar's wife wondered if Agatha realized how odd her story sounded. Yes, she had tried to marry James before but had forgotten to tell him that she did not know whether her husband Jimmy Raisin was alive or dead. Yes, Jimmy had turned up and cancelled the wedding ceremony. Yes, Jimmy was subsequently found murdered. No, relations between herself and James had not been very amicable. No, she did not know he had cancer. Mrs. Bloxby did not know that, numb and shocked as she was, Agatha was not going to admit she had learned of James's illness from Melissa.

Mrs. Bloxby knew that videos of the concert would be scanned and people interviewed to establish Agatha's alibi. Could they establish from the blood-stains when James was attacked? Villagers often walked their dogs along Lilac Lane. If the attack had taken place in daylight, surely someone would have seen something or heard something. Melissa was more of a suspect than Agatha. She was the other woman. What did anyone in the

35

village know of her? She was a fairly recent incomer. She must have been very keen on James to have had an affair with him in such a small village.

The questioning went on and on. Agatha's in bad shock, thought Mrs. Bloxby. They must know that.

At last, Agatha signed her statement and the interview was over. She was cautioned not to leave the country and to hold herself in readiness for further questioning.

When they emerged from police headquarters it was to find Charles waiting for them. "I've been grilled as well," he said cheerfully. "Fancy some lunch?"

"I must get back," said Mrs. Bloxby. "Alf will be wondering what's happened to me."

"That's all right," said Charles. "I'll take her home. We'd better talk."

Mrs. Bloxby looked doubtful. She drew Charles aside. "Be very careful," she whispered. "Mrs. Raisin has had a bad shock."

"I'll deal with her."

He took Agatha's arm and she allowed herself to be led across the square and into Mircester.

"When did you eat last?" he asked Agatha.

"I can't remember. I meant to have a late supper after the show." She plucked nervously at his arm. "The concert! I should get the newspapers."

"Forget it. We've got more important things to talk about." Charles suddenly saw Melissa walking in front of them. "In here," he said, dragging her into a place called Pam's Pantry. "I'm sure the food is good."

They sat down at a corner table. "I'll order us something," said Charles. The menu was of the snack variety. He ordered two club sandwiches and a bottle of mineral water.

"Now, Aggie," he said. "What on earth could have happened?"

"I don't know," said Agatha. "I've thought and thought. I'm

36

sure if I had been a better wife, he would have told me things. He didn't even tell me he had cancer."

"Absence *is* making the heart grow fonder," said Charles brutally. "Snap out of it. We won't get anywhere if you start blaming yourself for everything. The trouble is that James is a tight-arsed tick. That was what caused the problems in your marriage. It would help if you could get angry. I was asked if I knew anything about his affair with Melissa. Was he really having an affair with Melissa?"

"She says he slept with her a couple of times since we were married. I asked James if he had slept with her and he denied it."

"So he's an adulterer and a liar. You worked on some murder cases with James before. Anyone from the past likely to have surfaced?"

"I thought about that. They're all still locked up or dead."

"Maybe relatives? Friends?"

"Could be."

"Here's your sandwich. Eat."

"I can't."

"So what are you going to do to help James? Sit wallowing in some unreal world where it's all your fault?"

"Charles!"

"Snap out of it, sweetie. Martyrdom is ruining your looks."

Agatha glared at him. "My husband is missing, maybe dead, and all you can do is insult me?"

"That's what friends are for."

Agatha proceeded to tell him between bites of sandwich exactly what she thought of him.

Charles listened amiably and, seeing she had finished eating, called for the bill. "We'd better get back," he said. "There may be more news."

James Lacey stumbled in a daze along the waterfront at Bridport in Dorset. Night was falling. His head throbbed and he had no

37

idea how he had got there, only that he seemed to have been wandering for days.

Suddenly a squat little woman wearing a yachting cap appeared in front of him. "Why, it's James, James Lacey! You look a mess."

Somehow his dazed mind registered her identity. "Harriet," he said.

"We're about to set sail for France. Tubby's on the yacht. Look at your head. There's dried blood in your hair. What have you been up to?"

"Bar fight," said James, fighting away a memory of a swinging hammer and crashing furniture. "I'll be all right."

He knew some awful memories of what had so recently happened to him were about to come flooding back. And in that moment he remembered a monastery he had visited once in Agde, in the south of France. He remembered the cloistered peace, the sun slanting through the cloisters. He suddenly felt if he could get there, he would be safe.

"Can you take me to France?"

"I think you should go to a doctor and get that head examined."

"It's just a bit of blood. Worse than it looks. I'd really like to get away, Harriet."

"Got your passport?"

James searched in the inside pocket of his jacket. "Yes, I have," he said with something like surprise. He tried to remember why he had his passport but could not.

"Luggage?"

"No luggage. I sent it on ahead," said James, improvising.

"You look as if you've been sleeping in those clothes. It's a good thing I know you to be a respectable gentleman or I would start to think you were on the run from the police."

"Not from them," said James. Harriet looked up at him curiously and then gave a little shrug.

"Come along, then. We're nearly ready to set sail."

THREE

✝

THREE weeks had passed since the disappearance of James. Agatha had railed at the police. In these days of modern communications, someone must have seen him somewhere. He had not packed any clothes, although his passport was missing. He would have to buy clothes somewhere, draw money. There must be a trace of him.

But there was nothing.

It had been established that the blood in the cottage and in the car belonged to James. Bill told her they were still waiting for the results of further tests on hairs and threads and other bits and pieces carefully scooped up by the forensic team, but these days, he said, the lab was overloaded.

It is not only the police who suspect the nearest and dearest of murder. When Agatha went to the local pub or shopped in the village store, she could sense an atmosphere when she walked in.

She sank even deeper every day into depression. She had barely the energy to get out of bed, and when she did, she wandered around in a shapeless house-dress. From time to time, she would feel with a stab of deeper pain that she should be out roaming the countryside, looking for James. Then she would remember that the police were looking for him with all their resources, and sink back down into helpless misery again.

James's relatives had given up phoning. His sister and his aunts all seemed to imply that such a worrying, disgraceful thing would not have happened if he had refrained from marrying Agatha. She had finally unplugged the phone from the wall.

At the end of the third week, Agatha reluctantly answered the summons of her doorbell. "I've been trying to ring you," said the vicar's wife, pushing a strand of grey hair away from her mild face. "No reply. I thought you'd gone away."

"Come in. Like coffee?"

"Tea, please."

In the kitchen, Mrs. Bloxby looked anxiously at Agatha. "I just wondered if you had had time to clean up James's cottage."

"I haven't had the heart," said Agatha dully.

She placed a mug of tea in front of Mrs. Bloxby, who picked it up, and then put it down, untasted, and said, "I really think, my dear Mrs. Raisin, that you should take some sort of action or you are going to make yourself really ill."

"What can I do that the police can't?"

"You've never let that stop you before. You see, I could help you tidy up the cottage next door. You could go through James's papers—oh, I know the police have been through them— but there might be something there that they have missed."

"Still can't see much point in it," said Agatha, lighting a cigarette.

"I cannot see much point in you letting yourself go to seed. One would think James was dead."

"How do you mean, go to seed?" demanded Agatha.

"I shall put it bluntly. There are bags under your eyes, you have a moustache and hairy legs."

A small spark of humour gleamed in Agatha's bearlike eyes. "It's women's lib," she said. "We only shave ourselves because of men."

"I shave my legs because they get scratchy and itchy when the hair grows," said Mrs. Bloxby. "I thought your friend, Charles, would have been round to help you."

"He tried, but I didn't feel like seeing him."

"Mrs. Raisin, are we going next door, or what? I haven't got all day. There are other people in this parish in need of my help!"

Agatha blinked at her in surprise. She had hardly ever heard her friend speak to her sharply before.

"Okay. I'll get the keys."

"Clean yourself up first, there's a dear."

Agatha trudged upstairs. For the first time, it seemed, in ages, she took a good look at herself in the long mirror in her bedroom. She was appalled at the ageing mess that looked wearily back at her.

Downstairs, Mrs. Bloxby waited patiently. If Mrs. Raisin was taking a long time, then it meant she was tidying herself up, and Mrs. Bloxby was still shocked by the deterioration in Agatha's appearance.

At last, Agatha appeared, neat and tidy in a shirt blouse and skirt, her smooth legs in tights and her smooth face under a light mask of make-up. "Thanks for waiting," she said gruffly. "Let's go."

"Haven't you been to James's cottage before?"

"Just on and off," said Agatha, remembering nights she had cried into his pillow and days where she had sat with her face buried in his favourite old sweater. "I just couldn't get round to straightening things, although the police did quite a good job after they had finished."

They walked out into the sunshine. How odd that the world should look so normal, thought Agatha. Fluffy clouds, like clouds in a child's painting, hung in a deep-blue Cotswold sky. The first roses were tumbling over hedges and the air was sweet and fresh.

Agatha unlocked the door of James's cottage. Mrs. Bloxby stood back and looked at the roof. "The thatch needs done," she called. "I can put you in touch with a thatcher. You might want to wait and see if he comes back. It's an expensive job."

She followed Agatha in. "I'll draw the curtains back and open the windows."

Soon sunlight was flooding the cottage. Mrs. Bloxby looked round. There was a thin layer of dust on the furniture and the carpet was still marked with blood-stains. "Perhaps if you start with his papers," she said, "I'll begin with the cleaning."

Agatha went to the old roll-top desk in the corner where James kept his accounts and letters. The police had taken everything away to examine and the plastic bag holding all the papers they had returned lay on top of the desk. The fact that Agatha had taken some sort of action was beginning to send a little surge of energy through her.

Behind her, she heard the reassuring clatter of cleaning implements as Mrs. Bloxby fetched what she needed from the kitchen and got to work.

Agatha began going through piles of bills to make sure they had all been paid. Then she began on the little pile of mail which had been lying on the doormat when she walked in. New bills. Electricity, gas, water. Junk mail. One letter addressed in large looped handwriting addressed to James. She took up James's silver letter opener and slit open the envelope.

It was dated the Friday of the previous week. "Dear James," she read. "We really must sit down and talk. I hope you're back by now. I'm sorry I told Agatha about your illness, but how could I possibly guess you had not told her yourself? You must come and see me. We have been intimate together, you've made love to me, you can't just walk away and not see me again. Do please ring me, darling, or come round. Your Melissa."

Agatha's hands shook as she read the letter. A great wave of fury swept through her. She had almost been sanctifying James since his disappearance, crediting him with affections and little tendernesses that he had never demonstrated, blaming herself bitterly for everything. Despite what she had previously said, she had come to the conclusion that James had never been unfaithful to her. Such a straight, upright man would not. But now here it was. Proof. She forgot about his cancer. She only thought that he had cheated her. By God, she had to find him and tell James Lacey exactly what she thought of him. He could even be lying about having cancer! The police had checked every hospital in Britain without finding a sign of him.

"Everything all right?" called Mrs. Bloxby.

"Yes, sure," muttered Agatha. "Just some bills to pay."

"You do those and I'll get on with this." Mrs. Bloxby thought it would be better if she scrubbed out the blood-stains herself.

Agatha took out James's cheque-book. No reason to pay the damn bills herself. But of course she could not sign one of his cheques. They didn't have a joint account. Bastard. She should let his gas, water, and electricity get cut off.

She went to her cottage and collected her own cheque-book and returned. "Don't you think James would need money?" she called over her shoulder. "I mean, the police must have been watching to see if he cashed any cheques or used one of his credit cards."

"Mmm," was the only reply she got. Mrs. Bloxby scrubbed busily, thinking sadly that if James did not need money, then James was dead.

Agatha finished signing cheques and joined Mrs. Bloxby in cleaning and dusting.

Then they went back to Agatha's cottage for a coffee. "Have you seen anything of Melissa lately?" asked Mrs. Bloxby.

Agatha flushed, well aware of that crumpled letter in her handbag. "No, and I don't want to."

"Perhaps she is feeling very guilty. She did not attend the ladies' society meeting last night. And she's usually always there. No one has seen her for over a week. Her car is still outside."

"Why don't you phone her?"

"I tried, but there was no reply."

I'll go and see her the minute I've got rid of you, thought Agatha, engulfed by a wave of anger.

The phone rang. Agatha looked startled and then remembered she had plugged it back in before they had left to clean James's cottage as a sort of gesture to belonging to the world again.

"You answer it. I'll be off," said the vicar's wife.

As Mrs. Bloxby waved good-bye, Agatha picked up the phone. "Hello, Aggie," said Charles's voice. "How are things? I've been trying to get you."

"I'm all right," said Agatha. "Still miserable and shocked, as a matter of fact."

"No news?"

"None." Agatha thought about that letter and the desire to tell someone overcame her. Sometimes she found Mrs. Bloxby almost *too* good. Mrs. Bloxby might have sympathized with Melissa and Agatha could not have borne that.

"Well, just one thing," she said. "I went along to James's cottage to clean up and found a letter from Melissa on the door-mat. It was delivered last week. They had been having an affair."

"I thought you'd accepted that."

"NO, I HAD NOT!" howled Agatha.

"Careful. You'll break my ear-drum. You said—"

"I know what I said. But James assured me they had not been sleeping together and I believed him. More fool me. I'm going to find him."

"That's more like the Agatha I know. I'm bored. I'll be over in half an hour or so."

"But—" Agatha had been about to put him off because she was dying to confront Melissa, but he had rung off. May as well wait for him.

When Charles arrived, he found the cottage door open and walked in. Agatha was in the back garden, playing with her cats.

"Oh, it's you," she said, getting to her feet and brushing grass from her skirt.

"You don't look too bad," said Charles, surveying her critically. "I was afraid you might have gone to pieces. So where do we start? With James's family?"

Agatha shuddered. "I've had enough of James's family, what with his aunts and sister implying that if he hadn't married me he would be all right."

"So what about Melissa?"

"So what about her?" demanded Agatha truculently.

"I think you should swallow your pride and we'll go and see her. I mean, he did tell her he had cancer and didn't tell you. He may have told her other things."

"I was going to wait until your visit was over and then go round there and give her a piece of my mind."

"Won't do. You'd never get anything out of her that way. I mean, do you want to find James or not?"

"I want to find him and ask for a divorce."

"All right, then. Let's go."

"I hate this."

"Better than not knowing. Come on, Aggie. Let's get it over with."

Agatha walked with him through the village, aware of twitching curtains at windows and curious stares. I am the victim, not James, she told the watchers silently. I have been betrayed and abandoned. Then she thought of the cancerous tumour in James's brain and groaned inwardly.

Melissa's cottage, like Agatha's, was thatched. But where Agatha did not bother much about the little garden at the front of her house, Melissa's was a riot of roses, pink and yellow and red, tumbling over a white-painted fence. The white-painted door had a brass knocker. Agatha noticed the knocker was dull. That's odd, she thought. Melissa liked to pride herself of being a first-class housewife.

She seized the knocker and rapped loudly. As they waited, it seemed as if the whole village waited. It was very quiet. No cars drove along the road, no dogs barked, no tractors buzzed around the fields above.

Charles leaned round her and twisted the doorknob and gave the door a tentative push. It swung open.

"Agatha," whispered Charles. "I don't like that smell."

"Drains?" suggested Agatha, although her face had turned white as she sniffed a sweet, rotting smell.

"I really think we should stop where we are and phone the police," said Charles.

But a new burst of rage against Melissa engulfed Agatha. "Let's see. She probably went away and left some rotting food in the kitchen. Damn it, the bitch probably knows where James is and has gone to join him."

"Agatha, please stop . . ."

But Agatha walked straight into the cottage, calling, "Melissa!"

The smell was getting stronger but fury drove her on. She opened the kitchen door and stood stock still. Melissa was slumped over her kitchen table. Flies were buzzing about her dead body: heavy flies, sated flies. Charles peered over her shoulder. "Get the police, Aggie."

"Police," whispered Agatha through dry white lips. "She may just have died."

"Under the flies, her head has been bashed in." Charles gave her a push. "Go, phone."

Agatha stumbled into the sitting-room. She dialled 999 and gasped out the address and demanded police and an ambulance. Then she lurched out into the front garden and took in great gulps of fresh air. "Morning," said an old man, peering over the fence at her. "Lovely day."

"Yes, lovely," said Agatha. He looked at her curiously for a moment and went on his way.

Oh, James, thought Agatha, what have you done?

They were gathered in Agatha's sitting-room later that afternoon, Wilkes, Bill Wong, another detective, and a thin, serious police-woman.

Agatha gave them the letter and she explained her reaction and her desire to confront Melissa. She did not say anything about trying to find James herself. Asked about her movements during the previous days, she said honestly that until Mrs. Bloxby had called, she had been too depressed to move much at all.

"I've heard it's almost impossible to pin-point the exact time of death," said Charles.

"The corpse was cold but not stiff, which means she had been dead over thirty-six hours," said Wilkes. "Of course, I'm sure the flies will give us some clue."

"Flies?" asked Agatha.

The policewoman, who had not previously spoken, suddenly threw back her head, closed her eyes and began to recite, "After death the body begins to smell, and attracts different types of insects. The insects that usually arrive first are the Diptera, in particular the blowflies, and the flesh-flies, or Sarcophagidae. The females will lay their eggs on the body, especially around the natural orifices and in any wounds. Flesh-flies do not lay eggs, but deposit larvae instead.

"After about a day, depending on the species, the eggs hatch

47

into small larvae. These larvae live on the tissue and grow fast. After a short time, they moult, and reach the second larval stage. They continue eating and moult to the third stage. This takes about four to five days. When the larvae are fully grown, they become restless and begin to wander. They are now in their pre-pupal stage, about eight to twelve days after the eggs were deposited. Typically it takes between eighteen and twenty-four days from the eggs to the pupae stage. The exact time depends on the species and the temperature in the surroundings, so by estimating the age of the insects, scientist can estimate the time of death."

She closed her mouth like a trap. "Are you for real?" demanded Agatha.

"*Thank you,* Constable Morrison," said Wilkes. "But I think this is neither the time nor place for a forensic lecture." He turned to Agatha. "The hunt has now intensified for your husband."

"You think James did it, don't you?" said Agatha. "I thought so at first. But why?"

Constable Morrison threw back her head again. "Crime of passion," she said.

"We don't know who did it," said Bill Wong. "We have to look into Melissa Sheppard's background, see what, if any, enemies she had. Mr. Lacey's disappearance and her death may not be related."

The following day, Harriet Comfrey, her rotund figure bulging over a swim-suit, was relaxing on the deck of the *Sleeping Princess* in the harbour at Honfleur.

She saw her husband coming along the harbour, clutching a sheaf of newspapers. When he joined her, Harriet said crossly, "You've broken our holiday agreement. No newspapers!"

"I didn't mean to buy them," said Tubby, "but James's face is all over the front page. Look!"

Harriet picked up the *Daily Express*. There, sure enough, was a photograph of James Lacey. She quickly scanned the story.

Some woman called Melissa Sheppard had been found battered to death. Police were anxious to contact Mr. Lacey to help them with their inquiries. Mr. Lacey had disappeared some weeks ago after evidence of a fight in his cottage at Carsely, Gloucestershire. He was wounded and believed to be suffering from a brain tumour.

Harriet raised shocked eyes to her husband's face. "And we helped him out of the country! We'd better go to the police. Anyway, we may do him some good. We can tell them he left with us before this murder."

"Who's to say he didn't go back?" said Tubby gloomily. "I mean, he got me to row him ashore at that rocky beach down the coast. Imagine what the police will say. Why didn't you come forward before? You say he had a wound in his head? Aiding and abetting a criminal. All that stuff. Bang goes our holiday."

Harriet bit her lip. "Better say nothing about it, then. I mean, he didn't go through any passport control."

"But they're bound to get him. Then they'll ask him how he got to France and he'll say it was us."

His wife's face took on a stubborn look. "Let's just forget about it. We don't want to be involved. And no more newspapers, Tubby."

The press and television had come and gone. Carsely settled into a summer torpor. James had not been found.

Agatha and Charles had tried to get information about Melissa out of Bill Wong, but all he would say was that it was more than his job was worth to tell them anything. His bosses said they had suffered interference from them in the past. He was instructed not to tell them anything.

"The newspapers might have something," said Agatha, two weeks after the murder of Melissa. "I mean, I've got to get something. I'm still a suspect. Even Bill looks at me in a funny way. They say she must have been lying there dead for five days. We don't have a milkman round here anymore, and she picked up her papers from the village shop. If we still had milk delivered around here, then people would have noticed bottles piling up on the step."

"What do you mean, the newspapers might have something?" asked Charles. "We've read them all, day in and day out."

"What I mean is this. A couple of days after Melissa's murder, there was that awful shooting at Mircester School. Five children dead. Awful. But it wiped Melissa's murder off the papers. Now some reporter may have been working away at the background and then gets told to drop it. We could go to the *Mircester Journal* and ask."

"Sounds a bit far-fetched."

"You forget, I worked with the press for years. Anyway, it's better than doing nothing."

Charles made a steeple of his fingers and studied them while Agatha waited impatiently. It was at times like this that she wondered if she really knew Charles at all. Self-possessed as a cat, expensively tailored, sensitive face, but unreadable eyes under smooth fair hair.

"All right," he said. "It's better than sitting here."

The editor of the *Mircester Journal* looked more like Agatha's idea of an accountant than an editor. Mr. Jason Blacklock was dry and precise, with strands of brown hair combed neatly over a pink scalp and gold-rimmed glasses perched on the end of a long thin nose.

"I gather you want my help, Mrs. Raisin," he said, addressing Agatha. "I agreed to see you because there might be a story in it for us."

"If you help us," said Agatha, "we'll give you an exclusive when we're ready. Deal?"

"All right. So what is it you want?"

"I gather you would have had a reporter or reporters working on the murder of Melissa Sheppard."

"Of course."

"And pulled them off it when the shooting at the school happened?"

"Yes."

"We wanted to find out a bit about Melissa's background and wondered if one of your reporters would have something."

"Why? Are you playing at detectives?"

"We're not playing at anything," said Agatha sharply. "I am still a suspect, as is my husband. I want to know if there was anyone in Melissa's past life who would want to harm her."

Mr. Blacklock suddenly bellowed, "Josie!"

A skeletal girl appeared. She was wearing a purple spangled top over a long black skirt and huge boots.

"Where's Colin Jaeger?"

"Down the pub," said Josie laconically.

"Right. Will you take Mrs. Raisin here and Sir Charles Fraith down to the Ferret and Firkin and tell Colin he's to fill them in on the background of the Sheppard murder."

"Okey-dokey."

Agatha and Charles followed the thin figure of Josie out and down the stairs. Out in the street, Agatha said to Josie, "You should eat more."

Josie flicked back her lank hair and stared insolently at Agatha's stocky figure. "You should eat less, Granny."

"You insolent little pig," snarled Agatha. "Why, I'd like to stuff your skinny, undernourished form down the nearest drain."

"Ladies, ladies," pleaded Charles. "It's too hot for a row. Here is the pub. Josie, fetch this Colin and then you can go back to work."

Josie muttered something under her breath but she thrust open the door of the pub and let it swing back in Agatha's face.

"You asked for it, Aggie. Calm down. You should know better than to comment on someone's personal appearance." Charles opened the door for her.

Josie was talking to an untidy young man who was standing at the bar holding a tankard of beer. She jerked a thumb in their direction and then walked away, brushing rudely past them.

"Colin Jaeger?" asked Agatha. He nodded. "I'm Agatha Raisin and this is Sir Charles Fraith. Did that drippy child tell you we need background on Melissa Sheppard?"

"Something like that."

"So can we sit down at, say, that table over there, or have you got notes back at the office?"

Despite the heat, he was wearing a shabby tweed jacket. He pulled a notebook out of one pocket. "Got most of it here."

Charles bought Agatha a gin and tonic and himself a whisky and they joined Colin at a table. He flicked through his notebook. "Look at that," he said. "Perfect shorthand. 'You need shorthand,' says the editor. And what happens? Well, these days, everyone's got a dinky little tape recorder. Still, must admit it's a good way of keeping a lot of information."

"So what have you got on Melissa?" asked Agatha eagerly. "Is there a Mr. Sheppard?"

"Easy, now. You paying me for this?"

"Paying your editor," lied Charles quickly, seeing that Agatha was preparing to give him a lecture. "So you'd better get on with it."

Colin sighed. "Where are we? Pages and pages of school shooting. Ah, here we are. Background. Married Luke Sheppard in 1992. Divorced a year later, amicably."

"And did you talk to this Mr. Sheppard?" asked Charles.

"I was about to when the shooting started."

"Address?"

"Parson's Terrace, number fourteen, Blockley."

Charles made a note. "Anything else?"

"When she married Luke Sheppard, she was a Mrs. Dewey."

"Blimey. Two of them. What of Mr. Dewey?"

"Lives in Worcester. Turnpike Lane, number five."

"And how long was she married to him?"

"Three years. Let me see, 1988 to 1991."

"Are there any other husbands?" asked Agatha.

"None that I got around to finding."

"Got anything else?"

"All the stuff on you, Mrs. Raisin, and your . . . er . . . un-happy marriage."

"You mean, on Melissa?"

"No."

"My marriage was not unhappy," said Agatha through gritted teeth.

"Have it your way, but that ain't what the neighbours say. Raised voices, flying plates, all that stuff."

"Can we get back to Melissa?" said Charles. Agatha looked about to burst with rage.

"There's not much to get back to. I say, you pair might at least offer me a drink."

"First tell us about Melissa," said Charles.

"There isn't much more to tell. That's about as far as I'd got. Got as far as previous husbands and addresses and got called off the story."

"Come along, Agatha," said Charles, pulling her to her feet. "Better get going."

"What about my drink?" demanded the reporter.

"No time," said Charles, urging Agatha out of the pub.

"You are cheap, Charles," said Agatha. "I didn't like the little ferret, but you could have at least bought him a drink."

"Maybe next time," said Charles vaguely. "Blockley first. That's very near Carsely. He could have nipped over there and bashed her, after bashing James first in a fit of jealous rage."

James Lacey lay in a narrow white bed in the Benedictine mon-astery of Saint Anselm in the French Pyrenees, drifting in and out of sleep. He had arrived the day before, suffering from heat exhaustion. He knew from his previous visit that it was a closed order. Before, he had been allowed a cold drink of water and a rest in the cloisters before continuing on a walking tour. This time, to his request to join the order, he had been told he was obviously a sick man. He should rest and recover and then they would see.

After leaving Tubby and Harriet, he had slowly made his way south, resting in fields, eating little, always stumbling on, driven by worry and guilt, and fear of the monster he felt was growing in his brain.

He thought briefly of Agatha, but closed his eyes again and willed himself to sleep.

FOUR

✝

BLOCKLEY, though now a village, was once a thriving mill-town. The mills are now residences, and property prices, sky-high. The village is dominated by a square-towered church, and by Georgian terraces of mellow Cotswold stone. The long straggling main street used to be full of little shops, but only the many-paned shop windows, lovingly preserved, remain to show where they once stood.

It is one of the more picturesque of the Cotswold villages, but, because of an absence of craft shops, thatched cottages, and a museum, is mostly free from the tourists and tour buses which crowd other, more popular, places such as Bourton-on-the Water, Stow-on-the-Wold, and Chipping Campden.

Charles and Agatha drove down into the village from the A-44. "Poor Blockley, it must have the worst roads of anywhere around here," said Charles.

"Why is that?" asked Agatha idly. She was experiencing a rare peace, because at last she was doing something, and did not want her mood shattered by dwelling on thoughts of James's infidelity.

"The trucks grind through it on their way to Northwick Business Park," said Charles. "They chew up the two main roads down into the village and leave big pot-holes, and then all that happens is two men fill the holes up with tarry stones, which soon sink back into pot-holes under the weight of the trucks."

"I think they need a big-wig of some kind, a member of Parliament, someone like that, to complain. Where's Parson's Terrace?"

"Don't know. There's a post office. We'll ask there."

As in Carsely, the post office was also the general store. The woman behind the counter told them to turn left as they went out of the shop, left and left again. They would find Parson's Terrace at the top of the hill.

"We may not find him at home," said Charles. "May be out at work."

"We can try. A lot of people work at home in these villages, computer stuff," said Agatha vaguely.

Parson's Terrace was a row of very small cottages. "This is it," said Charles, parking outside.

"I wish we had some sort of official badge we could flash," mourned Agatha.

"Well, we haven't. Here goes."

Charles knocked at the door. "Someone at home anyway," he said, hearing someone approach.

When the door opened, at first they thought they were facing a teenager. She had black hair pulled back in two bunches and tied with red ribbons and was wearing a short print frock, ankle socks and sandals. Her eyes were large, seeming to fill the whole of her small face.

"We're hoping to talk to Mr. Sheppard," said Agatha in that

56

slightly cooing voice in which those who don't have children and don't much like them either address the species.

"Luke's out at work. Can I help you? I'm Megan Sheppard."

"Ah, what time will your father be home, dear?"

Those eyes widened in amusement. "I am Mrs. Sheppard and you are that Agatha Raisin I read about in the newspapers."

"May we talk to you for a little?" asked Charles.

"Come in. I was just about to have some coffee. We can have it in the garden. It's a lovely day."

They followed her through the dark little cottage—narrow kitchen, poky living-room and out into a pretty garden, where a table and chairs had been set out on a patio. "Have a seat," said Megan. "I'll get the coffee."

When she had gone, Agatha hissed, "How old do you think she is?"

"Late thirties?"

"Can't be!"

"It's the bobby socks, Agatha. She's a lot older than she dresses."

When Megan came back with a tray of coffee jug and cups, which she set down on the table, Agatha studied her face. In full sunlight, Megan's face now revealed thin lines around the eyes, but she still seemed remarkably young.

"I did not know Mr. Sheppard had married again," said Agatha. "There was nothing about it in the papers."

"There wouldn't be, would there?" said Megan, pouring coffee. "They only print the name of suspects."

"I am Charles Fraith," began Charles, accepting a cup of coffee from her. It was a china cup, decorated with roses. "Why wouldn't your husband be a suspect? I mean, she was married to him."

"But he had nothing to do with her. Everyone knows that." Somehow Megan's voice implied that they should have known it, too.

57

"Why did he divorce her?" asked Agatha. "Did he discover she was being unfaithful to him?"

"With your husband, you mean?"

"No," said Agatha sharply. "With someone else."

"Oh, no. He fell in love with me, you see." She smiled blindingly at Charles, who smiled back.

"And what does your husband do?" asked Charles.

"He owns The Well-Dressed Gent. It's a shop in Mircester. You are rather cheeky, you know, to ask all these questions. You're not the police."

"Mrs. Raisin is desperate to find the whereabouts of her husband. We're asking everyone connected with Melissa. Did you know her?"

"Of course not. Why should I?"

Agatha was becoming increasingly irritated. Among other things, the childlike Megan with her doll's house, and doll's china, was beginning to make her feel old and huge and lumbering.

"Well, for a start, I thought Melissa, knowing he was leaving her for you, might have called on you."

"Oh, no. More coffee, Charles?"

"Thank you. It's excellent."

She refilled his cup.

Agatha was suddenly anxious to leave. Megan could not help them. They should be on their way to Mircester to interview the husband. She realized they would really need to know what kind of person Melissa had been. They would need to find out if there had been anything in her behaviour or character to promote murder. In her heart of hearts, Agatha could not believe James had had anything to do with it. Whoever had attacked him had surely gone on to kill Melissa. She looked impatiently at Charles, but he was smiling and relaxed in the sunshine.

"How did you meet your husband?" Charles asked.

"I was working in the shop, as an assistant. We started going out for a drink together after work, and one thing led to another. He wasn't happy with her."

"Why?" demanded Agatha.

"Oh, you'll need to ask him and see if he wants to tell you anything."

"We'll do that," said Agatha. "Come along, Charles."

"Come back any time," said Megan, but she addressed the invitation to Charles. "Can you see your way out?"

"Little bitch," said Agatha as they drove off.

"Oh, I don't know," said Charles. "Seemed very charming to me."

"For heaven's sake! There's something wrong with a woman who wears ankle socks and her hair tied up like a child."

"It suited her."

"Anyway, we'd better go to Mircester. You know, Charles, I was thinking in there that we don't really know what Melissa was like. I mean, what sort of person was she?"

"Then we should call on Mrs. Bloxby first. Melissa went to that ladies' society thing, didn't she?"

"Yes."

"So let's ask Mrs. Bloxby's opinion of her. She must have formed some sort of opinion."

Agatha felt an irrational stab of jealousy. She prided herself on being a great judge of character. What could Mrs. Bloxby tell them? If she, Agatha, had not sussed out anything strange or odd about Melissa, how could the vicar's wife manage to do so?

More coffee in the vicarage garden. With scones, this time, light as feathers. Being a city mouse down to her bones, Agatha often envied the skill of the country mice. Not for them the quick-fix dinner in the microwave. Not for them the instant garden with plants bought fully grown from the nursery.

"You were asking me about Mrs. Sheppard," said Mrs.

Bloxby. "Do have some of my cherry jam on your scone, Sir Charles."

I wish I could produce homemade jam, thought Agatha. Of course, I could buy the good stuff, steam off the labels, and put my own on, and who would know the difference? Yes, I might do that.

"I thought, you see," said Charles, spooning jam onto a scone, "that with Melissa being such a regular member of the ladies' society, not like Aggie here, you might have formed some sort of opinion."

"I don't like to speak ill of the dead," said Mrs. Bloxby. "I suppose that's silly, now I come to think of it. Surely much worse to speak ill of them when they are alive. I suppose it comes from some old superstition that one might spoil their chances of getting to heaven."

"If she's got there, she's there by now," said Agatha, shifting impatiently on her garden chair.

"I hope so." And only Mrs. Bloxby, thought Charles, could say something like that and really mean it.

"Your garden is lovely," he said, looking about him with pleasure.

"Thank you. The wisteria was a bit disappointing this year, however. Usually, we have a great show but a wicked frost blighted the blooms."

"Melissa," prompted Agatha. "The reason we want to know what you think is because we want to know if there was anything in her character that would make her what Scotland Yard calls a murderee—you know, someone who would incite people to violence."

"Having an affair with someone else's husband in an incitement," said Mrs. Bloxby.

"Yes, but that would mean Aggie would have to have done it," said Charles, "and she didn't, and I don't believe for a moment it was the absent James. Besides, married women have affairs the whole time and no one bumps them off."

"I think married women are a lot more faithful than you give them credit for, Sir Charles. Let me think. Mrs. Sheppard. Well, she was quite hard to get to know, considering she was a very chatty lady."

Charles reached for another scone. Agatha, despite a tight feeling at her waistline, which she quickly assured herself must be psychosomatic, followed suit.

"What do you mean, chatty?" asked Charles.

"She would talk a lot about the weather, about recipes, about flowers, about village life—you know, the decline of the small village shop and all that—but nothing personal."

"Did she have a close friend in the village?"

"No. I would see her about the village, talking to this one and that, but she was not friendly with anyone in particular."

"Did you like her?" asked Charles.

"Well, no, I did not."

"Why?"

"I felt she was acting the part of the village lady. I felt she was restless and discontented and vain. I felt she was afraid of losing her looks. I felt—oh, I don't know—that she had a craving for excitement. Now, having an affair with James perhaps was her way of making herself feel like a desirable woman. She may have behaved in the same way with other women's husbands, but I don't know if she did. She probably enjoyed the power and excitement of an adulterous relationship."

"We've just been to see the present Mrs. Sheppard," said Agatha. "Funny little woman who dresses like a child."

"Quite attractive, in fact," murmured Charles, and Agatha threw him a filthy look.

"I was not aware he had married again. But then, I did not know him. Mrs. Sheppard moved to this village after her divorce from him. Is there any news of James?"

Agatha shook her head. "And I find that very odd. Particularly because of his cancer. You would think he would show up at some hospital somewhere."

Charles delicately licked a piece of jammy scone from his fingertips. "I think we'd better go to Mircester, Aggie, and see that husband. May I use your bathroom first?"

"You know where it is? Down the corridor and on your right."

When he had left, Mrs. Bloxby looked seriously at Agatha. "Have you considered, Mrs. Raisin, that you have been under a great deal of stress lately? That perhaps if you went away on holiday and tried to relax, it might be better for you?"

"Why?" asked Agatha, surprised. "You know I've got to find out about this murder. Apart from anything, James is still the prime suspect. I've got to keep asking questions."

Mrs. Bloxby wanted to say that she feared Agatha might find out more about James than she wanted to hear, but she said, "Just be careful. You have put yourself in danger before."

"I'll be careful. I wish you could meet the present Mrs. Sheppard. I didn't like her at all."

"Did Sir Charles?"

"Oh, him! He was all over her like a rash."

"Oh, well."

"I am not jealous of her," snapped Agatha. "I do not care what woman Charles fancies."

"If you say so. Ah, here is Sir Charles. Can I expect you at our ladies' society meeting tomorrow night, Mrs. Raisin?"

"I suppose so," muttered Agatha, wishing she had never joined in the first place. She had only signed up when she had first arrived in the village as part of playing some sort of role as a villager, like trying to bake and going to church.

"I wonder if they've bugged your phone," said Charles, as they headed towards Mircester.

"Would they do that?"

"Seems likely. I mean, they'll be hoping he'll get in contact with you."

"I don't like that idea. Charles, do you really think James is dead?"

"No. If James was dead, we'd have had a report by now. He can't hide away forever. And when he comes back, you'll need to face up to the fact that you should never have married him."

"We were working things out. It would have worked out. He'll need nursing, taking care of."

"I can't see you as a ministering angel, Aggie."

"Then you've never been in love."

"I think you fell in love with a dream James who does not exist."

"I am not a fanciful person!"

"I think you are, under that crusty exterior."

"Shut up and drive, Charles."

They completed the rest of the journey in silence.

"I wonder if he's handsome," said Agatha as she walked across the main car-park with Charles.

"Luke Sheppard? You mean because Melissa was an attractive woman?"

"If you like stringy, faded blondes and itsy-bitsy little middle-aged women who dress like schoolgirls."

"Late thirties isn't middle-aged these days. If it is, you're ancient, Aggie."

A tear rolled down Agatha's cheek and she gave a choked sob. "Here, now!" said Charles, alarmed, handing her a handkerchief as Agatha attempted to brush the tear away on her blouse sleeve. "You're falling apart. Do you want to go somewhere for a drink? Something to eat? We've only had scones."

Agatha blew her nose defiantly. "I'm all right. It's just that I keep wondering and wondering how the hell James could cheat on me like that."

"Maybe if I thought I were dying, it might affect my morals."

"Couldn't. You haven't got any."

"That's more like my Aggie. Come on. Here's the gents' outfitters. Oh, God, just look at that awful blazer with the improbable crest on the pocket."

A slim dark-haired woman was arranging piles of shirts at the back of the shop. She was dressed all in black—short black skirt, black stockings, and low-cut black blouse. "Maybe the third Mrs. Sheppard," murmured Charles.

Agatha sailed forward. "We're looking for Mr. Sheppard."

"I'll get him. You are . . . ?"

"Agatha Raisin and Sir Charles Fraith."

She undulated into the back shop. They could hear the murmur of voices and then Luke Sheppard appeared. He was a small, powerfully built blond-haired man with small red-veined blue eyes and a large thick-lipped mouth. His broad chest was encased in one of the crested blazers that Charles despised.

"How can I help you?" he asked.

"Are you very busy?" asked Charles. "Is there somewhere we can go and talk?"

"There's the pub next door. Can you take care of things, Lucy?"

"Of course, Luke," said the dark-haired assistant. She gave him a languorous smile.

They walked together into the beer-smelling darkness of The Green Man next door. The pub was nearly empty. Charles said he had left his wallet, which Agatha did not believe for a moment, but she paid for their drinks and then they all sat down around a table. "I assume this has to do with the death of my former wife," said Luke Sheppard. "What have you heard?"

"Nothing new," said Agatha. "You see, my husband is under suspicion and I am anxious to clear his name."

"I don't see how you plan to do that. Can't think of anyone else with any reason to have done it."

Agatha looked ready to flare up, so Charles said quickly, "It's just that we're trying to build up a picture of Melissa. No one seems to have known her very well. You see, if we get an idea what she was like, we might think of a reason why she was murdered."

"The reason," said Luke, "is that she was messing around with James Lacey."

"Humour me," said Charles. "What was she like?"

Luke's accents, which were a sort of refined Midlands, suddenly coarsened. "She was a bloody actress, that's what she was. She lived in a private soap opera. In fact, she watched as many soap operas as she could. I went to see her about a month before she was killed. She wanted more money. God knows why. She had enough of her own. I pointed out that when we divorced, she'd settled for a lump sum. She was playing at being the perfect villager, rambling on about recipes and plants and how to make loose covers. She was even wearing an apron!"

"So why did you marry her?" asked Agatha.

"Because the act she was playing when I met her was lady-tart. She promised everything." He nudged Charles. "Know what I mean?"

"And she wasn't?"

"She thought she was good in bed and she was lousy."

So what did James see in her? wondered Agatha.

"Doesn't help us a bit," mourned Charles. "Just because a woman's a bit of an amateur actress doesn't mean she would necessarily inspire someone to murder her."

Agatha covertly studied Luke Sheppard. She did not like him, and yet she had to admit he exuded a strong air of animal sexuality.

"I've got to get back to work," said Luke, draining his glass. "If I think of anything, I'll let you know."

65

"Here's my card," said Agatha.

He stood up and then said, "Why don't you pair let the police do the work?"

"I've managed to solve cases in the past," said Agatha.

He gave a bark of laughter. "Melissa did that as well. When she wasn't watching the soaps, she was watching Miss Marple or Morse on the telly. Another of her fantasies." He strode off before the fulminating Agatha could answer him.

"So that's put you in your place," said Charles. "Let's grab a bite to eat. Give me some money, Aggie, and I'll get it."

"No," said Agatha. "*You* get it."

"I told you, I forgot my wallet."

She leaned across quickly, thrust her hand inside his jacket, and pulled out his wallet. "There you are."

"Bless me, I was sure I had forgotten it."

"Good try, Charles. Get food."

He came back with two ploughman's, those bread-and-cheese rolls which are the cheapest thing on a pub menu.

"So we haven't got very far," said Charles. "Except maybe for the Miss Marple bit. I mean, what if Melissa, fancying herself a detective, had dug up something that someone didn't want her to know?"

"Could be," said Agatha, opening up her roll and looking gloomily at a piece of sweating cheese and a leaf of limp lettuce. "It all seems hopeless, but I've got to go on. Somehow, if I stop ferreting around, I'll sink back into misery again."

"I know," said Charles. "When we finish this, we'll call in at police headquarters and ask for Bill. Maybe he's heard something."

Agatha ate what she could. Charles finished his and then ate what she had left on her plate.

"Getting hot," he said as they emerged into the sunlight.

They walked to police headquarters, asked for Bill Wong and were told to wait. Some attempt had been made a long time ago to brighten up the reception area, but various potted plants were dying or dead and the magazines on the scarred table in front of them were years old.

Finally the desk sergeant called them over and pressed a buzzer so they could go through to the back. Bill was waiting for them in the corridor. "We'll use this room," he said, pushing open the door of an interview room. When they were seated, he asked, "What's new?"

"We came to ask you that," said Agatha.

He spread his hands. "Nothing. No news of James at all. His photo's been in all the newspapers and on television. We've checked the ports and airports. Nothing."

"Are you concentrating solely on him?" asked Agatha. "I mean, if you do that, you'll be letting the real murderer escape."

"We've interviewed everyone we can think of. I mean, we don't understand it. Those villages like Carsely are gossip shops. Yet, we get this murder, Lacey is attacked, no one sees a thing. Agatha, are you sure you didn't just have one of your rows with James and throw something at him?"

"No, I did not. And I was away all that evening."

"So you were."

"You bugging my phone?"

"If we were, I wouldn't tell you. But I don't know. I'm still too low down the ranks to know that sort of thing. If someone's phone is bugged, they need to get permission from the Home Office."

"We've got a likely suspect," said Agatha.

"I thought I told you pair not to interfere. Anyway, who is it?"

"Luke Sheppard."

"Oh, him. He's got an alibi for the time James was attacked. We cannot exactly pin-point the time of Melissa's death, but it was sometime during the night five days before her body was found."

"And what was Luke Sheppard's alibi for the evening James disappeared?"

"He was at a Rotary Club meeting all that evening."

"And the night Melissa was killed?"

"He and his missus were having a romantic night in the Randolph Hotel in Oxford. It was her birthday celebration."

"Rats!" Agatha stared at him moodily.

"We were trying to build up a picture of Melissa," said Charles. "You know, trying to find out if there was anything in her character or behaviour that would cause someone to murder her. Did you find out anything?"

"Only that she was regarded as the perfect village lady. Divorced two times and both amicable divorces."

"What we did find," said Charles, "was that, according to Sheppard, she was a fantasist, acted out roles she saw on television. She was addicted to soaps and detective series, and fancied herself as bit of a Miss Marple. She may just have dug up something that someone didn't want her to find out."

"It's a possibility, but a remote one. If only we could find James Lacey, we might have a clearer picture. But we are trying. We haven't given up on the case. So keep out of it."

"You didn't used to be like this before," said Agatha mournfully. "You used to be glad of my help."

"That was before you nearly got yourself killed on several occasions. You may not realize it, but I am fond of you, Agatha."

"Now you've done it," said Charles, as fat tears began to spill down Agatha's cheeks.

"What did I say?" asked Bill, as Agatha mopped her face.

"She's a bit fragile. Come on, Aggie, let's get going." Charles put a hand under her arm and helped her to her feet.

Turnpike Lane, Worcester, where Melissa's first husband lived, turned out to lie in the outskirts of the town in a modern housing development. "You want to go on with this?" asked Charles, as he parked outside number 5.

"Yes, I'm all right."

"You've got a soft centre after all, Aggie."

"How many times do I have to tell you not to call me Aggie? My husband may be dead, he is suspected of murder, and that's enough to upset anyone. Now are we going to talk to this man or not?"

They got out of the car and stood looking at the house. It was raw-looking, the stone a harsh yellowish colour, and was surrounded by identical houses. "He hasn't bothered much about the garden," commented Charles, looking at the weedy earth in front of the house, which was still dotted with bits of builders' rubble.

Charles rang the white bell-push on the white-painted door. Agatha was once more struck by the fact that there were no children playing about. Children rushed indoors after school these days to surf the Internet or watch television or play computer games.

A woman walking a dog stood at the garden gate and studied them. "Want anything?" called Agatha.

"I represent Neighbourhood Watch in this area," she said, "and I haven't seen you before."

"Well, now you have," snapped Agatha. "And I've got a gun. Bang, bang, you're dead!" She turned back and stared impatiently at the closed door.

She was just about to say to Charles that it did not look as if their quarry was at home, when the door opened a crack and one pale eye surveyed them.

"Mr. Dewey?" said Agatha.

"I'm not buying anything."

"We're not selling anything," said Agatha crossly. "I am Mrs. Agatha Raisin and this is Sir Charles Fraith. We would like to talk to you."

"What about?"

"Melissa Sheppard."

"Oh, her." The door swung open.

"Everything all right, Mr. Dewey?" called the woman at the garden gate and her dog gave a shrill bark.

"We're only here to shoot him," called Agatha to the woman. She turned back. "Do let us in, Mr. Dewey. We can't talk on the doorstep with that tiresome woman watching us."

"Come in."

Charles took a look back down the garden path and saw the representative of Neighbourhood Watch pull a mobile phone out of her pocket. He felt he should say something, but Agatha was already walking into the house, so he gave a shrug and followed her.

The small living-room into which Mr. Dewey led them was as characterless as the outside of the house. Fitted brown carpet covered the floor. There was a new three-piece suite, the sofa having a shell-shaped design. One coffee-table in plain wood. No pictures, photographs, books or magazines softened the starkness of the room. Agatha wondered if he lived in the kitchen.

"Mr. Dewey," she began when they were seated.

"John," he said. "You may call me John."

A small, slight man with closed features and gold-rimmed glasses, he was wearing a white T-shirt, jeans with ironed creases down the front, glittering white sneakers and, over his clothes, a plastic apron decorated with fat roses which reminded Agatha of Megan's cups.

"Well, John," she said, "you may have read about us in the papers."

"Yes, you're that woman whose husband killed Melissa."

"That's just the point. We don't think he did. Before he disappeared, he was attacked and we think that whoever attacked him killed Melissa."

"I don't see the point of these questions," he said. "I mean, I've told the police all I know."

"We're asking a different sort of question," said Agatha. "We would like to find out what Melissa was really like. I mean, if there was anything in her character that would drive anyone to murder her."

"She was just an ordinary sort of person, bit irritating."

"But you divorced her."

"No, she divorced me. We didn't quarrel about it, you know. I didn't argue. I bought this house after the divorce. Suits me to have my own way. She was a cluttery sort of person."

"Cluttery?"

"You know, she always had some fad or other—dressmaking one day, flower-arranging the other, house full of bits and bobs. She was a bad cook."

"She must have changed since she left you," said Agatha. "Everyone in Carsely praised her cakes."

"Oh, that. She probably did what she did when she was married to me."

"Which was?"

"She'd find a good bakery and buy cakes and then put home-made wrappings on them and say she had baked them herself. I mean, only rather sneaky and mean people would do a thing like that."

Charles glanced at Agatha's face, for Agatha was notorious for trying to pass off shop goods as her own work.

"Was she unfaithful to you?"

"Stands to reason, she must have been. She married Sheppard right after the divorce. She would say she was going out to some flower-arranging class or cookery class or something. Come to think of it, she was one hell of a liar." He gave a nervous giggle and put one well-kept hand up to his mouth. "Pardon my French."

The wail of police sirens approaching sounded from outside the house.

"Thank you," said Charles, getting to his feet. "Come along, Agatha."

"No, wait a bit, Charles. This is getting interesting. I mean—"

She broke off, suddenly aware of the sirens, the screech of tyres. Then a stentorian voice called, "The house is surrounded. Come out with your hands above your head."

John Dewey threw them one terrified look, darted out of the living-room and locked the door behind him.

Charles looked out of the window. "It's the police, Aggie. That damn woman took you seriously when you said you were going to shoot Dewey."

"How can we get out?" said Agatha, tugging at the door. "He's locked us in."

"We'd better get out through the window," said Charles, "before they break down that door and start spraying us with CS gas."

He began to tug ineffectually at the window. "Would you believe it? They're painted shut. He never opens them."

Agatha picked up a brass poker from beside the empty fireplace, where obviously no fire had ever been lit. She began smashing at the glass. "We're coming out!" yelled Charles, seeing a police marksman taking aim. "Don't shoot!"

When Agatha had smashed out all the glass, they climbed out into the glare of police lights and television lights. "Down on the ground," yelled a voice.

"Do as they say, Aggie," said Charles wearily, "or we'll never get out of here."

They were both handcuffed and led to the police cars. Agatha looked out of the window of the police car and saw the triumphant face of the Neighbourhood Watch woman. She was talking avidly to a television reporter.

• • •

"What a mess!" groaned Agatha when they finally emerged from Worcester police station several hours later. "I'll pay half your lawyer's fee, Charles, considering he represented me as well."

"You should pay the whole bill. Whatever possessed you to tell that woman we were going to shoot Mr. Dewey?"

"It was a joke!"

"That backfired. I'll drop you off home."

"Will I see you tomorrow?"

"Not tomorrow. I've got things to do."

"Oh." He's sick of me, thought Agatha. Now I'm on my own. With a great effort she managed to stop herself from crying.

To her surprise, she slept deeply that night and woke, for the first time since James's disappearance, feeling strong and well.

She made herself a hearty breakfast, fed her cats and let them out into the garden and then wondered what to do with the rest of the day. She heard her doorbell ring. Charles, she thought with a feeling of gladness that he had not abandoned her.

But it was Bill Wong who stood there when she opened the door.

"Come in," said Agatha. "I suppose you've learned all that fuss about nothing last night in Worcester."

"It's a good thing Charles dug up a hot-shot lawyer or you might both have been charged with wasting police time. That Neighbourhood Watch woman, Miss Harris, has, fortunately for you, a record of seeing villains behind every bush. You're interfering again, Agatha. I warned you."

"Have coffee, sit down, and listen," said Agatha. "Despite the police interruption, I felt I was getting somewhere."

"Oh, yes? We'd already interviewed him."

"But what did you ask, eh? Usual police stuff, where were you on the night of, and so on. What I'm trying to find out is what Melissa was *like*. I told you about that. I mean, surely that would give us some idea. If I could find out what she was like

73

and who she knew, then I might be able to find out who murdered her."

She handed Bill a cup of coffee. He studied her, his almond-shaped eyes curious in his round face.

"So what did you find out?"

"That she lived in a fantasy world and thought she was a detective, among other things, but I told you that. She was also prepared to cheat to maintain the fiction of being a perfect house-wife. She would buy cakes and then say she had baked them."

Bill laughed. "Do you remember how we first met? You'd entered a quiche in a baking competition, the judge dropped dead eating it, and we found out that you'd bought it and tried to pass it off as your own baking."

Agatha flushed.

"So you'll need to do better than that."

"Why did you call, Bill?"

"I've been sent along to find out what you're up to. Now, Wilkes, he says, give her her head. She's blundered around before and unearthed a murderer. But I don't want you to do that."

"I'll be all right. I can't do anything the police can't do, Bill. But you can't stop me asking questions. Do you remember that television game, 'What's My Line?' When they would call something like, 'Will the real airline pilot stand up?' That's how I feel about Melissa. Will the real Melissa Sheppard please stand up?"

"How are you and Charles getting along?"

"As usual. He's good company, but, well, you know, light-weight. Can't really rely on him. He comes and goes. He reminds me of my cats. I think they like me, especially when I'm feeding them. I think Charles likes me, particularly on the occasions when he says he's forgotten his wallet and I pay to feed him."

"You're just bitter. He's a better friend than that."

"If you say so." Agatha suddenly felt weary. "How's your love life?"

"All right. I'm taking it slowly this time. No pressing her

for too many dates. No rushing her home to meet the parents."

"Good plan," said Agatha, who had met Bill's parents and thought they were enough to kill any budding romance. "Anyway, I think Charles has dropped out. I got a very good cheque for my PR work on that boot. Would you believe it? The boss, Mr. Piercey, thought for a bit that I had arranged the police arrival to give the whole thing maximum publicity."

"So what are you going to do today?"

"Oh, potter about. Got the ladies' society tonight. I thought I'd take a cake along."

"Not baking one, are you?"

"I might try. It can't be that difficult."

Agatha played safe, or thought she had, by buying one of those cake mixes which said, just add water. But the oven must have been too hot, for the chocolate cake she had intended to produce came out crisp on the outside and soggy and runny on the inside. She scraped it into the bin and then went next door to James's cottage to check his answering machine, but there were no messages. She sternly resisted going upstairs to bury her face in his pillow. All that did was bring savage waves of hurt. Any decent worries she might have about his brain tumour always seemed to get swamped out by feelings of rejection and loss.

She prepared herself carefully for the evening at the Carsely Ladies' Society, putting on a pretty summer dress with slits up each side to reveal what Agatha considered her last good feature, her legs.

When she sat in the vicarage garden, balancing a cup of tea and a plate with a wedge of cake, she listened with only half an ear to Carsely's unmarried mother, Miss Simms, read the minutes of the last meeting. Unmarried mothers in villages were hardly unusual, but Agatha always found it amusing that Miss Simms should have been elected secretary by this bunch of very conventional, middle-aged and middle-class ladies.

Mrs. Bloxby, who was now chairwoman—no PC rubbish about chairpersons in Carsely—rose to put forward the arrangements for the forthcoming village fête. For once, Agatha did not volunteer to do anything. She was tired of village affairs and felt she had done enough in the past.

The other women there did not cut her dead once the business part of the evening was over. But they would ask her if she had any word of her husband and then move quickly away. Only Miss Simms pulled up a chair next to Agatha and said, "Wouldn't you feel better doing something at the fête, dearie? I mean, we need someone for the tombola. Take your mind off things."

"The way I feel at the moment," said Agatha, "a village fête would be incapable of taking my mind off things."

Miss Simms tugged ineffectively at her short skirt, which was riding up over her lace-topped stockings. "Anything I can do to help?"

"I keep trying to find out what sort of person Melissa Sheppard really was."

"Bit of a tart, if you ask me."

"How come?"

"Went up to London with her a couple of months ago. I don't have a gentleman friend at the moment, and she says there's this singles' bar with good talent and why don't I come along. So I did. Well, it was really rough stuff, if you get me. I like my gents in suits and with their own car. We get tied up with three bikers, all leather and medallions, and Melissa, she says, 'We're all going back to Jake's place,' Jake being one of the blokes. I take her aside and say, 'What you on about, Liss? They're a bit common and there's three of them.' She'd drunk a bucketful, pretty quick, and she says, says she, 'The more the merrier.' So I got the hell out of there and had to find me way to Paddington and pay for me fare home, 'cos we'd come up in her car. I asked her later how she'd got on, and she says, 'Okay, and I didn't take you to be a Miss Prim,' so I never spoke to her again."

At last I'm getting somewhere, thought Agatha. "I'd like to speak to those bikers," she said. "Would you like to go to London with me and spot them for me? Did they seem like regulars?"

Miss Simms looked at her doubtfully from under a pair of improbably false eyelashes. "They did seem to be regulars, but . . ."

"Don't worry," said Agatha. "I'll pay for everything, even for your baby-sitter, and I'm not looking for a fellow."

"Right. You're on."

"What time did you turn up there before?"

" 'Bout nine in the evening."

"Right. We leave about seven. Should make it in good time. The rush-hour traffic should be thinning out by then."

Shortly after Agatha got home, the phone rang. It was Charles. "How's it going?" he asked.

Agatha, glad that he had not abandoned her after all, felt relieved and told him about the singles' bar.

"I'll come with you."

"Okay," said Agatha after a little hesitation. "It's a bit rough, so don't look too posh."

He laughed. "As if I could."

And he really believes that, thought Agatha. How odd.

FIVE

†

HAD London always been so dirty and shabby? wondered Agatha. Surely not. The singles' bar was off Piccadilly Circus, and not, as Agatha had guessed, in some dreary suburb. Certainly it was a hot summer which always gave the city a tired, exhausted air. Charles managed to find a space in an underground car-park a short walk from the bar.

Agatha was wearing a silk trouser-suit which had looked very sophisticated and smart in her bedroom mirror at home. But as they walked through the crowds, she noticed women wearing floaty summer dresses, or very short skirts and brief tops, and began to feel like a frump. She was wearing flat gold leather shoes and wished now she had worn heels. Miss Simms teetered along in very high heels and a skirt that verged on the indecent as she was showing her usual glimpses of stocking tops. Charles was dressed in a soft blue cotton shirt, chinos, and moccasins. Agatha felt she was the only one who didn't fit in with the cosmopolitan atmosphere.

Miss Simms' singles' bar turned out to be a disco called Stompers. "Are you sure this is the place?" asked Agatha. The young people trooping in ahead of them all looked trendily dressed.

"Yeah, this is it," said Miss Simms, clutching Charles's arm. "Not my sort of place."

Agatha paid the entrance fee and they went downstairs to a large room where couples gyrated under darting strobe lights. The music was loud, horrendously so. It beat upon their ear-drums and made conversation impossible.

They made their way to the bar and in a brief moment when the music ceased, Agatha said, "Do you see them?"

"Not yet," said Miss Simms. She hitched herself up on the bar-stool and the resultant display of lace stocking tops and frilly knickers meant that she was immediately asked to dance.

Agatha put her mouth to Charles's ear and shouted, "Waste of time."

As dance number followed dance number—hadn't they moved on from The Village People?—Agatha began to get angry. Miss Simms hadn't returned. This was not a singles' bar. It was a disco for young people. She was feeling hot and tired and deafened.

She was just about to shout to Charles to go and collect Miss Simms and get them out of the noise and into the fresh air when Miss Simms suddenly appeared in front of them accompanied by a burly young man. " 'Ere's one of them," she roared.

Charles took the young man aside and shouted something. Then he jerked his head at Agatha and they all made their way out of the club.

"Thank God for that," said Agatha, taking in great gulps of polluted air. "This here is Jake," said Miss Simms. "He was one of them that was with Melissa."

Jake did not look like a bit of rough stuff to Agatha. He was wearing a black T-shirt, black trousers and enormous boots, but he had a pleasant-enough face.

"What's all this about?" asked Jake when they had managed to get a table at a nearby pub. "I read she'd got topped. Nothing to do with me."

"The thing is," said Agatha, "my husband's missing and he's suspected of having committed the murder. I don't know what Melissa was really like. I mean, what did you make of her; what really happened?"

"Well, for a start, you can't tell with the lights in there and she was heavy made up, you see. When we got back to our flat, and I got a good look at her, I thought; blimey, I thought, I ain't reduced to screwing someone as old as my mum. Besides, she was as pissed as a newt. Must have been drinking a lot in the club."

"She was," interjected Miss Simms.

"So me and the others had a confab in the kitchen and my mates, that's Jerry and Wayne, they says, get rid of the old bird. So I go back in and tells her, 'You'll need to go, we've got a date later with our girl-friends.' She says she could teach us a few tricks, like we didn't know. Disgusting, it was." He grinned cheekily at Agatha. "Don't know what the older generation's coming to." Miss Simms giggled and sipped at a blue drink which seemed to be full of fruit and decorated with small paper umbrellas.

"Told her she wasn't on. No way. 'Get the hell out,' I said. She asks for a drink for the road, so I gives her one and goes into the kitchen to tell my mates I'll soon have her out and I go back and the old bird's passed out on the sofa. So we all carry her downstairs and sit her on the pavement with her back to the railings and then we all went back to the club. When we got back—oh, 'bout two in the morning—she'd gone."

Charles looked at Jake thoughtfully. "Let me get this straight," he said. "I can understand you mistaking her age and

81

going off with her, but why bring your mates along? Did you all mean to have her?"

"What sort of blokes do you think we are?" demanded Jake truculently.

"We're not the police," said Agatha, "and we're not interested in your motives. Can I tell you what I think? There's one thing I do know about Melissa and that is she was a fantasist. So what would get you all to go along? And I don't think any of you made a mistake about her age. Drugs! The silly cow probably told you she knew where to score."

"Do I look like a junkie?" demanded Jake.

"Come on, tell us," pleaded Agatha. "We won't go to the police. I just have to know how far she would go with lying."

"It's worth fifty pounds," said Charles suddenly.

Jake sat with his head down. Then he said, "How can I trust you?"

"Simply because we're not the police," said Charles. "You don't look like a junkie. So what was it? Pot?"

He shrugged and then said, "Yeah, that was it. Told us her lover was a dealer and she could get us the best Colombian. She said she would phone him from our place. When we gets there, she starts to come on to us, and I mean all of us. It was right disgusting. 'Phone your friend,' we says. She keeps saying, 'Later, let's have some fun.' So we leave her with the whisky bottle and have that confab in the kitchen and we decide she's lying and when we go back in, she's passed out, like I said, and so we leave her on the pavement, like I said. Silly old trout." He focused on Agatha. "I saw your picture in the newspapers. She was knocking off your old man, wasn't she?"

Agatha averted her eyes.

"Forget about that," said Charles. He turned to Miss Simms. "You didn't know anything about this?"

"No. You can't hear a thing in that club."

"What about my fifty pounds?" demanded Jake.

"Could you pay, Aggie?" said Charles. "I'm a bit short."

"I paid the entrance fees to that disco."

"I've got me cheque-book with me," said Miss Simms with all the misplaced generosity of the poor.

"No, that's all right." Charles stood up and took out his wallet. He peeled off notes and handed them to Jake. "Give him your card, Aggie. Ring us if you think of anything else, Jake."

"Right. I'm off then." Jake stood up and then looked down at Miss Simms. "I'm going back to the disco. You coming?"

"Certainly not," said Miss Simms primly. "I'm going home with my friends."

Miss Simms looked disapprovingly after Jake's retreating back. "Cheek!" she said. "I like my gentlemen to be more mature. In fact, Eddie's back again."

"Who's Eddie?" asked Agatha.

"He's the one before last," said Miss Simms. "Ever so nice. In bathroom fittings in Cheltenham. His wife's left him. Not for me. They never find out about me. I'm not a tart, like some I could mention. No, she left him for a man in surgical goods."

After they had deposited Miss Simms at her home, Agatha and Charles sat in the kitchen of Agatha's cottage and mulled over the little information they had. "You know what hurts?" said Agatha. "It's just that the more we find out about Melissa, the more horrible it seems that James had anything to do with her."

"I think men under sentence of death will do things they might not otherwise have contemplated. Then James was always a violently jealous man."

"James!"

"Yes, James."

"I never really thought of him as being jealous," said Agatha. "I was always so violently jealous myself."

"Agatha admits to a fault! Goodness me."

83

"Never mind that. What about this business of Melissa saying she had a lover who was a drug dealer?"

"That was sharp of you to guess about drugs. What put you on to that?"

"Just a wild guess. And all this nonsense of Miss Simms about rough trade. I mean, she's very genteel. I thought it would be a real dive, but it seemed a respectable Piccadilly disco. It wasn't even a singles' bar either. What took Melissa there?"

"Sex?"

"I don't know. I'm beginning to think she was a real murderee. I mean, those lads could have turned out to be dangerous. Anyway, to get back to the drug-dealer lover. If only that would turn out to be true. It would supply a motive."

"I can't believe in this drug dealer. If Melissa coerced Miss Simms into going up to London with her, maybe she got friendly with someone else in the village."

"She probably mistakenly picked on Miss Simms," said Agatha bitterly, "because she thought her morals were as loose as her own. No one else in the village fills that bill."

"There might be someone. I mean, on the face of it, Melissa was just the perfect village housewife, apart from her fling with James. You know, Aggie, we can't keep leaving James out of the equation."

"He didn't do it!"

"But he got involved in something that meant he was attacked and probably by the same person who killed Melissa."

"That might bring us back to the husbands. We never really got to talk to Mr. Dewey properly."

"Let's leave him alone for a bit," pleaded Charles. "Gosh, I'm tired. Mind if I stay the night?"

"You know where the spare room is."

"I'll get my bag out of the car."

Agatha watched him go, half amused, half exasperated. In the past, Charles had sometimes moved in with her. It was always because he was bored, or because the elderly aunt who lived with him had decided to hold a charity party and he wanted to stay out of the way until it was over. She knew that if Charles was courting some girl—for he was ever hopeful of getting married—he would disappear from her life for months. The fact that he never managed to secure any sort of lasting relationship Agatha put down to his being tight with money. Then, people who were tight with money were also inclined to be tight with emotions. Not much giving, emotionally or physically.

"What are you brooding about?" Agatha started. She had been so immersed in her thoughts, she had not heard Charles coming back into the kitchen.

"You," said Agatha.

He sat down and looked at her, amused. "What about me?"

"I was wondering why you never had a permanent girlfriend."

"And what do you think is the reason?"

"I think it's because you're mean about money. What woman is going to put up with someone who takes her out for dinner and forgets his wallet, or, in your case, pretends to forget it?"

"What a funny woman you are. That reminds me. You owe me half of that fifty quid."

The next morning Agatha arose late and to the smell of frying bacon. She was half-way down the stairs in her night-gown when she remembered that Charles was staying. She retreated up the stairs and quickly showered and dressed. When she went back down again, it was to find Charles eating breakfast and chatting to her cleaner, Doris Simpson.

Agatha and her cleaner were two of the few women of Carsely who called each other by their first names. "Hullo, Agatha," said Doris. "Just about to get started. If you're finished upstairs, I'll begin with the bedrooms. Late night?"

Her eyes slid from Charles to Agatha.

"A celibate late night," said Agatha firmly. "We've been up to London, trying to find out more about what a sort of person Melissa was."

"I cleaned for her, you know," said Doris, her voice muffled as she bent down to take out more cleaning material from a kitchen cupboard.

Agatha and Charles stared at each other. "Sit down, Doris," said Agatha. "I didn't know you cleaned for her. You didn't say anything."

Doris sat down reluctantly. "Didn't like to, given the circumstances. Didn't think you'd want to hear her name mentioned. And you've been looking so ill. I was right worried about you."

"We're trying to establish what sort of person Melissa was," said Charles. "You see, that way we might figure out why she was murdered."

"I don't know if I'm supposed to talk about this," said Doris. "It was all hush-hush. But, then, she's dead."

Agatha and Charles looked at her eagerly. "What do you mean, hush-hush?"

"She told me," said Doris, looking over her apron shoulder and dropping her voice to a whisper, "not to touch anything on her desk. She said she was working on a secret project for the government. I should've told the police."

Agatha sighed. "The one thing we have found out about Melissa was that she was a fantasist and a liar. But how long did you work for her?"

"Just a day a week."

"Until she died?"

"No, I quit before then."

"Why?"

Doris turned an uncomfortable red. "Do I have to tell you?"

"I think you'd better."

"I went along one morning. She wasn't around. She had

86

given me a key, so I got started. I thought I would do the bedrooms first."

She stared at Agatha.

Agatha sighed wearily. "You found her in bed with James."

"Yes."

"I gave her a piece of my mind and handed the key back and got out of there."

James, James, how could you, and with such a woman? mourned Agatha.

Aloud, she said, "Forget about that part, Doris, and the hush-hush business. What else did you think about her?"

"She was very fussy. She would check up on my work. I said if she wasn't satisfied, I'd quit, and she laughed and said that one time she used to have a lot of servants, butler and footmen and all that, and she was used to supervising and checking. Funny, I didn't believe her. I mean, no one outside a few and the Queen has servants like that these days. But I didn't think much about her one way or the other."

"Even though you believed she was working for the government?" asked Charles.

"I didn't think much about that. I mean, the Cotswolds are full of retired military people who like to hint they were in intelligence during the war. 'I worked for the little grey men of Whitehall, for my sins.' And then you find they had some sort of minor desk job. I thought maybe she was doing some typing for a local MP, something like that. But the reason I didn't tell the police was because she had made me promise not to tell anyone and there could have been some truth in it. I sometimes reckon I'm too cynical. You get that way cleaning houses. I'd better get on, Agatha."

When Doris had gone off upstairs, Agatha said, "Typing. I wonder what she was typing? Who inherits? We didn't ask Bill."

"Let's ask Mrs. Bloxby. Did Melissa have any children?"

"Don't know that either."

"So let's get along to the vicarage."

"After I've had something to eat. You might have made me some breakfast as well, Charles."

"You were asleep."

"Oh, I'll fix something."

Charles watched, amused, as Agatha took a packet of frozen curry out of the fridge and put it in the microwave. "You're surely not going to eat curry for breakfast?"

"Why not?"

Charles waited while Agatha took the curry out of the microwave when it was ready and ate the unappetizing-looking mess, accompanied by strong black coffee, with every appearance of enjoyment.

Then she lit up a cigarette. "Can I have one of those?" asked Charles.

Agatha gave him a steely look.

"Have you heard of enabling, Charles?"

"Sounds like therapy-speak."

"I mean you can buy your own. I may smoke but I do not encourage other people to do so, particularly when they show every sign of being able to do without it."

"You'll be a saint yet, Aggie. And talking of saints, let's go and see Mrs. Bloxby."

Mrs. Bloxby was watering the vicarage garden. "So many greenfly and aphids," she mourned. "It's these warm summers. Said on the radio it would be cooler today, that it would go down to about seventy degrees Fahrenheit. I never thought I'd live to see the day when seventy degrees in England was considered getting cooler."

"There's rain forecast," said Charles. "We're still on the hunt for Melissa's character."

Mrs. Bloxby turned off the hose and joined them at the garden table. "What have you found out?"

They told her all they knew. She listened carefully and then she said, "I've been thinking a lot about Mrs. Sheppard since I saw you last. My first impression of her, I remember, was that she was a psychopath."

"What!" exclaimed Agatha. "You mean like a serial killer!"

"No, no. There are different degrees of psychopathy. It was something about the eyes. She often had a blank fixed stare which reminded me of someone I once knew. I thought at the time I was being over-dramatic, but what you have told me seems to add up to the character of a certain sort of psychopath—the compulsive lying, the total lack of conscience. Also, looking back, I don't really think Mrs. Sheppard liked anyone at all."

"That's interesting," said Charles. "Why we came to see you was we wondered if anyone had inherited her cottage?"

"I heard through village gossip that she had not left a will and that there are no children."

"I would like to have a look inside," said Agatha. "I'd like to see what she was typing."

"It's probably at Mircester police headquarters in an evidence box."

"I'd still like to get inside that cottage."

"Mrs. Simpson cleaned for her. She may still have a key."

"She says she gave it back."

"Maybe I shouldn't tell you this," said Mrs. Bloxby, "but Mrs. Simpson was always worried about losing clients' keys and she once let slip that she always makes a copy."

"Bingo!" cried Agatha. "Come on, Charles. Let's go back and see Doris."

Doris Simpson insisted mulishly that she never would dream of copying her customers' keys, until Agatha shouted at her that they damn well knew she did. Doris said huffily that, well, perhaps she might still have a key to Melissa's cottage, and was promptly bundled into Agatha's car and driven to her home and asked to find it.

"I feel we're doing the wrong thing," said Charles, as they walked to Melissa's cottage.

"Why?"

"Because if Fred Griggs comes strolling past, we'll be in bad trouble if we're caught." Fred Griggs was the local policeman.

"Look," said Agatha as they parked outside. "No police tape. It's been removed. We can just say she borrowed something of mine and I wanted it back."

"And Fred will say, 'What's all this? Why didn't you ask the police?' "

"And I'll say that we know the police are too busy. Stop *worrying*, Charles."

They walked up to the cottage door. "See. It's just a simple Yale key," said Agatha, inserting it in the lock. "Anyone could break in."

"That awful dead smell is still hanging about," said Charles. "There's still fingerprint dust over everything. If we touch anything, Aggie, they'll have clear marks of our fingerprints. We haven't got gloves."

"We just look. If she was typing something, she'd need to have a desk. Not in the living-room. Maybe she used one of the bedrooms as an office."

They went up the stairs. "I don't like this," muttered Charles.

"Oh, do shut up. You're making me nervous. What could possibly happen?"

They gingerly pushed open doors: bathroom, a double bedroom, a box-room, linen cupboard; and then, finally, a small room containing a desk and a computer was revealed.

"This is it!" said Agatha excitedly. "Let's see what we've got."

Too eager to find clues to worry about fingerprints, she jerked open the desk drawers. "Nothing," she said. "Must all be still at Mircester."

"I hate to suggest this, but there might be something in the computer."

"Right!" Agatha sat down in front of the screen and switched it on. "Let's see what we have on file. Would you believe it? Just one file headed 'Chick-fic.' "

"Bring it up," said Charles. "She might have been writing a book. Chick-fic are those women's books, all shopping and bonking. You know, where everyone gets laid in Gucci and Armani."

Agatha moved the mouse. "Here we are. Plot."

They both read. "Bitch!" said Agatha. The plot concerned a beautiful and sophisticated woman who comes to live in a Cotswold village and falls in love with a handsome man who is married to a cold and domineering wife. The description of the man, although badly written, was definitely that of James.

"Is that supposed to be me?" demanded Agatha, stabbing a finger at the screen. Charles peered over her shoulder. " 'Mrs. Darcy,' " she read, " 'was a squat bullying woman with no dress sense and beady little eyes.' "

Charles stifled a laugh. "Surely not."

Agatha stiffened. "What's that? I heard something drawing up outside."

Charles looked out of the window. "It's a removal van and a woman getting out of a car who looks a bit like Melissa and around the same age. She must have had a sister. We've got to get out of here without her finding us." He jerked up the window and said over his shoulder to the stricken Agatha, "Shut that bloody computer off!"

He hung out the window. "There's a creeper. I'll go first and catch you if you fall."

Agatha switched off the machine and hitched a leg over the sill just as she heard the door opening downstairs. She edged down, clutching handfuls of creeper. She felt her tights rip.

"A bit more," she heard Charles whisper. The creeper gave

way and she tumbled into his arms and flattened him into a soft flower-bed.

"Come on," urged Charles as she rolled off him, panting. They scrambled up and ran to the bottom of the back garden, which was surrounded by a high wall. Charles pushed her up and she grabbed wildly at the top of the wall and, with a groan, heaved herself up until she was straddling the top of it. Underneath was a bed of nettles. She shut her eyes and jumped and then stifled her screams as she landed among the nettles.

Soon Charles joined her and they stood in the lane which ran along the back of the cottage.

"I'm stung all over," said Agatha. "What a mess I am. I'd better get home and put some ointment on."

"You do that," said Charles, "and I'll stroll round to the front of the cottage and chat her up."

"I'm coming with you."

"She'll wonder what you've been up to," said Charles. "You've got nettle stings all over your arms and legs. Your tights are torn and your blouse has green streaks on it from the creeper. I'm a bit dusty, but my clothes are dark. Go on, Aggie. I'll be along soon."

Agatha reluctantly started to walk home, but was less reluctant as she neared her cottage and felt the pain from the stings increasing.

Once inside her cottage, she went upstairs and stripped off her clothes, showered and covered her stings in anti-histamine cream. She donned clean underwear and a loose cotton dress, applied fresh make-up and went downstairs to wait for Charles.

She waited and waited and then, growing impatient, decided to walk up to Melissa's cottage and find out what was going on.

When she got there, removal men were carrying out furniture. "Where's the lady of the house?" asked Agatha.

"Gone off with some fellow to the pub for lunch," said the foreman.

Agatha swung round and headed for the Red Lion. She was very angry. Charles should have phoned her and asked her to join them.

Charles was sitting with a woman who bore a family resemblance to Melissa. Her hair was dark, probably the real colour of Melissa's hair, thought Agatha.

"I was waiting for you, Charles," said Agatha truculently.

"About to phone you," said Charles. "Just getting to know Julia here. Julia Fraser is Melissa's sister."

"Sorry to hear about your loss," said Agatha.

"Are you?" she said coolly. "I wasn't."

Agatha sat down. "Do you want something to eat?" asked Charles. "We're having egg and chips."

"That'll do," said Agatha. When Charles went to the bar to give her order, Agatha looked curiously at Julia. "So you didn't like your sister?"

"No."

"Why?"

"She was a lying bitch. She made a dead set for my husband and I told her I never wanted to see her again."

"Oh. But she left you everything in her will?"

"Yes, that was a surprise. I'm cleaning that cottage out and then I'm going to sell it."

So there had been a will! Mrs. Bloxby didn't know everything after all, thought Agatha with a certain degree of satisfaction.

"So who are you?" asked Julia.

"Sorry. I forgot to introduce myself," said Agatha as Charles came back to join them. "I'm Agatha Raisin."

"Poor you. I heard Melissa got her claws into your husband. Read a bit about it in the papers. Any word of . . . who is it?"

"James Lacey. No."

"Have you reverted to your maiden name?"

"No, I've always done business under the name of Raisin

93

and so I kept using it. Have you any idea who would have wanted to murder your sister?"

"Lots of people. Your husband, for one."

"He can't have done it. He was attacked and we think it was the same person who killed your sister."

"I can't think of anyone in particular. She was always trouble. Do you know, my father had her sectioned once?"

"No, what for?"

"She was in her late teens and she was on drugs."

Drugs again, thought Agatha.

"She was diagnosed as a psychopath. She was a compulsive liar and just didn't know right from wrong. She liked to get control of men and manipulate them. She was a bit of a chameleon. She would try to be everything she thought some man wanted her to be and they always fell for it and then soon found out their mistake, but she could never sustain an act for long. And it was never her fault. I was amazed that she'd actually gone to the trouble of making a will. She was the sort that thought she would live forever. I know I must sound hard. But she drove out any affection. When I heard she was dead, my first thought was one of relief. I hate to think there's some murderer out there, but on the other hand, she could drive people batty and she had a vicious tongue."

"Did you know her husbands, Sheppard and Dewey?"

Julia shook her head. She pushed away her barely touched plate of egg and chips. "I'd broken off relations with her ages ago. Look, thanks for the food and drink. But I'd better get back. No, don't move. I feel like a walk."

When she had gone, Agatha turned accusing eyes on Charles. "Why didn't you let me know you were both going to the pub?"

"I was getting on so well with her and I thought it would take you ages to clean yourself up."

"Well, don't try to cut me out again. That's what you were doing. Oh, Lord!"

"What?"

"That open window in the office. What if she reports it to the police?"

"I shut it. When I got there and we'd been chatting for a bit, I asked her if I could use the loo, and when I was upstairs I shut it."

"Clever you," said Agatha, mollified.

"So am I forgiven?"

"I suppose. Don't do it again. You know, all that stuff about Melissa being a psychopath makes it worse. There must be so many suspects and we haven't got a clue who did it."

"I don't know much about psychopaths. I thought they were people like Hannibal Lecter."

"When you've finished eating, we'll go home and look it up in the encyclopaedia."

After looking it up in the encyclopaedia and running reams of information off the Internet, Agatha groaned, "Why can't they use simple language?"

"It seems to me," said Charles, "as if psychopath was a sort of blanket diagnosis until fairly recently. It seems as if our Melissa, sectioned at a later date, would have been diagnosed as ha. ng ASPD, antisocial personality disorder. Here are some of the features, apart from not having a conscience: lack of empathy, inflated and arrogant self-appraisal, and glib, superficial charm. Tendency to be hooked on drink or drugs or both and . . . um . . ."

"What?"

"Never mind."

"What are you keeping from me?"

"Deviant sexual practices."

"I don't love James any more," said Agatha in a shaky voice.

95

"Not one bit. How could he even spend a minute with such a creature?"

"Never mind. Here we are knowing lots and lots about ASPD and not a bit nearer finding out who did it or where James is."

James Lacey was feeling strong and well. His headaches had gone. He now attended prayers and worked in the extensive vegetable gardens of the monastery. He felt a miracle had happened and that somehow his brain tumour had gone. But his counsellor, Brother Michael, knew nothing of this. He only heard of James's desire for a quiet religious life. He knew James had spent most of his years in the army. But James mentioned nothing of his marriage or what had made him flee. If any thoughts of Agatha entered his mind, he banished them quickly. He blamed the brain tumour on the mess of his old life. In the monastery, with its rigid discipline, it was rather like being in the army again. He intended to serve a period of probation and then join the order. Somehow, sometime in the future, he would tell Brother Michael the truth about his life. But not yet.

SIX

†

THE following day, Agatha said, "We've got to try Mr. Dewey again."

"We've only got to show our faces near his house and that damned woman will start shouting for the police."

"I don't think so. She's already made a fool of herself."

"Oh, really? I thought it was you who had made a fool of yourself, saying you had a gun."

"Never mind that. I paid Dewey a generous amount to repair his window. Let's try. I can't just sit here and worry about James."

"I thought you didn't love James any more."

"I just want to get my hands on him and give him a piece of my mind. Come on, Charles."

As they drove towards Worcester, Agatha said, "Now there's this new bypass, I miss seeing Broadway. I keep thinking I must turn off one day and see what the old place looks like."

"Tell you what. If we ever find out who did this murder, I'll treat you to dinner at the Lygon Arms." The Lygon Arms was Broadway's famous and expensive hotel.

"I wish you hadn't said that," remarked Agatha. "You promising me an expensive dinner makes me think you don't believe we'll find anyone."

"Oh, I'm sure we'll just blunder about in our usual way and unearth something."

They were approaching Evesham when Charles muttered something and pulled over by the side of the road and got out. "What's up?" asked Agatha when he got back in the car.

"Slow puncture. Anywhere around here can fix it?"

"Don't you have a spare?"

"No, I used that last year and forgot to get a new one."

"Well, if you go round that next roundabout and into the Four Pools Estate, there's a place called Motorways. They'll fix a new wheel in minutes."

By the time they parked at Motorways, the wheel was nearly flat. They sat down in the office and waited. A mechanic came in and said, "Your other tyres are nearly bald."

Agatha fixed Charles with a steely glare. "Do get all your tyres fixed. What if one blew out when we were speeding along some motorway?"

Charles said he would like all new tyres and one spare. "I like seeing you spending money," said Agatha with a grin.

The man behind the counter said, "The coffee in the machine over there is free, if you'd like some."

Charles brightened visibly, as if the thought of something free had allayed some of the dismay he had felt at having to shell out for new tyres.

Agatha sat nursing a cup of coffee and staring dreamily about her. It was funny, she thought, not for the first time, how one never got the city out of one's bones and how even industrial waste had a certain sort of comforting beauty. The rain had started to fall outside and she breathed in that old familiar smell of rain on hot dusty concrete. In the village, she was surrounded by flowers: lavender and hollyhocks, impatiens, roses, delphiniums, gladioli, and pansies, and yet she could still see beauty in willow-herb thrusting up out of the cracks in an industrial estate.

She was almost sorry when the car was pronounced ready. "Seriously, Charles," she said as he drove off, "how did you get to be so mean? It's not as if you're short of a bob."

"I suppose it all started with death duties," said Charles. "And my father had let the land go to rack and ruin. The farms weren't paying. It was a hard fight to turn things around, getting a good stockbroker so that money could make money. I couldn't bear to lose the house and land. I got used to economizing on everything I could and the habit's stuck, I'm afraid. I even took a diploma in agriculture and a course in bookkeeping so I could do the accounts and save the expense of an accountant. For a while I even opened the house to the public."

"Don't want to run down your home," said Agatha. "But it's a great Victorian pile, hardly an architectural gem."

"I invented a ghost," said Charles. "I engineered an occasion for dry ice to leak out through the walls of the library. Gave the visitors no end of a thrill. They used to come in coach-loads. But the minute I got solvent, I stopped the house tours. That stockbroker is a whiz. He made me a fortune."

"Mine's pretty good, too," said Agatha, and so they talked comfortably about stocks and shares until they reached the outskirts of Worcester.

"We may not be lucky enough to find him at home this time," said Agatha.

And this proved to be the case. No answer to the doorbell, but at least the Neighbourhood Watch woman was nowhere in sight.

"Let's try next door," said Charles. "I saw a curtain twitch."

"No, let's not," said Agatha hurriedly. "The neighbour

probably last saw us being carted off by the police. I saw a newspaper shop just outside the housing estate. They might know where he is. We forgot to ask him if he worked at anything."

The Pakistani shopkeeper volunteered the information that Mr. Dewey kept an antique shop in The Shambles opposite the back of Marks & Spencer in the centre of Worcester, and so they drove into the main car-park by the river, where swans sailed majestically up and down. The rain was quite heavy now. Charles produced a large golf umbrella from the boot of the car and under its shelter they walked up and across the main street and through to The Shambles.

It turned out to be a very small shop selling nothing but antique dolls. They stood for a moment looking in the window. "There's something scary about old dolls, I always think," said Charles. "All those watching eyes. I sometimes think a bit of the personality of each child who loved them is still there inside them."

They entered the dark shop and walked in. Mr. John Dewey was sitting at a small table at the back of the shop. He rose to meet them. "Oh, it's you again," he said.

"I hope you got my cheque," said Agatha.

"Yes, thanks."

"Our conversation was interrupted."

"I can't think of anything else to tell you. Do you mind if I go on working?"

He sat down at the table and picked up a large Edwardian doll with only one blue eye. "Just getting a new eye for her," he said. He had a tray of glass eyes in front of him. "It's a matter of getting just the right colour and the right size," he said.

"Ah, perhaps this." He picked out an eye and carried it to the window. "Mmm, I think this will do." He returned and sat down and held the doll on his lap. "Soon have you seeing the world again," he said. With one deft movement he removed the head. "I fix it from the inside," he said, looking up at them.

He looked so small and neat and absorbed in his work that Agatha blurted out, "How could you marry someone like Melissa?"

"I sometimes ask myself that," he said. "I'd never bothered much about the ladies before. But then she seemed to have such a knowledge of antique dolls. Wait, I'll show you something." He put down the doll he was working on and went into the back shop.

"He's *weird*," muttered Agatha. "If he comes back swinging a hammer, run for it."

"What made you think of a hammer?" asked Charles. "They never found a weapon."

"I always thought of a hammer, I don't know why."

Mr. Dewey came back carrying a doll. "This is my favourite. Eighteenth-century. Do you notice these old dolls often have human faces?"

The doll had a leather face and green eyes. The hair was powdered and the dress was panniered silk. Agatha looked at it uneasily. She thought the doll had a mocking, knowing look. "What's this doll got to do with Melissa?"

"Everything. We had been talking in the shop for a few weeks and then we occasionally had lunch, always talking about dolls. Then she said she had two tickets to a fancy dress ball in the town hall and would I come? I was very shy and said I didn't dance, but she said it would be fun to dress up and watch the costumes."

"What did you go as?" asked Agatha.

"I went as Blackbeard, the pirate," he said. Agatha tried not to laugh, he looked so neat and prim, cradling the doll in his arms. "I said I would meet her there. It's only a short walk from here to the town hall. I must say, I felt quite different in my costume. I even swaggered a bit. When I got there, I looked around for her and what I saw first was not Melissa but this doll, my precious. She had copied this gown and had her hair powdered. I fell in love on the spot. I was dazed. I asked her to marry me before the evening was over." He sighed.

"And how did the marriage break down?"

"As soon as we were wed, she stopped talking about dolls, showed no interest in them. And she wouldn't ever wear the dress again. I asked her to wear it in the house, just for me, but she wouldn't. She seemed to have become a different person, hard and brittle. I immersed myself in my work. But I wanted to save our marriage. It had been dragging on in a terrible way for over three years. I pleaded with her one more time to wear the dress and she said, 'That's it!' and she got a pair of kitchen scissors and she said she was going to cut my favourite doll to ribbons.

"My heart was beating fit to burst but I forced myself to speak in a calm and reasonable voice. I told her she didn't have a key to the shop, that the metal shutters were down over the window and door and the burglar alarm set. I told her I would never ask her to wear the dress again. I told her to sit and I would fix her a drink. She drank a lot. I said I would mix her a special cocktail. I did. I opened up several of my sleeping pills and mixed up some concoction from the cocktail cabinet. I remember her eyes were hard and glittering as she drank it down. When she passed out, I tied her arms and legs very firmly. With wire."

Agatha moved close to Charles.

"When she recovered, I said I was going to take her eyes out and replace them with doll's eyes. Did I say I had gagged her as well? No? Well, I did. I told her I wanted a divorce, I wanted her to leave immediately. I told her to nod her head if she agreed. She nodded. I wanted to frighten her so much, you see, that not only would she leave me and divorce me, but that she would not attack me when I released her. As soon as she was free, she packed and left."

Agatha looked at him, her eyes gleaming. "But you must have still loved her."

"Why?"

"You learned somehow that she was having an affair with my husband, so you attacked him first, but he escaped, and you then killed Melissa."

He gave a gentle little laugh. He did not seem at all upset by Agatha's accusations. "I am not a violent man. Oh, if you could have felt the relief I felt when she had gone. Did I say I could not dance? I meant, I was too shy to dance. But when she had gone, I waltzed around the house." He took the doll's tiny hand in his and waltzed round the shop.

Just then a customer walked in and he stopped dancing. "I will be with you in a minute," he said. He retreated to the back shop with his doll.

"Let's get out of here," muttered Agatha.

They walked outside. The rain had stopped and patches of pale-blue sky were appearing among the ragged grey clouds far above them.

"We should tell Bill about this," said Charles.

"Phew!" Agatha clutched his arm. "I could use a drink."

They went into a pub. Agatha asked for gin and tonic and Charles had an orange juice. "Didn't Bill say he had an alibi?" asked Agatha.

"No, he said Sheppard had an alibi. He didn't say anything about Dewey and we didn't ask. I think we should tell him this. The man's mad."

Agatha took out her mobile phone. But she was told when she dialled police headquarters in Mircester that Bill had gone home.

"I hate seeing him at home," mourned Agatha. "Those parents of his!"

"We'd better try anyway. Drink up!"

The Wongs lived in a builder's estate much like the one inhabited by Mr. Dewey. Bill's father was Hong Kong Chinese, and his mother, from Gloucestershire. Mrs. Wong opened the door. She stared at them and then shouted over her shoulder, "Father, it's that woman again!"

She was joined by Mr. Wong, who shuffled forward in a pair of carpet slippers. "May we speak to Bill?" asked Agatha. "It's very important."

"You should've phoned first to make an appointment." He stood in the doorway with his wife at his side and neither of them showed any signs of moving. How could Bill ever hope to get married, thought Agatha, living as he did with these possessive parents?

She suddenly shouted, "Bill!" at the top of her voice, and was relieved to hear his answering voice, "Agatha?"

Reluctantly his parents backed away from the doorway and then Bill stood there, beaming. "Come in, come in. Perhaps we could all have some tea, Ma?"

"I'm not making tea for nobody," grumbled his mother.

"Can we go into the garden, maybe?" suggested Agatha. "We've got some news that might interest you."

"Sure." Bill led the way through the house into the garden at the back, which was his pride and joy. They sat down at a garden table surrounded by a riot of flowers.

"What have you got for me?"

Agatha described John Dewey and then related the story of his marriage, ending up with asking, "Did he have an alibi?"

"There are witnesses to testify that he was working late in his shop the night Melissa was killed, and that Neighbourhood Watch woman saw him returning home around midnight. Of course, we can't pin-point the exact time of death. He could easily have driven over to Carsely. We'll keep an eye on him. Anything else?"

Agatha told him about the visit to the disco, about learning that Melissa at one time had been sectioned for a drug addiction and diagnosed as a psychopath. Then she said, "Of course, there is the other husband, Sheppard."

"But Luke Sheppard and his wife spent that night at the Randolph in Oxford."

"Still, that's not far. He could have driven to Carsely, done the deed, and driven back. It takes about three quarters of an hour to get to Oxford. Half an hour if someone broke the speed limit."

"We checked. The night staff didn't see him leave."

"It's impossible," groaned Agatha. "It could well be someone from way back in her past. She told my cleaner she was engaged on secret work for the government. Now I know that's another of her lies, but what prompted that lie? Could she have been tied up with some MP or army man?"

"Like James?" suggested Bill, and then regretted saying it as a haunted look appeared in Agatha's eyes.

"Is there no word of him, Bill?"

"Not a thing. We regularly check to see if he's drawn any money, but there's nothing. Look, why don't you stay here and relax and then we'll all have dinner."

Agatha repressed a shudder. His mother was a dreadful cook and his parents would grumble about their presence all through the meal. She was always amazed that Bill could not see how awful they were, but he obviously adored his father and mother and could see no fault in them. "No, thanks," she said. "We'd better get on."

"Thanks anyway for your news. We may pull in Dewey for questioning again. If he could tie her up like that and threaten to take her eyes out, then he could easily have killed her."

"Where to now?" asked Charles. "Call it a day and go for dinner?"

"I'm tired. But we could just catch Luke Sheppard again before he closes his shop."

"And what can we ask him we haven't asked him already?"

"We could tell him about Dewey. I mean, ask if he'd ever met Dewey. Ask him whether Dewey ever called on Melissa."

"All right," said Charles amiably. "We'll give it a try."

Agatha looked at him with a sudden burst of affection. "I don't know what I would do without you, Charles!"

His face took on a tight, closed look. Damn, though Agatha. Rule number one. Never tell a man you need him. In a moment or two, he'll tell me he wants to go home and pack. But to her surprise, he drove steadily and said nothing until they drove into the main car-park at Mircester.

"I feel our Sheppard is a bad-tempered man," said Charles. "Let's hope he doesn't exercise it on us."

"You could buy something," suggested Agatha. "That would put him in a good mood."

"From that shop? You must be joking."

"A thought, that's all." As they walked along the street where Sheppard's shop was situated, they saw him outside, pulling down the shutters. They quickened their step and came up to him. "Oh, it's you pair," he said ungraciously.

"We wondered if you could spare us a minute," said Agatha.

"Okay, but a minute is all I've got. Let's go to the pub."

Once inside, Agatha asked him what he wanted to drink, not wanting Charles to start on one of his tales about a missing wallet.

She carried the drinks over to the table. She had bought an orange juice for herself as well as Charles. She would offer to drive them home.

Agatha told Luke Sheppard about their meeting with John Dewey and then asked him, "Did Melissa ever talk about her previous marriage? Or did Dewey ever try to see her?"

"She said he was weird. She said he loved his dolls more than humans. But she didn't volunteer much else except it was one marriage she was glad to get out of."

Agatha was disappointed. "She didn't say anything about being frightened of him?"

"No, I saw him once. Curiosity, you know. I went to that shop of his. Insignificant little chap, if you ask me. Wouldn't hurt a fly. She didn't have any trouble divorcing him."

Charles said, "But he forced her into a divorce. Didn't she tell you?"

He looked genuinely surprised. "No, she told me he had agreed to the divorce without a murmur."

"Here's what really happened," said Agatha, and told him about Dewey's drugging Melissa and threatening her.

He goggled at her. "She never said a word. But she was secretive. She had a lot of money of her own. But she never discussed it with me. She kept her bank-books and bank papers locked up. Mind you, that didn't bother me much. I wanted rid of her after the honeymoon."

"What happened on the honeymoon?" asked Agatha eagerly.

He glanced impatiently at his watch. "I'll make it quick. It was like this. We went to Paris. It was August and there weren't many French people around. All gone off on the annual holiday. She was a great know-all. Had memorized the guidebook. We trudged round everywhere—Notre Dame, Versailles, Sacre Coeur—you name it. I don't speak French. She said she spoke it like a native. I said, 'How come then the natives don't understand a word you're saying'? She'd dropped the act of hanging on my every word, being the perfect partner. She demanded attention the whole time and not only from me, from about every man who crossed her path. I often wondered how she would get on in a roomful of men with different personalities, trying to be all things to all of them. I'm telling you, by the time we got back, I *detested* that woman."

"So how did you get her to agree to a divorce?"

He looked again at his watch. "I've really got to go."

"Quickly," said Agatha. "Did you ask for a divorce and did she agree to it just like that?"

"Yes, something like that." He got to his feet. "See here, I've given you pair enough of my time. Don't come round here again."

"Where were you living when you were married?" asked Charles.

He half-turned. "Why?"

"Just wondered."

"Oxford."

"Where in Oxford?"

"Jericho. Pliny Road."

He marched out of the pub.

"What did you make of that?" asked Charles.

"I think," said Agatha, resting her chin on her hands, "that he threatened her just like Dewey."

"I think you're right. That's why I asked for his old address."

"Why?"

"Because we will go there tomorrow and ask the neighbours about Sheppard and Melissa. I wonder, why Oxford? It's an hour-and-a-half's drive at least from Oxford to Mircester."

"We should have asked Melissa's sister more questions."

"We can still do that. I've got her card. She lives in Cambridge. The other university town."

"Do we need to go all the way there? It's quite a drive."

"Maybe we'll phone her. Let's get out of here and have some dinner."

"Come home and I'll make us something."

"Anyone who eats microwaved curry for breakfast is not to be trusted with dinner. Plenty of good restaurants in Mircester."

A wave of black depression hit Agatha as soon as she awoke the following morning. She had been dreaming about James, and in her dream they had been walking along a sunlit beach together and he had been holding her hand. Where was he? Was he alive? Did he ever think of her? Why was she going to all this trouble to clear his name?

She mumbled that thought to Charles when he came into her bedroom, demanding to know why she wasn't getting up.

"Because we are out to clear your name as well, sweetie. Or had you forgotten? Your alibi is only for the evening James disappeared. You've got nothing to prove your innocence when it comes to Melissa's murder."

"Can you bring me up a cup of coffee?"

"No, you'll drink it and lie in bed and smoke and gloom. Come downstairs."

Agatha climbed out of bed. Her knees were stiff and she stared down at them. Here was another bit of body betraying her. She did some exercises and took a hot shower. By the time she had dressed, the stiffness had gone. But, she wondered, was this the beginning of the end? Good-bye healthy life and hullo rubber knickers and support hose? What would it be like to creak about on a Zimmer frame? She had a sudden craving for life, for excitement. She had an impulse to ask Charles to go upstairs to bed with her that minute. Then she thought, was this how James felt? If I can feel like this over a brief ache in the knees, what did he feel like when he learned he might die? He should have been making his peace with God, she answered herself. Would you? sneered a little voice in her head. Agatha slowly shook her head. The God she only half believed in had shaggy grey locks and wore open-toed sandals and disapproved of one Agatha Raisin.

"Agatha! Why are you standing there shaking your head and moving your lips?" asked Charles.

Agatha gave herself a mental shake. "I just wondered what thoughts were going through James's head when he learned of his cancer."

"Doesn't bear thinking of. I've made toast and coffee. Eat. Drink. Then let's get off to Oxford."

As they drove to Oxford, Agatha driving this time, she switched on the air-conditioning in the car. "The sun's so hot," she said. "Going to be one very hot day."

"Watch out for the speed camera just after Blenheim Palace," said Charles as Agatha drove through Woodstock. "You just get used to the camera facing one way, and then they come and turn it the other way and catch all the drivers who increase speed when they think they are safely past it."

"I never speed through towns or villages," said Agatha virtuously. A car ahead of her, unaware that the camera had turned, went slowly past it and then speeded up. There was a bright flash as he was photographed. "See what I mean?" said Charles with all the satisfaction of one motorist seeing another getting caught by a speed camera.

"I was thinking, Charles, that we have all these suspects whirling around our brains. Well, maybe two suspects, Sheppard and Dewey."

"Three."

"Who's the third?"

"Her sister. She inherits. Maybe she knew she was going to inherit. Melissa, it seems, had money of her own."

"Yes, but where does James come into it?"

"I'd forgotten about him."

"Why would the sister attack James?"

"We don't know what James was up to. Remember, he was like you when it came to trying to find out things."

"So three suspects . . ."

"Maybe more. What about Jake and his pals? No one's going to bother much about a bit of pot these days. But remember, Melissa had once been sectioned for drugs. Maybe she wanted some hard stuff and they were pushing."

"All possible. But we can't go to Bill with mere speculation. I can see both Sheppard and Dewey doing it, but I really can't think of a motive. They were both clear of her."

"Who knows? Maybe Melissa paid a visit to Dewey's shop and spat on his favourite doll."

"Which brings us back to where James came into it."

Charles groaned. "Okay, let's see if we can find out anything about Melissa and Sheppard when they were married that he hasn't told us. I mean, it took nearly a year for the divorce to come through, so he didn't start divorce proceedings immediately after the honeymoon."

"It's a pity we didn't get the number in Pliny Road. I don't know whereabouts in Jericho it is. I'll pull into the lay-by and have a look at the map. You'll find a street map of Oxford in the glove compartment. Jericho's that residential area between the Woodstock Road, Saint Giles' and the canal."

"I know," said Charles as Agatha drew the car to a stop. They spread out the map. "Let's see the index," said Charles. "Ah, here we are: Pliny Road, off Walton Street, just there."

"Doesn't look very long," said Agatha. "We'll just knock on doors."

"While we're in Oxford," said Charles, "do you think there's any point in asking questions at the Randolph? Maybe one of the staff saw something."

Agatha shook her head. "I've a feeling the police will have covered that thoroughly."

"Still . . . let's see how we get on in Jericho first."

"I hope the traffic's not too bad," said Agatha. "They've made Cornmarket a shopping precinct and for a while it's been chaos."

"Seems clear enough," said Charles as they drove along the Woodstock Road. He studied the map again. "Turn next right, Aggie."

"I thought for a while you'd given up calling me Aggie. I wish you wouldn't. Every time you call me Aggie, I feel as if I ought to be standing at the doorway of a terraced house in a mining area in some northern town with my hair in rollers, wearing a chenille dressing-gown and fluffy slippers, and with a cigarette stuck in my mouth."

"Sounds like you."

"I'm driving or I'd hit you. Where now?"

"Turn right on Walton Street and next left."

"It's residents' parking only."

"So risk it."

Agatha parked in Pliny Road, and they got out. Tall Victorian houses lined either side of the road. "Where should we start?" she asked.

"Let's try the middle, although sod's law probably has it that they lived at the end. You take the left side and I'll take the right."

After ringing several doorbells, Agatha began to wonder if she was going to have any success. Perhaps Oxford was like London and people didn't know their neighbours.

Then she heard a shout from across the road and turned round to find Charles waving to her. He came to meet her. "A woman in that house," he said, jerking a thumb over his shoulder, "remembers them, because she sometimes chatted to Melissa at the corner shop. They lived at number fifteen."

Number 15 had a poster for the Green Party in the window. Agatha rang the bell. A thin woman with an arrogant face answered the door. She was wearing a long red dress of Indian cotton and vinyl sandals. She was very tall. "What is it?" she demanded. A waft of incense floated out of the house.

"I am Agatha Raisin," said Agatha. "I am anxious to find out what I can about the Sheppards. Did you buy the house from them?"

"I don't like reporters. If you ask me, the capitalist press is the ruin of this country."

"I am not a reporter," said Agatha. "You see . . ."

Charles moved forward and smiled pleasantly. "I am Sir Charles Fraith. Haven't we met before?"

The change in her was almost ludicrous. "I d-don't think . . . Oh, *do* come in, Sir Charles."

"How kind," murmured Charles. Agatha followed him, muttering, "Snobby cow," under her breath.

"I'm Felicity Banks-James," their new hostess trilled over her shoulder as she led them down to the basement and into a kitchen which looked as if it had been taken straight from one of those photos in glossy magazines urging you to try "a French provincial kitchen look." Bunches of dusty herbs hung from the ceiling. A brace of pheasant hung from a hook near the cooker, which Agatha gleefully recognized as being stuffed, the kind the taxidermist in Ebrington sold to yuppies. Huge copper pans lined one dresser, looking as if they had never been used. An enormous scrubbed table surrounded by plain wooden chairs dominated the centre of the room. On another dresser, blue-and-white plates stood in rows, also looking as if they had never been used, to judge from the film of dust covering them. A pile of Marks & Spencer's frozen dinners was stacked on a corner of the table. "Just got back from shopping," she said, opening a giant fridge and hiding the evidence of un-chic microwave cooking. "Coffee?"

"That would be nice," said Charles, beaming at her.

"It's decaf. I do think caffeine is so . . . *What are you doing?*"

"Sorry," mumbled Agatha, stuffing her packet of cigarettes back into her handbag.

"Decaf will be all right," said Charles quickly. "What a charming house you do have. You did buy it from the Sheppards?"

"Yes, he wanted to sell me the furnishings as well. Oh, my dear, ghastly three-piece suites, horrible paintings, the kind Boots used to sell, I don't know if they still do. You know, that woman with the green face and waves on the shore and little kiddies and puppies. They even had a fuzzy pink toilet tidy in the bathroom. Ugh. 'Get it all out before I faint,' that's what I told him. Then I had to rip up all their nasty fitted carpets. And then I found in a suitcase in the basement . . . Well, you'll never believe it."

"A body?" asked Agatha sourly.

She ignored her and said to Charles. "It was a *fox* coat!"

"What horror!" said Charles, accepting a green mug of coffee.

"Exactly. To think of all the effort I and my friends have

gone to, to sabotage the hunt. I phoned up Sheppard. He's a *shop-keeper*, gents' outfitting, how quaint. She, that woman who was killed, Melissa, it was she who came to collect it."

"Mrs. Banks-James—" began Charles.

"Oh, do call me Felicity, Sir Charles."

"Just Charles will do. Felicity, what did you make of her?"

Agatha and Charles had seated themselves at either side of the table. Felicity sat down beside Charles and went on as if Agatha weren't there.

"Came as a shock, actually."

"In what way?"

Agatha stood up abruptly. "Do you mind if I go out into your backyard there and have a smoke?"

"Be my guest," said Felicity, not taking her eyes off Charles.

Agatha stumped off. Felicity waited until the door had closed and murmured, "What a grumpy woman, if you don't mind my saying so, Charles. Not exactly one of us."

Charles bit back the remark he was about to make, which was, "What do you mean, one of us, you pretentious raddled bitch?"

Instead he said mildly, "You were saying you were surprised about Melissa."

"Well, my dear, after all that *ghastly* furnishing, she was not what I expected at all. She was very pleasant-looking and very smartly dressed. After introducing herself, she said, 'I've come to rid you of that horrible coat.' You could have knocked me down with a feather. She said he had bought it for her and she couldn't bear to wear it without crying when she thought of all those dead little foxes. We had a long chat. She said she was so glad to be free of him. And then she began to cry and she said it had been a nightmare. After she had pulled herself together, I said I was surprised that such a sensitive person—I am very sensitive myself, some people say I am psychic—would have such furnishings, and she said he had chosen it all himself. She said he *beat* her. I told her to take him to court, but she said now that she was free, she just wanted peace and quiet. She promised to come out with the hunt saboteurs and left me a phone number, but when I tried it, it didn't exist. She was so upset, she must have made a mistake. So I phoned Sheppard and asked him if he knew his ex-wife's phone number and he snarled, 'Get lost,' and slammed the phone down. He did it, mark my words.

"Oh, Agatha Raisin! That's the woman whose husband is missing. Poor her. No wonder she looks so fierce."

"We really must be going," said Charles. He felt he had suffered enough of Felicity's company.

"Oh, must you . . . ?" she began but Charles was walking to the kitchen door, which he jerked open and said, "Come on, Aggie."

Felicity led the way up the stairs. "Charles, dear," she cooed, "do give me your phone number and we can have a further chat about poor Melissa."

"I'm living with Agatha at the moment," said Charles smoothly.

"And my phone's been disconnected," said Agatha. "Come along, Charles."

"Right with you, dear heart. 'Bye, Felicity." Charles trotted after Agatha and muttered to her, "Back to the car."

He repeated everything Felicity had said, doing a very good impression of Felicity's voice until Agatha was helpless with laughter. After she had recovered, she said, "I bet you Melissa did furnish that house. She was doing her chameleon bit, changing to suit whoever she was with. I bet she wore that fur coat as soon as she could. She probably hid it in the basement so that Luke Sheppard wouldn't give it to his new wife."

"We'll wait here for a bit and then, when we're sure Felicity isn't looking, we'll try the neighbours. I feel we're getting somewhere at last."

"I wonder what it would be like to live in a street like this," mused Agatha. "So peaceful."

"Lot of car crime in Oxford. You'd probably lose that expensive radio that you've got in yours and never play. Why don't you play it?"

"I like popular music when I'm driving, but the BBC's going in for disc jockeys, particularly in the afternoon, who shout at you in estuary English, talk too much and sometimes sing along with the records."

"Get your head down! Felicity's coming out."

They both crouched down in the front seat.

After a few moments, Agatha whispered, "I'm getting cramp. Has she gone?"

"Wait a bit longer."

Agatha counted to ten, then twenty. She had nearly reached thirty when Charles said, "All clear."

"Ooof!" Agatha straightened up with a groan.

"Let's go. I think I saw someone behind the curtains in that house to the right of Felicity's."

They walked down the street, keeping a careful look-out in case Felicity should come hurrying back. They mounted the steps to the neighbour's door and rang the bell. A thin, stooped man opened the door.

Agatha went through the introductions and the reason for their visit. "Come in," he said. "I am William Dalrymple. I'll tell you what I know, but it isn't much. Can I offer you something?"

"No, we're all right," said Agatha. He ushered them into a pleasant sitting-room on the first floor. It was lined with bookshelves. There was a desk by the window overlooking the garden, piled high with books and papers.

"Do you teach at the university?" asked Agatha.

"Yes, history."

How James would have loved to meet him, thought Agatha. James, where are you?

They sat down. "What precisely do you want to know?" asked William.

"We want to know," said Agatha, "if you met Melissa Sheppard. What impression did you get of her, and were there any rows?"

"I can't help you about the rows, because the walls of these houses are very thick. But Melissa called round several times until I told her not to."

"Tell us about it," said Charles.

"Shortly after they had moved in, Melissa came round and asked if she could borrow a screwdriver. I invited her in and went to look for one. When I came back, she had taken one of my books off the shelf, Arthur Bryant's *Age of Elegance*, and was reading it. She asked if she could borrow it. I warned her that I thought it was in places a rather glamorized version of early-nineteenth-century history. She said she liked glamorous things and flirted a bit. I am an old bachelor and I must confess I was flattered. But I sent her on her way with book and screwdriver.

"She came back a few days later to return them. She said she had found the book fascinating, and asked if I had anything on Marie Antoinette. I realized then that she probably was only interested in history in the Hollywood sense—you know, Joan of Arc, Mary Queen of Scots, that sort of thing. I said I didn't have what she wanted but I was sure Blackwell's could find her something. She began to talk about herself. She said she believed in reincarnation and was sure she had been Josephine—you know, Napolean's missus, in a previous life. I said it was amazing how people who believed in reincarnation always believed they had been someone important in a previous life, like Cleopatra or someone; I mean, never a scullery maid. We were both sitting on the sofa and she put a hand on my knee and said, 'Oh, William, can you see me as a scullery maid?' I removed her hand and said rather testily that I had a paper to prepare. I thought that would be the end of it. But she came back one more time.

"It was late at night. I heard the bell ringing and ringing. I opened the door and she flung herself into my arms and said her husband did not love her and could she stay with me.

"I thrust her away and told her never to call on me again. I slammed the door in her face. I thought she was mad. I mean, look at me! I've never been the sort of man that women go for."

Agatha, looking at his gentle face, his droopy cardigan, and his other-worldly air, thought that before Melissa threw herself at him, there had probably been many approaches made to him which he had not even noticed.

"It's all I can tell you," said William. "Except I was not surprised to read of her murder. She was intensely narcissistic."

"Do you happen to know if she was friendly with anyone else in the street?" asked Charles.

"She did say during her mad reasoning on incarnation that a Mrs. Ellersby at number twenty-five shared her views."

"Right, we'll try her."

Agatha felt suddenly weary of the whole thing. She would have liked to stay longer in William's pleasant sitting-room. "I was sorry to hear about your missing husband," said William as he walked them to the door. He gave Agatha an awkward pat on the back. "Don't worry. I always feel that no news is good news. Live people can hide, dead people usually get found."

When Agatha and Charles had said good-bye to William and were walking down the street, Agatha suddenly said, "But why would James want to hide from me?"

"Guilt," said Charles. "Guilt about his fling with Melissa. Let's go and talk to the dotty Mrs. Ellersby."

SEVEN

†

MRS. Ellersby looked perfectly sane when she answered the door to them. She had grey hair worn curled and shoulder-length, thick glasses, and a face where all the wrinkles seemed to run downwards to a turtle-neck. Agatha surreptitiously felt her own neck and mentally planned to visit her beautician soon.

After introductions and explanations, she led them down to her kitchen. These tall Victorian houses, thought Charles, would once have had maids and a cook. Now the residents, if they were lucky, made do with a cleaning woman. The kitchen was neither pretentious nor weird. Fittings, thought Agatha, casting an expert eye around, by Smallbone of Devizes. Must have money.

"So you want to know about Melissa?" said Mrs. Ellersby. "Before we start, can I get you anything? Tea? Coffee?"

Both shook their heads. "I met Melissa at a class on Buddhism. I was very taken with her. So full of energy. So anxious to learn all she could. I lent her my books on the subject and we had interesting discussions."

"Where is this class?" asked Charles.

"It's been disbanded. So sad. It was in a church hall in Saint Giles'."

"So you found Melissa a perfectly nice person?" asked Agatha.

"At first. Then I was disappointed."

"Why?"

"She turned out to be rather silly. She was interested in re-incarnation. But only because she was sure she had been someone famous in a previous life. You see, at the beginning, she would listen to me as if she was fascinated by everything I had to tell her, and I must admit I was flattered. When I really got to know her, I was startled that I had not previously for a moment guessed at the sheer shallowness of her brain. She appeared to have a fixation that she had been the Empress Josephine in a previous life."

"Did she ever talk about her husband?"

"Not to me. She talked about herself as Josephine, saying that Napoleon had given her a hard time and on occasions beat her up. I must say, I wondered if she might be referring obliquely to her own husband. I did not like him one bit."

"Did you know him?" asked Agatha.

"Oh, yes. I had a party and I felt obliged to invite both of them. I had gone off Melissa, but she was still so friendly, I felt trapped. How can you say to someone, 'I wish I had never be-friended you'? I had invited some friends. The Sheppards behaved very badly. She kept making pointed little jokes at his expense. You know, that awful type of married woman who humiliates her husband in public. He drank too much, and then he suddenly shouted at her in front of everyone, 'I must have been mad to marry you.' I decided after that to have nothing more to do with her. The next time she called, I hid downstairs in the kitchen, waiting for her to go away. But she must have walked down the steps at the front of the house. I was sitting at the kitchen table, holding a cup of coffee. I looked up and saw her face pressed to the glass. We stared at each other for a long time. Then she went away and I never saw her again."

"Do you think Sheppard could have murdered her?" asked Charles.

"Oh, easily," said Mrs. Ellersby. She turned her mild, myopic gaze on Agatha. "But your husband was attacked, was he not? I can imagine Sheppard attacking her, but not anyone else."

"But my husband had been having an affair with Melissa," said Agatha through gritted teeth.

"I read about that. But she was divorced. It would take a very jealous man to do that, and it is my opinion that Sheppard hated her so much, he would probably be sorry for any man who became involved with her. Do not think too badly of your husband, Mrs. Raisin. You must wonder how he could ever have become involved with such a person. But she had great charm when one first met her. She exuded enthusiasm and energy and warmth. I've always prided myself on being a great judge of character, and yet I was initially taken in by her very easily."

"Thank you," said Agatha. "I needed to hear that."

"Is there any news of your husband? I gather from the newspapers that he was ill."

"Yes, he had a cancerous tumour," said Agatha, "but the police have checked all the hospitals. He took his passport with him, but there is no record of him having left the country."

"Which hospital was he being treated at?"

Agatha looked at her and frowned. "I don't think he had started his treatment."

"But he knew he had a tumour, so he would need to be diagnosed."

"It would be Mircester General Hospital."

"Perhaps if you ask there, you can find out perhaps how bad

the tumour was, or if he let slip any of his plans. A lot of people are terrified at the idea of chemotherapy. He may have said something to his doctor."

"I never thought of that," said Agatha eagerly. "We can try there."

They said good-bye to Mrs. Ellersby. "I'm hungry," complained Charles, "and I'm not dashing off to Mircester and neither are you. Let's leave the car where it is and walk up to Brown's on Saint Giles' and eat hamburgers."

"All right," said Agatha. "I'm suddenly weary."

Brown's, as usual, was very busy, but they got a table in the smoking section after only a ten-minute wait. "So many young people," said Charles when they were seated. "Doesn't it make you feel old, Aggie?"

The honest answer to that was that she had been feeling old all day, but Agatha only grunted by way of reply.

Charles ordered two hamburgers and a bottle of wine. "I'm driving," said Agatha.

"So you are. All the more for me."

"I would have thought something plebeian like beer would go better with hamburger and chips."

"You're only saying that because you can't have any."

"I can have a glass. That's below the limit."

"Cripes! Look over there. No, don't stare. Do it casually. The table over in the corner on your left."

Agatha took a covert look.

Then she turned back and hissed, "By all that's holy, it's Sheppard and his would-be child bride."

"Wonder what they're doing back in Oxford?"

"Probably just in for a meal," said Agatha. "James and I often drove into Oxford for a meal. Do you think he likes her dressed like that?"

Megan Sheppard was wearing a short black dress with a white Peter Pan collar.

"She looks quite fetching, Aggie. She can get away with the girlish look."

"Humph!"

"Oh, oh, he's seen us and he doesn't look too happy. He's coming over."

Sheppard loomed above them, clenching and unclenching his fists. "Are you following me?" he demanded.

"Why on earth should we do that?" said Charles mildly. "We're having a meal here, just like you."

He stood staring at them, his face dark with anger. Then he strode away. Agatha swivelled round to see what was happening. He bent over his wife, and then jerked her up by the elbow. He threw some money down on the table and then strode out of the restaurant, practically pulling his small wife after him.

"Now there's a man with a guilty conscience," said Agatha, turning back, her eyes gleaming.

"Have you ever thought that he might be perfectly innocent," said Charles, "and that we frighten him?"

"Us? Why?"

"If you were questioned and then apparently pursued by two people, one of whom is married to the prime suspect and she herself is suspect number two, wouldn't you get nervous?"

"Only if I had done the deed myself," said Agatha stubbornly. "I swear that man's a killer."

"You had Dewey down as number-one suspect yesterday."

"Oh, well, I mean, that was different."

"How?"

"He was scary, telling us about threatening to take her eyes out. But I mean, striking someone with such a savage blow, like what happened to Melissa, is just the sort of thing Luke Sheppard would have done."

"Don't let your imagination keep running away with you.

We have to dig up some hard facts. All we've got at the moment is speculation. We set out to find out all we could about Melissa. We felt sure if we really got to know her character, that would lead us to the murderer. But what have we got? A shifting, changing, manipulative woman who, quite frankly, could have been killed by anyone. And the main piece of the jigsaw is James. Without James, we haven't a clue."

"We'll just need to go on, however," said Agatha, "as if we're never going to find James. You say, maybe if we clear his name and wherever he is, he reads it in the newspapers, he may come back."

"To you, Aggie? Not still hoping for a happy marriage?"

"I just want to know that he is still alive," said Agatha, staring down at her plate and not meeting his eyes.

"So what's our next plan of campaign?"

Agatha racked her brain. She did not want to tell him she was at a dead end, in case he would pack up and go home and she would be left with her own company. What had happened to the old Agatha Raisin, who had not needed anybody? Maybe I did, she admitted ruefully to herself, and wouldn't admit it.

Then her face cleared. "Of course. The hospital! At least as his wife I can ask the doctor what his condition was."

"All right. We'll go tomorrow." Agatha heaved a sigh of relief. "But before we do, I think we should sit down and start to make notes, put everything in order. Oh, and then there's Melissa's sister, Julia. I really think we should make the effort and go to Cambridge to have another word with her. We've been looking at sex and passion and forgetting about the other prime motive, and that's money."

Agatha was up early the next morning and anxious to leave for Mircester, but Charles insisted, "Notes first."

Agatha switched on her computer. Her cats were in a playful mood that morning and were insisting on doing what cats like to do, namely jumping up on the keyboard and jumping on the keys. Charles carried them out into the garden and returned to sit down beside Agatha.

"Let's start with Sheppard," said Agatha. "He has a good alibi for the night of Melissa's murder and that in itself is suspicious. Usually innocent people do not have any alibi. Motive? Melissa may have known something about him that he did not want anyone else to find out."

"So where does James come into it?"

"Rats! James. Well, Melissa might have tried to tell him that something. James flees after avoiding being killed."

"So why not just kill Melissa and leave James alone?"

"I'll never get anywhere if you insist on playing devil's advocate."

"All right. Go on."

"Maybe Sheppard continued to hate her. Maybe—"

"I've a thought. Maybe James does not know anything about Melissa's murder. He shot off after he was attacked. He may have amnesia. He may not have read the papers."

"You mean, if he's alive, he may have information that would solve this case?"

"Something like that. Then what about what our genteel friend Miss Simms calls rough trade, Jake and his friends? She was sectioned for drugs. That's it!"

"What's what?"

"We ask the sister when she was sectioned, where, and what were the circumstances. Was she into really heavy mainlining stuff?"

"She certainly wasn't on anything last time I saw her," said Agatha. "No dilated pupils, no track marks on her arms. I really don't think we've enough at the moment, Charles, to make notes. Please let's go to the hospital."

"I know you'll never settle to anything until we do go. Come on, then."

• • •

Mircester General Hospital lay on the outskirts of the town, a gleaming modern building which had replaced the old Victorian hospital in the town centre, now a hotel. "Look at that!" said Agatha, outraged, as they drove into the hospital car-park. "We've got to pay for parking."

"I suppose they've got to try to make any money they can, these days. I mean, you must remember when the National Health Service started, Aggie." Agatha winced at this reference to her age. "It was going to be easy free treatment for everyone. Now it's all breaking down. And the reason it's breaking down, apart from sheer bad management, is all the new operations that everyone now expects—free hip replacements, free heart transplants, and all that costs a bomb."

"I still think it's a lousy trick forcing people to pay for parking," muttered Agatha. "How long do you think we're going to be?"

"Put in enough money for a couple of hours."

With Agatha still complaining, they walked into the hospital. To their request to see the consultant or doctor who had diagnosed James Lacey, they were told to wait. And they did. They waited and waited. Agatha flipped nervously through pages of old *Good Housekeeping* magazines, barely taking in what she was reading. She was just about to approach the reception desk and make a very Agatha-type scene, when a tall, thin man in a white coat came up to them. "I am Dr. Henderson. I was a friend of James. I am so sorry, Mrs. Lacey. I gather there is no news?"

"I'm afraid not," said Agatha. "I wanted to talk to you about his condition."

"Come with me. I can spare you a little time." He led them along gleaming hospital corridors to a small cluttered office. "Please have a seat. I can only tell you what you must know already, that he had a brain tumour. We were going to try chemotherapy. He was due for an appointment, his first treatment, when he disappeared."

"What was his state of mind when you saw him?" asked Charles.

"He was deeply shocked and upset. He asked a lot about alternative methods. He was very interested in mind over matter. He had heard that in California they have tapes which you play which train you to combat the illness mentally. He also asked about diet. I said that miracles sometimes did happen, but that in his case, I could only recommend chemotherapy. I am afraid I do not believe in miracles."

"But you said they sometimes do happen," pointed out Agatha.

"Not in my own experience, but some of my colleagues have experienced such. Sometimes people can have some leap of faith which seems to restore the immune system, but I am an agnostic, and I believe that it is down to coincidence. James did ask to see a psychiatrist. No doubt he was hoping to be instructed in some mental tricks."

"A psychiatrist? At this hospital?" said Agatha.

"A Dr. Windsor."

"May we see him?"

He picked up a phone on his desk. "A moment. I'll see if he is free."

He turned away from them and dialled an extension. "I have James Lacey's wife and a friend of hers with me," they heard him saying. "Can you spare them a minute?"

A voice quacked from the receiver. "Right," said Dr. Henderson. "I'll send them along."

He replaced the receiver. "You are lucky. He has fifteen minutes to spare between patients. If you go out of here and turn left, walk back along the corridor and through reception and follow the signs to the psychiatric unit, you will find a small reception area and he will be waiting for you."

They hurried off and, following his instructions, arrived at the psychiatric unit. Agatha had been expecting a stereotype psychiatrist, a heavy-set bearded man with a German accent, and was startled to be greeted by a small, slim man in a sports jacket who looked to her eyes far too young to be a psychiatrist.

"I am Dr. Windsor," he said, shaking hands with them. "Please sit down. Is your husband still missing?"

"I am afraid so," said Agatha. "We gather that James came to see you because he was interested in finding out if it might be possible to cure cancer by mind over matter."

"Actually, it was not that at all. I normally would not discuss any patient's business, even to the nearest and dearest, but his question seemed to me to be academic, so I do not think there is any problem in telling you what he wanted to know."

"Which was?" Agatha crouched forward in her chair, her bearlike eyes fixed on his face.

"He was asking me about the symptoms of antisocial personality disorder. He said he was not asking about anyone in particular. He needed details for a book he was writing."

"I am surprised you could give him your time when he wasn't a patient," said Charles.

"He was paying for my time. I saw him at my private consulting rooms in the town."

"We read up on that mental illness," said Agatha, disappointed, and slumping back in her chair. So James had diagnosed Melissa before they had. Big deal.

But Charles asked, "Was there any specific point he wanted clarified?"

"Yes, as a matter of fact, there was. He wanted to know that if such a personality were rejected by someone, would they stalk, would they chase after that person. I said, not often, for although such a personality does not suffer from guilt, he or she suffers from intense feelings of bitterness and resentment. He then asked if two such people could be friends. I said that two such people

128

might get together to aid and abet each other, but friendship, no. He wanted to see me again, but I refused."

"Why?" asked Agatha.

Dr. Windsor's face darkened. "I had a personal phone call while he was with me. I went into another room to take it. It was quite a long phone call. When I returned, he was sitting where I had left him. But after he had gone, I found several things that disturbed me. Two of the drawers on my desk were slightly open, as if someone had hurriedly tried to shut them, and several files in my cabinet—old files which I had removed from the hospital and kept in my rooms—I could swear had been disturbed. Papers were sticking out the tops of some of them. And yet the filing cabinet had been locked. I could not accuse my receptionist because she was having an evening off. Did I tell you it was evening? No? Well, it was because I could only fit him in after hours, so to speak. I phoned him up and accused him of having broken into my filing cabinet. He denied the whole thing, and very vehemently, too. But I said I could not see him again. I did not trust him. I was not long enough with him, but perhaps he, too, suffered from this mild form of psychopathy, and yet I am sure it must be almost impossible for anyone suffering from this form of mental illness to know they have it." He glanced at his watch. "That is all I can tell you."

Charles and Agatha walked out to the car-park. "*Two* of them," said Agatha excitedly. "What was James on to? And who's the other one?"

"Maybe one of the husbands."

"If only we could find out. Perhaps we could break in and have a look at—"

"NO! Absolutely not."

"Just an idea. It's early yet. If we went to Cambridge, how long would it take us?"

"Let me see," said Charles. "If we take the by-pass which will get us onto the A-40 to Oxford, then out to the M-40, then the M-25 and then the M-11 right up to Cambridge, maybe about two and a half hours." He fished a card out of his pocket. "Let's see where she lives. Boxted Road. Have you a Cambridge map?"

"No, but we can pick one up in Mircester before we set off."

Even though she was not driving herself, Agatha found motorway journeys wearisome. After they had left the outskirts of Oxford, she closed her eyes and thought of everyone who might be connected with the murder. She fell asleep and into a dream where Dewey was approaching her with a sharp knife, saying, 'Pretty dolly, you need new eyes.' She awoke with a start and looked around groggily. "Where are we?"

"M-11," said Charles. "Not far now. When we get to Cambridge, we turn off the Madingley Road, just before Queen's Road, go down Grange Road and turn off about the third street down on the right. Maybe we should have phoned first. I mean, she might not be home."

"We've come this far now. May as well try. I mean, if we'd phoned her, she might have put us off, particularly if she feels guilty."

They had left the sunshine behind in the Cotswolds. A uniformly grey sky stretched over the university city of Cambridge. "Cambridge is outstripping Oxford when it comes to brains," commented Charles.

"Why is that?"

"For years now, Oxford's gone in for inverted snobbery. They turn down bright pupils from private schools in order to favour pupils from comprehensive ones. Big mistake. It's not only the rich who pay for the children's education, but often it's caring parents who are prepared to take out a second mortgage to pay school fees, and caring parents produce bright children. But Oxford still holds a lot of charm for people. Must be the weather. It can be a lousy climate over here and in winter cold mist creeps in from the fens and blankets everything. Let me see, this is the

Madingley Road. Keep your eyes peeled for Grange Road."

"There it is," said Agatha, "over on the right."

"So it is. Here we go. One, two, three. Ah, here's Boxted Road. Very nice, too. You'd need a bit of money to live in one of these villas. What's the number?"

"Thirteen, and, no, I am not superstitious."

Charles parked the car and they both got out. "I wish I'd brought a jacket," said Agatha, hugging her bare arms. "It looks almost misty at the bottom of the street. You can't get fog in summer."

"You can in Cambridge," said Charles. "Let's see if she's at home."

They walked up a path through a front garden without a single flower. Only laurel bushes lined the brick path. "Sounds of activity coming from inside," said Charles. He rang the bell.

A young man opened the door. "Mrs. Fraser?" asked Charles.

He turned round and yelled, "Julia!" at the top of his voice. A door in the dark hall opened and Julia Fraser appeared.

"Good heavens, what are you two doing in Cambridge?" she asked. "Come in." She ushered them into a pleasantly cluttered sitting-room.

"Was that your son?" asked Agatha.

"No, I rent rooms to students. Now, I suppose you've come to ask more questions, and I think it's a bit thick. I know you"—she looked at Agatha—"must be anxious to find out about your husband, but I cannot help you any further. I told you it was years since I had anything to do with Melissa."

"It's not that," said Charles. "James Lacey seems to have been doing a bit of investigating before he left; we don't know why. You said your sister had been diagnosed as a psychopath. James asked a psychiatrist at Mircester Hospital if it was usual for two such personalities to get together."

"And you've come all this way to ask me if she had a mad friend? How would I know?"

Agatha looked around the pleasant but shabby sitting-room and heard the noise made by the resident students filtering down through the ceiling. "What interests us as well is how much money Melissa had. I mean, she seemed to have lived comfortably. She didn't need to take in students."

"I'll tell you what I can," said Julia, "if the pair of you will promise to go away and not trouble me again. You bring up things I would rather forget."

Charles looked at Agatha, who nodded.

"It's a deal," he said.

Julia leaned back in her chair and half-closed her eyes. "Our father . . . do you know about him?"

They shook their heads.

"He was a Colonel Peterson, a rich landowner with a big estate in Worcestershire. He was the law at home. My mother was dominated by him and had little say in our upbringing. From an early age, Melissa contrived to make me look like the bad child. Father adored her. He could see no fault in her. It was a blow to him when Melissa was found to be taking drugs. She was living in a flat in Chelsea that he had bought for her. My mother died when we were still in our early teens. Melissa was found to have taken an overdose. Father had her transferred from a London hospital to a pyschiatric unit at Mircester Hospital so that he could keep an eye on her. His disappointment in Melissa affected his health. Shortly after she came out, he had a massive stroke. He left everything to Melissa. He left a letter for me with his will, which he had recently changed. He said I had always been wicked and the fact that I had introduced his dear child, Melissa, to drugs had proved that I was evil. I challenged Melissa. I was incandescent with rage. I'll never forget that scene. She laughed and laughed until the tears streamed down her face. Of course she put the family home and the land up for sale."

"But surely her father was told that she was a psychopath?"

"Probably, but he probably thought it was the effect of the drugs that the wicked Julia had pushed on her. I was married by then. My husband wasn't very good with money. When he died, I really only had this house. That's why I started letting out rooms to make a living."

"But surely now you have inherited the money, you don't need to do that any more?"

"True. I'm still recovering from it all, so I haven't made any changes. Melissa had gone through very little money indeed. To be honest, I thought she would have squandered most of it."

"So how much did she leave?" asked Agatha eagerly.

"Mind your own business. I've told you enough."

"It's very good of you to give us this time," said Charles, bestowing a charming smile on her. "But you, too, must be anxious to find out who killed your sister?"

"Not really. Except to shake him by the hand. I hated Melissa from the bottom of my heart. I adored my father and she took his love away and she made my childhood a misery. But, no, I didn't kill her, and in case you are getting any ideas about that, I was here with my students the night she was killed. Please go, now."

"Is there anyone way back then, I mean around the time she was being sectioned, that she might have harmed? I mean, perhaps someone from her past murdered her."

"I did not know any of her friends. Come to think of it, she never seemed to have any. People would take to her, but as she could never sustain her act for very long except with Father, they soon drifted off. Now, I really do want you to leave."

As they walked down the path, Agatha said, "It's a pity she's got an alibi. What a motive!"

"I know," agreed Charles. "I say, look at the fog! Let's find somewhere to eat and see if it thins out."

He drove to the multi-storey car-park off Pembroke Street

and then they walked round into the main shopping area and found an Italian restaurant.

"So," said Agatha, after they had ordered pizza, "where are we? Not much further."

"If only this were a detective story," mourned Charles, "and we were ace detectives, dropping literary quotations right, left, and centre, we would prove that Julia placed a dummy of herself in the window of her sitting-room to fool her students while she drove to Carsely and murdered her sister. I mean, think of the money she must have got."

"We haven't even stirred anything up," said Agatha. "I mean, if one of the people we've been questioning were guilty, you would think they'd have shown their hand by now."

"You mean, like trying to kill you?"

"Maybe not that. Just warning us off."

"Julia more or less did that."

"No, by warning us off, I mean someone saying something like, 'Stop now, or it will be the worse for you.' We haven't rattled anyone. Gosh, why did we order pizza, Charles? This tastes like a wet book."

"Get it down you." Charles peered out of the window at wraithlike figures moving through the mist. "I think we're going to have to stay here the night, Aggie. We can't drive home in this."

But Agatha did not want to spend a night in a hotel with Charles. "We can try," she said. "I mean, you said Cambridge was a foggy place. I bet when we get to the outskirts, it'll start to clear."

Charles opted to take the road which went back through Milton Keynes and Buckingham, saying that he did not want to drive on the motorways in fog.

By the time they had crawled as far as the Bedford bypass, the fog was getting worse. "There's one of those road-house places," said Charles, swinging off the road. "We'd better check in for the night."

"I'll pay," said Agatha quickly. "You've done all the driving."

Once inside, she firmly booked two rooms. "Honestly," complained Charles, oblivious of the stare of the desk clerk, "a double room would have been cheaper. And more fun."

Agatha ignored him. She took the keys from the clerk and handed one to Charles.

"If you think of anything, let me know. I'll be in my room."

"I'm thinking of food for this evening. Have you a restaurant here?" he asked the clerk.

"Certainly, sir. You'll find it through those doors on the left."

"We'll go there at seven," said Charles. "That pizza didn't go very far."

Agatha, when she let herself into her room, was glad for the first time to be on her own. She undressed and had a leisurely bath and then washed out her underwear and dried it as best she could with the hair dryer.

Before she could get dressed again, there was a knock at her door. She whipped the coverlet off the bed and wrapped it around herself and opened the door. Charles handed her a sweater. "I just remembered I had a spare one in the car."

Agatha took it gratefully. "Any sign of the fog lifting?"

"No, as thick as ever."

"What time is it?"

"Going on for seven."

"Won't be long."

When he had gone, Agatha put on her damp underwear and clothes and then pulled Charles's sweater over her head. It was blue cashmere. James had one like it. She wished she could stop the sharp pain she felt every time she thought of James.

The restaurant was crowded with other stranded travellers. They managed to get a corner table.

"What now?" asked Agatha, after they had ordered fish and chips.

"I don't know," said Charles. "Bit of a dead end all round, if you ask me."

"If only we could prompt someone into showing their hand. I know, maybe we could see that editor again and give him a story saying we know who the murderer is and we are just trying to find one final bit of proof."

"Dangerous, that. Not only will he come after us, but the whole of Mircester police will be down on our heads. We'll be asked to explain ourselves and when they find out we haven't a clue, we'll look ridiculous and the murderer will feel safer than ever."

"Oh, well, maybe I will be able to think of something after a night's sleep. What time should we ask for a call?"

"Eight o'clock. Go straight off and have breakfast on the road."

But when they set out the following morning, Agatha could not think of any bright ideas at all. A weak sun was shining through a hazy mist, and the dreadful fog of the day before had gone. She kept racking her brains. She felt that if she did not come up with something, then Charles would leave. Agatha hated being dependent on anyone, and yet she was afraid that without Charles, she would give up the hunt and sink into a depression.

They decided not to stop for breakfast, but to go straight to Carsely. Agatha stifled a yawn. She had slept badly.

Then Charles said the words she had been dreading to hear. "I'd better go home and see how things are. I mean, we seem to have come to a dead end."

Agatha said nothing. Her pride would not allow her to beg him to stay, or ask him if he was coming back.

"So here we are," said Charles, pulling up outside Agatha's

cottage. "I'll get my stuff and be off. Don't worry about any breakfast for me."

"Charles," said Agatha in a thin voice, "the door's open."

"Doris Simpson?"

"It isn't her day for cleaning."

"I'll call the police."

"No, I don't think whoever did it would break in in broad daylight."

They got out of the car and together they went up to the door. "It's been jemmied open," said Agatha. "Look at the splinters."

"But what about that expensive burglar alarm system of yours?"

"I forgot to set it," wailed Agatha. "Oh, my cats. What's happened to my cats? I've got to go in."

She strode into the house and into her sitting-room. "The television set and the radio haven't been taken. Oh, look at this."

Charles followed her into the sitting-room. The drawers of Agatha's desk in the corner of the room were lying open and papers lay about the floor and her computer was still switched on.

"That's it!" said Charles. "We've finally rattled someone. They were searching your papers, Aggie, to see if you had come up with anything. Look for your cats and I'll call the police."

Agatha went through to the kitchen, calling for her cats. Then she noticed the kitchen door was standing open. Her cats were rolling on the grass in the sunshine. She crouched down beside them and stroked their warm fur.

Then she heard Charles calling, "Fred Griggs is on his way. I'll make some coffee."

Agatha went into the kitchen. "Should we touch anything? I mean, they'll want to dust everything for fingerprints."

"I don't think our criminal stopped to make coffee." Charles filled the kettle and plugged it in.

Fred Griggs loomed up in the doorway, making them jump.

"Anything been taken?" he asked, pulling out his notebook. "I've phoned headquarters. They'll be along soon."

"Maybe I'd better wait for them to arrive," said Agatha, "and it'll save me going over the whole thing twice. I haven't looked upstairs."

"I'll go with you," said Charles to Fred. "You make the coffee, Aggie."

After some time, they came back downstairs. "I had some papers in my suitcase, some farming accounts I meant to go over," said Charles. "They've been tossed over the floor. Your bedside table's been ransacked."

"What about Mr. Lacey's cottage?" asked Fred, and Agatha and Charles stared at each other in consternation.

"We'd better have a look," said Charles.

"Do you have a key?" asked Fred.

"Yes, I keep it on a hook by the stove. Oh, it's gone."

"Of all the stupid places . . ." began Charles, but Agatha was already hurrying out the door.

Fred and Charles followed her to James's cottage. "The door's closed," said Fred. He tried the handle. "And locked."

"The key fits the back door," said Agatha, "and whoever it was left my cottage by the back door."

They went round the side of James's cottage to the back door. It was standing open with the key in the lock. They crowded inside and through to James's sitting-room. Papers were spread everywhere. It had been ransacked, just like Agatha's cottage.

Agatha sat down suddenly and put her head in her hands. Fred heard the wail of sirens. "I think we'd better go back to your cottage."

Agatha rose, helped by Charles and followed Fred next door. Bill Wong came to meet them, his round face creased with anxiety. "What have you been up to, Agatha?"

"I haven't been up to anything!" said Agatha, her voice shrill with shock. "I've been burgled."

"Let's sit down and go over it," said Bill. He was flanked by a policewoman and a detective constable.

They all gathered round the kitchen table. Wearily, Agatha began to talk, explaining that she had forgotten to set the burglar alarm and yes, she had been stupid enough to leave a key to James's cottage on a hook in the kitchen. "What I can't understand," she said, "is how someone knew the burglar alarm wasn't set."

Bill nodded to the detective constable who went outside. After a few moments he was back. "The wires have been cut."

"And nothing of value has been taken?" asked Bill.

"Not at first glance," said Agatha. "Whoever it was must have been trying to find out if we knew anything about the murders."

"And had you?" asked Bill sharply. "Apart from what you've told me."

"Nothing more than that," said Agatha. Charles looked at her, wondering whether she had forgotten about the psychiatrist or was deliberately withholding that information.

They could hear cars drawing up outside. "That'll be the forensic team," said Bill, getting to his feet. "They can start with James's cottage." He turned to Fred Griggs. "Ask around the village and see if someone heard or saw something."

The phone rang. Agatha picked up the extension in the kitchen.

It was Mrs. Bloxby. "I heard you had been burgled. Is there anything I can do to help?"

"I don't think so," said Agatha, "unless you can ask around and see if anyone was seen lurking around Lilac Lane during the night."

"Where were you?"

"Cambridge," said Agatha. "I'll tell you later."

"So you were in Cambridge," said Bill when she put down the phone. "Asking the sister questions?"

"Just a chat," said Agatha, "and then the fog was so bad we had to stop somewhere for the night. The thing is, who would know that I wasn't coming home? It was a last-minute decision."

"Someone was lurking about and got lucky," said Bill. "It couldn't be the sister, because you saw her over in Cambridge and I cannot imagine she would drive through that dreadful fog and back again."

"Unless," said Charles suddenly, "she followed us. I didn't check whether anyone was following us. Why should I?"

"And why would she do that?" asked Bill patiently.

"She's got the best motive, and if she were guilty, she'd follow us to see if we were ferreting around Cambridge for more clues."

"Why? She's got a good alibi. The students who lodge with her swear she was there the whole time Melissa was being murdered."

"But would they really know? I mean, if she took off in the middle of the night, took the motorways, she could do it in two and a half hours."

"Each way," said Bill. "That makes five hours. A long time to be away."

"Students don't get up early," said Charles. "Say she left at two in the morning, and allowing time for the murder, got back at eight, say. Her students might not have noticed anything. I mean, if someone says good night to you and there they are again at breakfast time, of course you think they've been there all night. We were driving very slowly through the fog. She could have followed us easily and seen us turn off at that road-house."

"You could have been going for a meal."

"She could have waited in the car-park. There's a good view of the reception, all lit up, and despite the fog, she would have seen us making a booking."

Bill passed a hand across his face. "You'll need to do a lot better than that."

"What I can't understand," Agatha burst out, "is why you couldn't come up with at least one fingerprint or footprint when James was attacked and Melissa killed. I watch loads of forensic TV programmes and they seem to be able to tell from hair and fibres and footprints and fingerprints—"

"It takes a long, long time these days to get results back from the lab. But in all cases, the perpetrator wore gloves. In James's case, the footprints were scuffed; in Melissa's case, whoever did it was very thorough. The place had been wiped clean of fingerprints and vacuumed thoroughly."

"Maybe if you checked the vacuum bag, there might be—"

Bill shook his head. "Here's a thing. We have a feeling that whoever did it brought their own vacuum cleaner."

"This is getting madder and madder," wailed Agatha. "How could anyone lug a vacuum cleaner through the village without being seen?"

"It could have been one of those hand ones people use for cars," said Bill. "We get the feeling the murder was cold-blooded and calculated."

Agatha and Charles decided after the questioning was over to go and visit Mrs. Bloxby and leave the forensic team a clear field. "We'll probably find the place covered in fingerprint dust," complained Agatha. "I thought they used lights these days."

"Don't ask me," replied Charles. "It's all a closed book to me."

"I thought you had to be home today?"

"I'll hang on a bit longer. Things were getting a bit boring, but now they've picked up."

Agatha felt a pang of dismay. Although she often suspected that all she meant to Charles was a diversion, she didn't like to have it confirmed.

Mrs. Bloxby was just arriving back at the vicarage as they

walked up. "Oh, you poor things," she said. "Do come inside. I've just been visiting Mrs. Allan."

Agatha remembered vaguely that Mrs. Allan was a battered wife who lived on the council estate. "She back with her husband?"

"No, he disappeared. But would you believe it, she actually misses him and keeps saying he wasn't so bad and she should never have reported him."

"At least there aren't any children," said Agatha. "I hate it when children are involved."

"That reminds me," said the vicar's wife, ushering them in, "we have the concert and fête to raise funds for Save the Children in two weeks' time. I wondered if you could help, Mrs. Raisin. We're having a cake sale as well."

"I'm not good at cakes."

"But you are good at publicity. We need to get a lot of visitors."

"You've left it a bit late. I'll do what I can. Give me the exact date, time, and what's on offer and I'll see what I can do with the local papers."

"Perhaps that friend of yours, Mr. Silver, could help. He was awfully good before."

"It would mean inviting him down and he'd expect to be here for the whole weekend. Don't think I could face it at the moment. But I'll do what I can."

"And we have no one to man the white elephant stall, yet. Perhaps you, Sir Charles . . . ?"

"Sorry. I haven't been home for a bit and I can't stay away much longer. Besides, you know what these white elephant sales mean? People buy stuff one year to help out and then they put it in the next year, until no one really wants to buy anything."

"But with Mrs. Raisin doing the publicity and attracting visitors to the village, I'm sure it will be a big success."

"Sorry, not my scene."

"Sit down," said Mrs. Bloxby. "Did you have any breakfast?"

"No, we haven't had time with all this," said Agatha.

"I made some fresh rolls. I'll make you rolls and bacon."

When she had gone off to the kitchen, Agatha leaned her head back against the feather cushions of the old sofa and closed her eyes. "This can't go on," she said. "I don't think whoever broke in was bothered whether they would find me there or not. I keep thinking of some faceless man, armed with a vacuum and a hammer."

"I've a nasty feeling we're never going to get anywhere on this one, Aggie," said Charles.

"But we've got to! We've got to clear James's name." She opened her eyes and looked at him accusingly.

"Fact is," said Charles. "I really should be at home. Before we came along here, I phoned my aunt. She's got some people coming to stay today. They're bringing Tara with them."

"Who the hell's Tara?" grumbled Agatha.

"A very gorgeous girl."

"Imagine naming someone after a plantation in *Gone with the Wind*."

"Well, you know what parents are like. Boys get traditional names like John, Charles and David. But when it comes to girls, they call them really daft names."

Mrs. Bloxby came back bearing a laden tray.

Charles took an appreciative bite of a bacon roll. "Bliss," he said. "Will you marry me?"

"I might," said Mrs. Bloxby with a flirtatious laugh. Agatha glared at her. She was a vicar's wife. She should behave like a vicar's wife.

"So have you any idea who might have broken into your house?" asked Mrs. Bloxby.

"My money's on Sheppard," said Agatha.

"Oh, why?"

"I think he really hated her. He exudes an air of threat and violence."

"What about the other husband? Dewey," said Charles. "He's sneaky and creepy enough to have got into your cottage without being noticed."

"I just don't know," said Agatha.

"Don't you think you should move out of the village for a little?" suggested Mrs. Bloxby. "I do not like to think of you being there, a target for some murderer."

"I'll be all right," said Agatha. She was about to add, "I have Charles," and then remembered that the fickle Charles would soon be off in pursuit of some gorgeous girl called Tara and he would probably forget about her for weeks.

EIGHT

✝

ROY Silver was delighted to accept Agatha's invitation. He felt it was very trendy to tell his colleagues in the office that he was popping down to the Cotswolds for the weekend.

Agatha met him at Moreton-in-Marsh station on the Friday evening. "Not much of a glad welcome," said Roy, looking at her sour face. "What's up?"

"May I refresh your memory? James is God knows where and suspected of murder and I'm not in the clear myself. My house and James's were ransacked. The murderer is out there, and for all I know, I'm the next victim. Furthermore, Charles was supposed to help me in my moment of peril and he's buggered off to his estates."

Roy slung a thin arm around her shoulders. "Never mind, you've got me."

Agatha repressed a sigh. Roy looked thinner and weedier

and more white-faced than ever. He was wearing designer jeans and fake crocodile boots with high heels. She had not warned him about the fête, worried that if she did, he would not come, and she did not like being on her own.

"You must tell me all about the murder," said Roy, teetering on his heels towards her car.

"Aren't those boots terribly uncomfortable?" said Agatha.

"Yes, but they give me *height*."

"You don't need height. You're tall enough. Not really suitable for down here."

Roy paused, one hand on the car door, looking stricken. "You think so?"

"Great for London," said Agatha consolingly, "but not here. Sling your case in the back."

"I've got moccasins and sneakers in my case," said Roy, as Agatha drove off. "So who did it?"

"I don't know. But when we get home, I'll fix you a drink and tell you all I know."

They chatted about people they knew in the PR business, but as Agatha swung off the A-44 and down the Carsely road, Roy saw a large board: VILLAGE FÊTE.

"What a coincidence, sweetie," said Roy in a suspicious voice. "There always seems to be a fête on when I come down here."

"Isn't the weather hot and stuffy?" said Agatha.

She was conscious of Roy glaring at her. "The fête. You're working at it and you've put me down to work as well. Remember that time you had me dressed up as a jester and had me cavorting around? Never again."

"It's just the tombola stand," said Agatha soothingly. "Only an hour or two."

"Or three or four," said Roy waspishly. "And the prizes! Old tins of sardines, brunette hair shampoo, plastic flowers."

"Well, I'm doing the white elephant stall."

"I must say, that's worse."

"Not this year. I went round the rich of Gloucestershire and got them to contribute something worthwhile. It *is* for charity. The nouveau riche don't give a damn, but the old guard of the county always feel obliged to give something. Then I spread the word around that there were treasures to be found at the white elephant stall. The buyers will be turning up in droves, and not only them. So many people watch the *Antiques Roadshow* on telly, and think that they too can be the lucky one with the bit of priceless Staffordshire that they just managed to pick up at a boot sale. Cheer up, Roy. Gives you a bit of caché. I'll see if I can get you a write-up in one of the locals: 'Young London Exec Does His Bit at Village Fête.'"

Roy brightened. "That would do me no end of good at the office."

Agatha parked outside her cottage. "James's cottage looks as if it's about to fall down," commented Roy as he got out of the car.

"It's the thatch. Needs doing," said Agatha. "But thatching costs a mint, so I keep putting it off in the hope that he'll turn up and do it himself."

Once they were both settled in the sitting-room with large drinks, Agatha began to tell Roy about the murder and all she and Charles had found out.

"It's Dewey," said Roy, when she had finished. "Mark my words: it's Dewey. How creepy! I mean, the police think the murder wasn't committed in a burst of passion. Someone took the trouble to bring a vacuum with them, for heaven's sake. Look at the way Dewey drugged Melissa and then threatened her."

"But he was clear of her," said Agatha patiently.

"You don't know that," exclaimed Roy, wriggling with excitement. "I mean, she could have turned up to pester him, for all you knew. I would like to meet him. Why don't I go over to his shop tomorrow—"

"There's the fête."

"Let me off the hook. This is important."

"I can't let you back out now."

"Can't you just imagine I didn't turn up? They'd have to find someone else."

"Let's compromise," said Agatha. "You work at the fête and I'll take you to where Dewey lives. Or you can phone him on Sunday and say you're an avid collector and only down for the day."

"Oh, all right. What's for dinner?"

"I'll have a look in the freezer."

"I thought you'd moved on from the microwave."

"I've moved back."

Agatha rose and went into the kitchen and lifted the lid of the deep freeze. There were things down there, she thought, that must have been bought ages ago. She wished she had put labels on them. She decided to defrost two freezer boxes from the bottom.

"We're having pot luck," she called out, putting the two boxes into the microwave to defrost.

She set the kitchen table—Agatha hardly ever used the dining room—and then, when the microwave pinged, she took the two packages out and prised open the lids.

"Jackpot," she said cheerfully. She remembered Mrs. Bloxby giving her an enormous casserole of savoury stew and dumplings and she had put the remainder into the two freezer boxes. No need for Roy to know she hadn't cooked the stew herself. She tipped the contents into an attractive oven dish she had never before used and lit the oven. Then she put two baking potatoes in the microwave and joined Roy.

"Won't be long," she said. "I was only joking about the microwave. I've been slaving away all day over a casserole on your behalf. It's a recipe I got from Mrs. Bloxby."

Roy admitted that dinner had impressed him. Agatha, after

she had stacked the dishwasher, was anxious to return to talking about the murder because during dinner they had chatted about old times, but all Roy would say was that he was sure Dewey had done it, and did not want to discuss Agatha's favourite—Sheppard.

At last, Agatha suggested an early night because they both had to get up in time to set up their stalls in the morning. She set the newly repaired burglar alarm, and with a feeling of relief that she was not alone in the house, fell into a deep and refreshing sleep.

In the morning, murder and mayhem seemed very far away. It was a perfect English summer's day, bright sunlight and not too hot. After breakfast, she and Roy walked to the church hall. To Agatha's relief, Roy was so depressed at the idea of working at the fête that he was wearing an old pair of jeans with a shirt and sweater and sensible shoes. She herself was wearing a pale biscuit-coloured trouser-suit with high-heeled strapped sandals. A warning voice in her head was telling her she would regret the high heels before the end of the day, but she had a nagging dream that the missing James would walk into the fête and she did not want the frumpish feel that flat shoes always gave her.

The white elephant stand was next to the tombola. While Roy made acid comments about the cheapness of the items contributed to his stall, Agatha unpacked her collection, putting the usual old recycled Carsely junk to the front of the stall and the good items at the back. As she had guessed, the collectors and antique dealers were circling around early. Agatha unpacked slowly. She had invited the local press and did not want to start selling until they had arrived. She unpacked a box from a local manor-house that had been contributed at the last minute and so far she had not had time to examine the contents. There was a small dark oil painting of ships on the sea, badly in need of restoration. Agatha suddenly wished she knew more about antiques. The picture might turn out to be valuable. There were several china ornaments, most of them cracked or chipped, and then, at the bottom of the box, something wrapped in tissue. She took it out and unwrapped it—and then nearly dropped it. Looking up at her out of the tissue-paper wrapping was an eighteenth-century doll. It was either the twin of the doll that Dewey loved so much, or somehow he had decided to sell it to the owners of the manor-house and they had given it to the sale.

She called Roy over and showed him the doll. "This is the one Dewey is in love with," she hissed.

"Where did it come from?" asked Roy.

"A manor-house over Longborough way. Rats! I just knocked at the door and asked for contributions. Don't even know their name."

Roy looked excited. "Phone Dewey and get him over here. Can it be the same one?"

"It looks the same to me. But I can't imagine Dewey parting with it. Get me a phone book. There should be one over at the back of the church hall next to the kitchen."

She waited impatiently until Roy came back with the phone book. She scanned the pages until she found the number of Dewey's shop and phoned it. Roy fidgeted impatiently while Agatha spoke rapidly into the phone. When she rang off, she turned gleaming eyes to him. "It's not his but he's locking up the shop and coming over. I don't know the price of these things. I wish I knew more about antiques. I could be selling old masters for a few pounds, for all I know."

"Make it an auction," said Roy. "Announce that because there are valuable items on the stall, you will start the auction at eleven o'clock. Take that big card which says WHITE ELEPHANT STALL, turn it over and write AUCTION in big letters."

Agatha did as she was told and then waited and waited. Buyers circled around, trying to purchase things, but Agatha remained adamant. They would just need to wait until the auction started. She got Mrs. Bloxby to organize a microphone for her.

When the press arrived, she tipped them off—hopefully—that she meant to gain thousands from the auction and then introduced them to Roy, describing him as a top London executive.

Dewey arrived just before eleven o'clock. "Where's the doll?" he asked.

"You'll need to wait for the auction," said Agatha.

"Just let me see it!" There was a light film of sweat over his face and his eyes were glittering.

Agatha held it up. He drew in a sharp breath. "I'll give you two hundred for it."

"You'll need to wait with the others," said Agatha firmly.

On the stroke of eleven, Agatha started the auction with the oil painting. She felt like an amateur. She did not even know the name of the painter because the painting was so dirty, the signature was obscured. But she bravely spoke up. "Who'll give me one hundred pounds? Starting the bidding at one hundred."

The large crowd shifted and swayed. A man scratched his eyebrow. Was that a bid?

"As we have professionals here as well as non-professionals," called Agatha, "instead of signalling, I must ask you to shout out your bids."

Silence. Then the man who had scratched his eyebrow called out, "One hundred and fifty."

Silence again. Wasn't bad for a ratty old painting, thought Agatha, picking up her hammer, a kitchen hammer, as no auctioneer's gavel had been available. "Going, going . . ."

"Two hundred," called another voice.

The crowd around the white elephant stand began to get thicker. The bidding rose and rose. The painting was finally sold for twelve hundred pounds. Agatha guiltily hoped that the people who had given her the painting were not in the crowd.

And so it went on. Auction fever was gripping the crowd. Some of the villagers were bidding wildly for the rubbish they had ignored the year before.

At last, Agatha held up the doll. The bidding went up and up until Dewey suddenly called out shrilly, "Two thousand pounds!"

There was a startled silence. Dewey stared at Agatha, his eyes mad with longing. Agatha took pity on him. "Going, going, gone. Sold to Mr. Dewey," she said quickly.

After that, the excitement died down. Dewey wrote out a cheque and tenderly took the doll in his arms. "The money is going to a very good cause," said Agatha. Roy, who had persuaded Miss Simms to take over the tombola stall, came hurrying up. Agatha introduced him. "I'm ever so interested in antique dolls," gushed Roy. "Can we have a chat?"

"No," said Dewey harshly, "I shut up my shop to come to this auction. Got to get back."

"I'll come with you. I'm ever so madly keen on antique dolls and I must say, that one you got is the most fascinating and beautiful thing I've ever seen."

Dewey's eyes darted suspiciously from Agatha's face to Roy's. Then he said reluctantly, "All right."

Roy trotted off after him. Agatha longed to follow as well, but the remaining items which no one had seemed interested in bidding for might still be sold. New visitors were arriving. So she put price cards on the remainder and stood there patiently, her feet beginning to ache dreadfully. Where had the days gone when she could run around all day in very high heels and not even feel a twinge? Agatha felt the autumn of her life stretching in front of her.

She looked around the crowd, searching for a victim to take over the stand for her so that she could give in and find a pair of flat shoes. She saw Mrs. Allan, Carsely's battered wife, and called to her. Mrs. Allan came up to Agatha. Although she was only in her thirties, she had stooped shoulders, as if from a lifetime of warding off blows. "Could you take over for me?" asked Agatha.

"I dunno. I ain't never auctioned nothing."

"The auction's over. I've put the price tickets on everything. I'll give Mrs. Bloxby the cheques."

"Oh, all right, then," said Mrs. Allan. "Ain't it hot?" She removed a limp white cardigan and draped it over the edge of the stall. Underneath the cardigan, she was wearing a skimpy blouse. Agatha's eyes sharpened. There was a nasty bruise on one of Mrs. Allan's thin arms. "What happened there?" she asked, pointing to the bruise.

"Oh, that? Ever so clumsy, I am. Hit it on the door."

Agatha headed off to find Mrs. Bloxby and handed her a pile of cheques and notes. "There must be a fortune here, Mrs. Raisin," said Mrs. Bloxby. She turned to her husband, the vicar. "Alf, isn't she marvellous? Don't you just feel like giving Mrs. Raisin a great big hug?"

The vicar shied like a startled horse. "Good heavens, is that the time?" he exclaimed. "Got to see someone," and ran off as fast as he could.

"I've got to get home," said Agatha. "My feet are killing me."

"Such a pity. Those shoes look really glamorous."

Agatha smiled. Mrs. Bloxby had a knack of saying the right thing. A lesser woman would have said, "Why don't you wear sensible shoes?"

"I've left Mrs. Allan in charge. She's got a terrible bruise on one arm. Can it be the husband? He's out of the picture, isn't he?"

"As far as I know. But the trouble with that kind of woman—I don't mean to sound patronizing, but sometimes I despair—is that they get rid of one villain and pick up another."

"Why?"

"I've been told that women who don't think much of themselves gravitate to people who'll make them feel even worse about themselves. It's amazing how they get rid of one and then marry again, the same type."

"Has she got anyone?"

Mrs. Bloxby sighed. "Not that I know of, and if she has, there is nothing I can do about it but sit and wait until it gets too bad again and then step in and try to pick up the pieces. Off you go. You've done splendidly. The doll! What an enormous amount of money."

"That was Melissa's ex-husband, the one before Sheppard."

"Really? He looks quite mad. I hope he does not regret spending such a vast amount of money. But these antique dolls can be really valuable."

"I only hope that the people who donated the doll don't come after me and demand the money," said Agatha.

"Who was it?"

"Big manor-house. Over by Longborough. Big cedar tree outside."

"Oh, Lord Freme. I wouldn't worry. He's got millions."

"I'll be off then."

"Where's your young friend?"

"Gone off with Dewey to do a bit of detective work."

"Is that wise? He may be your murderer."

Agatha looked worried. "I'll wait a bit and then go after him."

She went home and massaged her aching feet after she had taken her shoes off. Her cats jumped, purring, onto her lap and she lay back in the armchair and stroked their fur, reluctant to return to the fête. But at last she let them out into the garden, put on flat shoes and walked back to the church hall.

"Sold anything?" she asked Mrs. Allan.

"A liddle jug thing. I put the money in the box."

"Thanks, Mrs. Allan. Why don't you go and get a cup of tea? I'll take over now."

Mrs. Allan slouched off. At the next stand, Miss Simms turned the tombola drum and called over, "Your young man not coming back?"

"Don't think so," said Agatha. "There's nobody interested in what I've got left, so I can take over for you."

"Ta. Where's Charles?"

"Gone home."

"All your fellows left you?"

"Looks like that," said Agatha sourly.

The day wore on. The morris dancers jumped up and down energetically, tourists took pictures, the cake-and-jam stall had sold out and the cafeteria was doing a roaring trade. Clouds were piling up over to the west and Agatha could feel the beginnings of a headache. Where was Roy? She began to worry so much that even when Mrs. Bloxby rounded off the day by making a speech of thanks to everyone who had helped in general and one, Agatha Raisin, in particular, she barely listened. As soon as the applause had died down, she ran home and got into her car and headed for Worcester.

When she arrived in Worcester, she realized she should just have waited at home for Roy to call. She had forgotten, he didn't have a car. He might even now be on the train, heading back to Moreton-in-Marsh. She glanced at the clock on the dashboard. Six o'clock! Dewey would have shut up shop, so she would have no way of finding out when Roy had left.

She decided to try the shop anyway. She parked the car and hurried over to The Shambles. To her relief, she saw the shutters had not been put up. She cupped her hand and peered in the window. Roy was sitting in a chair, looking like a scared rabbit. Dewey was talking forcibly and standing over Roy, brandishing a pair of scissors. Agatha was about to burst in, but then she thought that might urge Dewey to violence. She moved away from the window and took out her mobile phone and called the police, and waited, trembling and anxious, until a squad car roared up. "My friend is in there," she babbled to the first policeman, "being threatened with a pair of scissors." There were three policemen in all. They walked into the shop and Agatha followed them, glad to see that Roy was still unharmed.

"We have a report that you have been threatening this gentleman with a pair of scissors," said the leading policeman ponderously.

Dewey, whose face had been contorted with rage when Agatha had seen him through the window, immediately became transformed into a meek and bewildered shopkeeper.

"I do not know what you mean!" he said, putting the scissors down on the desk. He looked at Agatha. "It's that trouble-making woman again. I was merely giving this gentleman a lecture on antique dolls."

"Is that true, sir?" The policeman looked at Roy.

"Yes, I suppose he was," said Roy. "But he scared me. I've been here for hours and *hours*. He said I was checking up on him. He said I didn't know the first thing about dolls and he stood over me with the scissors in my face and went on and on."

"Do you wish to lay charges?"

"No," said Roy. "I just want to get out of here."

"If he threatened you with a pair of scissors, you should lay charges against him."

"I was defending myself, officer," said Dewey. "You will find that this woman and another man entered my home recently and said they had a gun."

Now the policeman looked at Agatha suspiciously. "You pestering this man?"

"No," said Agatha, and "Yes," said Dewey.

"Could we just let the matter drop?" pleaded Roy.

Dewey suddenly agreed. "Yes, let's just forget about the whole thing."

The police driver came into the shop. "Smash and grab out on The Walls, sir."

"Right." The policeman glared all around. "I'll let it go this time."

"Come on," hissed Roy, grabbing Agatha's arm. He obviously didn't want to be left with Dewey again.

"Phew!" said Roy as they hurried along the street. "Let's find a pub. I could do with a drink."

"Now," said Agatha when they had found a table in a quiet pub, "what happened?"

"At first it all seemed pretty matey," said Roy. "That was when we drove to Worcester. He was torn between joy at getting the doll and wondering whether he had paid too much over the top for it. He did all the talking. Things were fine until we got to the shop. He seemed to have taken a liking to me. He got us coffee and we sat down by the desk. I said I was a friend of yours and wasn't it dreadful about the murder of his ex-wife. He said, yes, it was terrible and then he grew cold and began to question me on my knowledge of antique dolls, of which I know zilch. He began then to accuse me of merely wanting to poke my nose into his affairs. I protested. I said I may not know much, but I was eager to learn as I was thinking of starting a collection.

"His eyes were all funny and glittery. He said I was just like Melissa, pretending to a knowledge I didn't have to ingratiate myself with him and do him harm. By this time he was waving the scissors around."

Roy took a gulp of his drink and went on. "That's when I said, all haughty-like, that he had hurt my feelings and I was leaving. 'Oh, no, you're not,' he says, pointing the scissors at my face and standing over me. 'You say you came here to learn, and learn you will.' Then two customers came in. He said to them, as pleasant and calm as anything, 'Excuse us a minute,' and digging those damn scissors into my side, he ushered me into the back room. 'Sit there quietly until I'm ready for you,' he said. 'Call for help and I'll kill you and say it was self-defence.' He went back into the shop and locked the door.

"There was no way out. The back door was locked and there was only a little barred window. I shook with terror. And I was surrounded by all those dolls, all those little staring eyes. I was in there so long, I thought he'd gone for the night, and I was just about to risk calling out when he opened the door and, still brandishing those damn scissors, told me to go and sit down in the shop. Then he started this long lecture. Don't ask me what it was about. I was so terrified I couldn't take in a word. Then you came. Agatha, he's certifiable, sweetie. Bonkers, a picnic short of a sandwich, raving. He did it, mark my words. The intensity of his rage was something awful."

"But how can we prove anything?" wailed Agatha.

"There must be something in his past. We'd best go and see that copper friend of yours. We need help."

"We'll go tomorrow. Let's hope Bill Wong's on duty. You wouldn't want to meet his parents. If you've finished your drink, let's go."

As they walked to the car-park, Roy kept casting nervous glances all around, as if expecting to see Dewey leap out at him.

When they got back to the cottage, Agatha phoned Bill. She told him briefly what had happened and asked if they could call on him the following day, but Bill said he would come over right away.

"We'd better eat something before he arrives," said Agatha. "Bill will already have had something."

"I'll fix it," said Roy. "I'm still nervous and I feel like doing something. Have you got eggs and cheese? I'll make a cheese omelette."

"I have both. I'll leave you to it."

While Roy worked in the kitchen, Agatha phoned Mrs. Bloxby and apologized for having run away from the fête.

"Did you catch up with Roy?"

"Yes," said Agatha. "I'll tell you about it later."

"Well, thanks again for a splendid effort. We raised a great deal of money. I told Alf we owe it all to you."

"And what did the vicar say?" asked Agatha, who knew Alf did not like her, but craved his good opinion.

"Oh, he agreed with me," said Mrs. Bloxby, although what the vicar had actually said was, "God moves in mysterious ways."

Agatha rang off. She poured herself a stiff gin and tonic and lit a cigarette. She had just finished both when Roy called her from the kitchen. As Agatha rose out of the deep armchair in which she had been sitting, she felt a slight stiff pain in her knee joints and her chest gave a distinct wheeze. She stood, alarmed. She took a deep breath, but the wheeze had gone. She remembered when she was in Wyckhadden that she had managed to give up cigarettes. It had felt good. Then she remembered Jimmy Jessop, the police inspector in Wyckhadden who had proposed marriage to her. She remembered him as safe and decent. She could have been Mrs. Jessop by now had Jimmy not found her in bed with Charles. Damn Charles. She would never, ever have gone to bed with him had not that fortune-teller told her that she would never have sex again. Now Jimmy was married. Was he happy? Maybe he was divorced.

"Agatha!" called Roy. "Your food's on the table."

She banished thoughts of what might have been from her mind and joined Roy in the kitchen.

"I've been thinking," said Roy, "about what we could do tomorrow."

"What?"

"You said this chap Sheppard lives in Blockley, which isn't far from here. We could drop over there tomorrow—"

"Are you mad? He'd be furious."

"Ah, but if we told him we're pretty sure it was Dewey, he might open up a bit."

"I don't know. Maybe." Agatha thought of that sinister pain in her joints. "Tell you what," she said. "I need exercise. If it's a fine day, we could walk over."

"All right. I could do with a bit of exercise myself."

Bill arrived just after they had finished their meal. He listened carefully while Roy described his adventures with Dewey and made several notes. When Roy had finished, Agatha said, "You see, we wondered if you had been digging into Dewey's past, if there was anything there."

"Nothing sinister that we've been able to find," said Bill. "He's the son of fairly wealthy middle-class parents. The father died young and he was very close to his mother. When she died, he had just finished at university. With the money she left, he bought that shop and started up in business. He really knows his stuff. He doesn't seem to have any friends. When he married Melissa, they didn't seem to socialize. I'll dig a bit deeper. I'll pull him in and have another go at him."

"Is there any news of James?" asked Agatha.

"Not a whisper. I would have told you if I had heard anything."

The following day dawned sunny and fresh. They set out to walk to Blockley, which meant climbing up the steep road out of Carsely, walking along the A-44 and then down the hill into Blockley. When they reached the village, Agatha felt that longing for a cigarette and fought it down. She had not yet lit up one that day.

"I don't feel very brave," she whispered to Roy as they walked up Greenway Road. "He's a very belligerent man."

"Maybe we should forget about the whole thing," said Roy uneasily. "I hear there's some good French cooking down at the Crown. We could walk about a bit and then have lunch."

But his cowardice spurred Agatha on. "Don't want to think we've walked all this way for nothing. If he's mad at us, he can slam the door in our faces."

Walking close together, they approached the door of the Sheppards's cottage. Agatha rang the bell.

After a few moments, Megan Sheppard answered the door. She was wearing a brief pair of hot pants over a gingham blouse. Her hair was tied in two bunches with pink ribbons. "Oh, it's you," she said. She called over her shoulder, "Luke, it's that woman from Carsely who's been pestering you."

Luke Sheppard loomed up behind her. "Get away from here," he growled.

"We thought you would like to know," said Agatha bravely, "that we're pretty sure it was Melissa's first husband, Dewey, who killed her."

What was that odd look that had flashed in his eyes? wondered Roy. Relief?

The truculence left his face. He said mildly, "You'd better come in and tell us about it."

They followed the Sheppards through the cottage and out into the garden. After they had all sat down round the garden table, Roy told them all about his visit to Dewey's shop.

"You poor thing," said Megan, looking into his eyes. "You must have been frightened to death."

"I tell you," said Roy, delighted to have such an appreciative audience, "I thought my last moment had come."

"So have you told the police all this?" asked Luke.

"Yes," said Agatha. "They are going to pull him in for further questioning. Did I ask you this before? Did you know Melissa was sectioned at one time?"

He looked genuinely surprised. "No. Was it drink?"

"Drugs."

"When was this?"

"A long time ago, when her father was still alive. Did you ever know her sister?"

"No, Melissa didn't have anything to do with her."

"Do you know if she had a friend from the past, someone she might have met when she was in the psychiatric unit?"

"No, come to think of it, she didn't have any real friends. I mean, she would strike up a friendship with someone but it would never last very long. People would go off her."

"Just like you, dear," said Megan, and stroked his hand. And yet Agatha noticed that one of Megan's smooth tanned legs was pressed against Roy's.

"Is there anything you can think of," pursued Agatha, "any little thing that might help us find out who murdered Melissa?"

"What's this?" The anger had returned to Luke Sheppard's face. "You told us it was Dewey."

"We're sure it is. But still—"

"I think you should get a life," said Luke.

"Don't be hard on her, dear," cooed Megan. "Some of these old village women lead empty lives."

Roy cackled with laughter and then put a hand over his mouth when he saw Agatha's furious face. But Luke went on as if she had not spoken. "Where do you get off, nosing around, poking around into people's lives? Get out of here."

Agatha stood up, her face flaming. "Come on, Roy."

They both marched out. The Sheppards stayed where they were.

"Insufferable man," raged Agatha, "and she's nothing more than a little bitch."

"Clever, though," said Roy. "Even if he hadn't lost his temper, her crack at you would have made you leave."

"I keep wondering where James fits into all this," said Agatha. "Oh, why doesn't he turn up? He should be getting treatment. He may be dead."

She began to cry. Roy put an awkward arm around her shoulders. "The living can keep out of the road of the police, Aggie. The dead find it difficult. Cheer up. Let's try the Crown for lunch."

After Agatha had taken Roy down to catch the London train that evening and returned to her cottage, she found herself thinking more and more about Jimmy Jessop, that police inspector in Wyckhadden she had so nearly married. Yes, at the time, she had hoped to make James furious and jealous. And if the wretched Charles hadn't turned up at a moment when she was weak and shocked, she would never have had sex with him. She thought of Jimmy's nice smile and the way his eyes used to light up when he saw her. Roy had gone, Charles showed no sign of coming back. She had a longing for masculine company.

Before she fell asleep, listening uneasily to the night sounds, things rustling in the thatch, the creaks as the old cottage settled down for the night, she decided that the next morning, she would get up bright and early and go to Wyckhadden.

As she drove out of Carsely the next morning, she turned on the radio. Stepping Out were still top of the pops with their rambling song. I wonder if they ever thank me for getting them fame, thought Agatha. Then she began to wonder if she should have tried to phone Jimmy first. The woman he had married instead of her had warned her in no uncertain terms not to come round again, so she couldn't have phoned him at home. Then his colleagues at the police station all loathed her and would no doubt lie to her and tell her he wasn't available. No, the best thing to do was to go to that pub where he usually had his lunch-time drink and see if he turned up there.

She remembered Wyckhadden as a seaside town plagued with extremes of weather and was quite surprised to find a pale misty sun shining down on a placid sea. She had left home at dawn and so it was an hour before lunch-time when she arrived. She walked along the pier and back again, and then followed the familiar route to the pub. She ordered a gin and tonic and sat at the table they had always sat at and waited, looking up hopefully every time the door opened. Outside, the street suddenly darkened as a cloud crossed the sun. What am I doing here? wondered Agatha. Was it because she was sure that James was still alive and that he had not contacted her because he did not want to see her again? Had she nourished some mad hope that Jimmy might still feel something for her, that he would get a divorce, marry her and give her a shoulder to lean on for the rest of her life?

She swallowed the last of her drink and reached for her handbag. The pub door opened and Jimmy walked in. He stood looking at her in surprise and then that old familiar slow smile lit up his face.

"Why, Agatha!" he said, sitting down opposite her. "This is a surprise. What brings you here?"

Agatha suddenly wanted to lie, to say she had just wondered if the place was still the same, but she found herself saying simply, "You. I came to see you."

"I'll get us drinks. Wait there."

Jimmy went to the bar, a tall, competent, *safe* figure.

He came back with a pint of beer for himself and a gin and tonic for Agatha. "I assumed you're still drinking the same," he said.

"Yes. Thanks. How's marriage?"

"Great. We've got a son, Paul. Apple of my eye. What did you want to see me about? Is it all this stuff about you I've been reading in the papers?"

"Yes, that's it. My brain's in a muddle. I seem to have a suspect, but I can't pin anything on him."

"You shouldn't go on like this," said Jimmy. "You should leave these matters to the police. Oh, I know you helped me down here, but still . . . You'll get yourself killed one of these days. Okay. Go on. Tell me about it."

Agatha began at the beginning. She left nothing out, all the rows with James, the bad marriage, his brain tumour, and then went on to what she knew about Melissa and her ex-husbands. Jimmy took out a large notebook and began to make neat short-hand notes.

When she had finished, he asked, "What sort of village is Carsely?"

"Normally old-fashioned, sleepy and quiet. Nice people."

"But a close-knit community?"

"Not exactly what it would have been in the old days. Cotswold villages get a lot of newcomers, people buying second homes and only using them at the weekends. There isn't the gossip and curiosity about each other there would have been not so long ago. It all gets a bit Londonified, you know, everyone minding their own business a little too much, but they do rally round if someone is in trouble. Do you mean, why when James was being attacked and Melissa murdered did no one see or hear anything?"

"That's it."

"Well, they didn't."

"I think," said Jimmy, "if I was on the case I would ask around the village again. In my experience, you'll find someone really did see something. Might be an idea to keep asking. It's infuriating the way people might come up with something like, 'I saw old Mr. Bloggs walking down the street about that time.' 'Why didn't you say anything?' 'Oh, it was only old Bloggs. Didn't seem worth mentioning.' That sort of thing."

"I'll try," said Agatha. "Now if you were making a guess as to who did it, who would you pick?"

He flicked through his notes. "Well, I would be thinking of the sister. I mean, forget all this mystery about psychopaths. There's money involved. And I should think a good degree of hatred."

"But why James?"

"He may have ferreted something out, told Melissa, she tells her sister and the sister tries to kill James."

"But Melissa and her sister weren't on speaking terms!"

"You only have Julia's word for that. If their father had a big estate and left all to Melissa, and by your report Melissa didn't use much of it, then it must have been some sum worth killing for. Then, if Melissa and Julia were supposed to be estranged, why did Melissa leave the money to her? You don't leave money to someone you hate."

"I know. But she did not have any friends. Husbands both finished with. Maybe when she was making out her will, she found Julia was the only logical person to leave it to."

"Still, it's odd. It would have been more like her to leave it to the cat's home to spite Julia. I think your first move should be to start questioning the villagers again. That's what police work is, Agatha," he added sententiously, "plod, plod, plod."

He glanced at his watch and gave an exclamation of dismay. "I've got to get back and I haven't even had any lunch. Need to grab something from the police canteen. Tell you what, I'll phone the wife. Why don't you spend a nice day pottering round the shops and come home with me for dinner?"

Agatha repressed a shudder. His wife would probably throw the dinner in her face. "No, I've got to get back. Got things to do."

They both stood up. "Well, as I've said before, Agatha, if it weren't for you, I wouldn't be happily married now." Jimmy smiled down at her.

Agatha felt like crying. But she said, "You deserve to be happy, Jimmy. You're a good man."

They emerged from the pub. The sky had clouded over and torrential rain was beating down. "Wyckhadden's the same as ever," mourned Agatha. "Dramatic weather."

"Where's your car?"

"Not far. In the central car-park."

"Give me your keys and I'll go and get it for you. You'll get soaked otherwise. Tell me the make and registration number."

Agatha was fishing in her handbag for her keys. She looked up and saw Jimmy's wife, Gladwyn, bearing down on them, her eyes glittering with rage. "Get it myself," gasped Agatha and took off, running as hard as she could. When she got to her car, she was soaked to the skin. She sat there miserably until the rain thinned and then stopped. She climbed out of the car and walked to a large department store which sold cheap clothes and bought herself a sweater and skirt, underwear and shoes, and, after she had paid for it all, put the lot on in the fitting-room and stuffed her wet clothes in a carrier bag. She was about to leave the store when she noticed it was raining again, so she retreated back in and bought a raincoat and umbrella. When she emerged, the sun was shining. "I hate this place," she said loudly, and several passers-by edged nervously away from her.

As she drove the long road home, she told herself severely that the next man she became involved with would be someone who really loved her, not someone she irritated every minute of the day as she had irritated James, or a fickle lightweight like Charles.

If Charles comes around again, she told herself, I'll tell him to get lost.

But when she turned the corner into Lilac Lane, and saw Charles's car parked outside her cottage, she experienced a feeling of relief. Not yet, she told herself. I'll tell him to get lost when all this is over.

NINE

✝

CHARLES had let himself in, having kept the spare key, and was watching television and drinking whisky.

"Back again," he said lazily. "Where have you been?"

"Just around. Oh, you may as well know—I went to Wyckhadden."

Agatha sat down with a weary sigh. Charles studied her. "I'd better not ask you why you went there. Whisky or gin?"

"Whisky with water." Charles rose and poured her a drink and handed it to her.

"I went to tell Jimmy—remember Jimmy?"

"Could I forget? Found us in bed together and broke off your engagement."

"I thought if I told him all about the case, he might come up with something."

"And did he?"

"He had an idea. He said usually in cases, people would say they had seen or heard nothing, but if we asked again, someone might come up with something they thought was too ordinary or insignificant to mention."

"He's got a point there," said Charles. "We never really questioned the villagers. That's all been left to the police. Oh, God, that means going from door to door."

"Maybe not. I've an idea. We could see Mrs. Bloxby and suggest a meeting in the church hall. Give them all sheets of paper and ask them to write down anything at all they might have seen or heard on the day James was attacked and on the night Melissa was murdered."

"That'd be a start. I can't help myself, Aggie. Did you actually go to Wyckhadden to kindle the old flame?"

"Of course not," said Agatha quickly. "What about Tara?"

"What about her?"

"What about this gorgeous creature you were straining at the bit to see."

"Didn't work out."

"What went wrong?"

"Well, I took her out for dinner. She said she was a feminist—she works for some magazine—and believed in women paying their own way, so we decided to split the bill. We went to Père Rouge, a new place in Stratford. When the bill came round, she gave me exactly half. I said, 'Wait a minute, you had the oysters to start, a whole dozen; I only had one glass of wine and you had the rest of the bottle; I had pasta and you had fillet steak; I didn't have pudding and you had crêpes Suzette;' so I took out my pocket calculator and worked out her share of the bill, which seemed fair enough to me. Then I worked out the tip; she hadn't even offered to cover that, and told her the total. She looked at me in a cold way and asked me if I was joking. I said I couldn't see anything funny. She got to her feet, said, 'Be back in a minute,' and then she didn't come back. So I had to pay the whole bill. Then when I got home, it was to find she had arrived before me in a taxi, kept the taxi waiting, packed her things and headed off."

"Oh, Charles, couldn't you just have left it? I mean, taking out a pocket calculator."

"What's up with that? She said she would pay her share and I wasn't going to let her get away with just paying a measly half when the greedy cow had gorged her way through the most expensive things on the menu."

"Charles, that meanness of yours will keep you a bachelor until the end of your days."

"I am *not* mean. I take people at their word. If someone says they'll pay their share, I expect them to do so."

"Never mind. Let me tell you what happened this weekend." Agatha told him about the fête and Roy's encounter with Dewey.

"Everything does seem to point to him. Did Jessop suggest anything else?"

"He did seem to think it was Julia. He said there were two good motives, money and hate. Also I still think it odd that Melissa left everything to Julia. And did Julia know about the will?"

Charles groaned. "I've a feeling we might have to make another trip to Cambridge."

"Let's try this village meeting first. We'll see Mrs. Bloxby in the morning."

The next day, Mrs. Bloxby listened carefully to their suggestion. "I do not see what harm it will do," she said. "Wait until I get the book and see when the hall is free. It had better be an evening, so that everyone will be back from work."

She returned with a ledger and ran her finger down the pages. "Let me see, next Saturday evening is free. I'm afraid Alf might expect you to pay for the rental of the hall."

"What! After all the money Aggie raised at the fête!" exclaimed Charles.

"That money went straight to charity," said Mrs. Bloxby.

"I don't mind," said Agatha. "I'll pay half and Charles will pay the other half."

Charles opened his mouth to protest but saw the gleeful look in Agatha's eyes and closed it again.

Mrs. Bloxby carefully entered the hall booking and said, "You are both going to have a busy day."

"Why?" asked Agatha.

"Because everyone will have to know there is a meeting. You'll need to run off fliers from your computer and post them through all the doors."

Agatha groaned. "Can't I just put up a notice in the village shop?"

"A lot of people shop at the supermarkets and might not see it."

"I know," said Charles. "The schoolchildren are still on holiday. We could get some of them to distribute fliers."

"I wouldn't do that," said Mrs. Bloxby. "It's been tried. They even get paid for it, but children are so lazy nowadays. One cottage usually ends up with several hundred fliers pushed through the one letter-box and then the little angels come round to the vicarage demanding their money."

"Oh, well," sighed Agatha. "I need the exercise."

She and Charles returned to her cottage. Agatha typed off a flier on her computer and ran off several hundred copies and then she and Charles split up, agreeing to meet at the Red Lion later.

As Agatha trudged from door to door, she felt a sudden sympathy with the lazy schoolchildren. It would be so easy just to hide a bunch of fliers or shove a hundred through the one letter-box and then be finished with the wretched things. She just hoped the same idea wasn't occurring to Charles.

She took a break for lunch and noticed from an egg-smeared plate lying in the sink that Charles had taken a break as well. Back out she went, ending up by posting the last flier in the village store's window. People she spoke to grumbled that they had told the police all they knew, and yet all seemed intrigued by the idea of the meeting.

Agatha wearily made her way along to the pub, where Charles was already sitting. She eyed him suspiciously. "You didn't cheat?"

"No, sweetie, as my aching feet will bear testimony. I ran like the wind from door to door. You *would* leave me to do the council estate. Loads of houses there. Oh, and I had to call the police."

"Why?"

"I was bending down—all the letter-boxes in those council houses are practically at ground level—when I heard a woman screaming. 'Leave me alone,' she was shouting, and then there was the sound of a thump and then another scream. So I called Fred Griggs."

"Was it a Mrs. Allan?"

"That's the one. Fred tried to get her to lay charges. The man is called Derry Patterson, a big rough fellow."

"But she wouldn't lay charges?"

"Nope."

"Why does she do it? She's just got rid of one brutal man."

"Seems they go for the same kind. Anyway, what next?"

"I think we should try to get Bill to tell us the name of Melissa's solicitor and also tell us how much she left in her will."

"Aren't wills published in the newspaper? We could ask that editor in Mircester. He might open up a bit. I know, we'll tell him about the village hall meeting, get a bit of publicity for it."

"Good idea."

The following day, the editor of the *Mircester Journal,* Mr. Jason Blacklock, surveyed them wearily. "You two again," he said. "You're not very good at supplying us with stories. It's just as well we don't cover Worcester, although I did get reports you've had the police out twice."

"The next thing that happens in your area, we'll let you know. I mean, I did send you an invitation to the fête," said Agatha. "I looked at your paper and you didn't cover it."

He sighed. "I decided to give Josie a break and sent her."

"What? Mircester's finest example of anorexia?"

"Yes, her."

"So what happened?"

"She told us nothing happened. She said it was just a tatty little village fête. When I read in the *Gloucester Echo* that an antique doll had gone for two thousand, I fired her."

"I suppose she didn't even bother to go."

"You suppose right. Now, what are you after?"

"Do you know how much Melissa left in her will?"

"Somewhere in the region of two and a half million."

Charles let out a low whistle. "That's surely an amount to die for."

"You mean to kill for," said Agatha.

"You think it was the sister?" said Blacklock. "But I gather she's got a cast-iron alibi."

"Seems that way," said Agatha. "Why we're here is we'd like to know how we can get hold of Melissa's lawyer."

"That would be Mr. Clamp of Clamp, Anderson and Biggins. They're round the corner in Abbey Way, number nineteen."

Agatha and Charles rose. "So, any story?" he asked.

"Not yet," said Agatha. "We'll let you know."

When they were outside the newspaper office, Charles said, "You'll never guess who I saw."

"Who?"

"The fair Josie, over in a corner of the office."

"But he said she was fired!"

"Maybe she's working out her notice, or maybe Blacklock doesn't want us to know he's got a soft spot for such a loser.

Let's go and see this lawyer anyway. He'll probably give us the usual spiel, can't reveal details of my clients, blah, blah, blah."

"Worth a try anyway. Come on."

They entered the law offices and left the busy world behind. It was an old building and they were immediately shrouded in dusty quiet. An elderly receptionist listened to their request and then creaked off into an inner office. Had she been with the firm a long time? wondered Agatha. It would be nice to think she had been employed recently. It would be great to think that one could still find work in one's declining years. Again she felt the pang of regret that she had not married Jimmy. She would need to see out the rest of her days on her own. Even cats did not last forever, and she knew that if anything happened to Hodge and Boswell, she would not replace them. And then she realized she had not thought of James. It was if she had finally accepted that she would never see him again.

The receptionist returned and inclined her grey head. "Mr. Clamp will see you now."

Agatha, because of the age of the receptionist, had expected an elderly man, but Mr. Clamp was small and round and comparatively young. He looked more like a young farmer than a lawyer. His face was a healthy outdoor red and he had very large, powerful hands.

"I have read about you, Mrs. Raisin," he said after Charles had made the introductions. "I gather you have come to inquire about Mrs. Sheppard's will."

"Not quite," said Agatha. "I am puzzled as to why she left everything to a sister whom she had not seen in years and did not even like. I wondered if you could tell me her state of mind."

He frowned and looked down at his desk.

"We are not asking for state secrets," urged Agatha. "And your client is dead."

He raised his eyes. "I suppose there is no harm in telling

175

you. She was agitated, nervous. She said, 'I always thought I would live forever.' "

"Did she say anything about Julia, her sister?"

"No, she just said something like she may as well make it easy and leave it all to the one person and then she laughed and said, 'I'd love to see Julia's face.' It was a very straightforward will. Everything to the sister."

"Something must have happened to make her think she had not very long to live," said Charles.

"I think that's perhaps being wise after the event," said Mr. Clamp. "She appeared in good health. A very attractive and charming lady, I thought her. As a matter of fact, she asked me out to dinner."

"Did you go?" asked Agatha.

"No, there is a Mrs. Clamp who would not look favourably on me going out for dinner with an attractive woman."

"You could have said you were working late at the office," said Charles with a grin.

Mr. Clamp was not amused. "I never lie to Mrs. Clamp."

He could not help them further. They walked back to the car-park, turning over in their minds what they had heard. "I'm damn sure someone threatened her," said Agatha at last. "I think that's why she made a will and left everything to Julia, of all people."

"Considering her treatment at the hands of Dewey, I'm surprised she didn't make out a will before," said Charles.

"Maybe it isn't Dewey. Maybe she knew Dewey so well that she knew he wouldn't really hurt her," said Agatha.

"I find that hard to believe. I mean, he certainly terrified Roy."

"But Roy hadn't been living with him. Besides, Dewey's tale of how he threatened Melissa may have only been a fantasy. Maybe the fact is she just got bored with him and got a divorce.

Maybe she did threaten to attack his pet doll and so he agreed to a divorce without any protest."

"If that's the case, bang goes suspect number one. And what about James? Are we ever going to find James?"

"I think he's dead," said Agatha. "Look, his council tax bills and water bills would go unpaid unless I paid them and James was always fussy about paying his own debts. He would have returned to clear things up if he could."

"I think if he was dead, he would have been found by now. The police don't give up easily. They'll have been looking all along. Did you get all his papers?"

"I suppose so. I dealt with the unpaid bills. He hardly ever got any personal correspondence, except from his publisher."

They both stopped and looked at each other.

"I never thought of his publisher or agent," said Agatha. "But the police wouldn't have missed that."

"Who's his agent?"

"Some woman called Bobby English, one-woman show, office in Bedford Street in Bloomsbury."

"The hunt is on again," said Charles cheerfully. "We'll go to London."

Agatha had never met Bobby English before and was taken aback when she saw her and then stabbed with jealousy. She was a tall willowy woman with a cloud of dark hair, very white skin, large dark eyes and a sensual mouth painted deep-red. She was wearing a power-suit and very high heels.

"Terrible for you," she said briskly, "but I don't think I can help you any more than I have helped the police."

Charles looked around at the framed book jackets on the office wall. Some of the covers were quite lurid. He pointed to one, entitled *The Beckoning of Desire,* which showed a voluptuous blonde with her dress down around her waist and said, "Forgive me for saying so, Bobby, but you don't seem the sort of agent to deal with dry military history."

"No, I'm not. But I met James at a party and we took a fancy to each other." Agatha scowled. "It amused me to push his book and he was delighted when I found a publisher for it."

"That's Greive Books, isn't it?" asked Agatha.

Bobby nodded.

"What is the name of his editor there?"

"Robin Jakes."

"I assume Robin is a woman," said Agatha sourly. Bobby nodded again. Agatha had always disapproved of women who affected men's names. Now she was beginning to positively hate them. Had James had an affair with Bobby?

She eyed the agent. "No, I didn't," said Bobby, "if that's what you're thinking. We were just friends."

"Did James ever let slip some part of the world that he particularly liked?" asked Charles. "I mean, do you have any idea where he might have gone?"

"No, he had travelled widely. I don't think he had any tie to any particular place. I really can't help you. When we met, we would talk about books, markets, possibility of sales, that sort of thing. You can try his editor, but I don't think Robin can tell you any more than I can."

To Agatha's relief, Robin Jakes turned out to be a pleasant, middle-aged woman with sandy hair and thick glasses. "I am so sorry," she said, shaking Agatha's hand. "It must be an awful time for you."

Agatha blinked back sudden tears. No one else, apart from Mrs. Bloxby, seemed to have thought that she might be suffering. To their questions, Robin said sadly that she had no idea where he could have gone. "He had travelled so much," she said. "I once suggested he might try writing a travel book, but his passion was military history. I was just his editor, you know. We weren't

178

friends." She frowned in thought. "There's something he said, oh, about a few months before he disappeared. What was it? Oh, I have it. I was asking him again to consider writing a travel book. He was . . . is . . . a good descriptive writer. He laughed and said he had an old diary of his travels. He said he might dig it out and have a look at it."

"A diary!" exclaimed Agatha. "The police said nothing to me about a diary."

"We'd better get on to them," said Charles. "They may have held it back."

Outside the publishing office, Agatha took out her mobile phone. "Better make sure you get Bill," said Charles. "If they have it, anyone else might not want to release it."

Agatha was told Bill was out and so, after a meal in London, they travelled back. Once home, Agatha got Charles to phone Bill at home, guessing that the formidable Mrs. Wong might be more prepared to bring Bill to the phone for a man.

When Bill answered, Agatha snatched the phone from Charles. "Bill, it's me, Agatha. I've just heard that James kept a diary of his travels. Do the police have it?"

"They kept back some papers, Agatha. It might be among them."

"Oh, Bill, I've got to see that diary. There might be something in it that would mean something to me and wouldn't mean anything to you."

"I'll ask. Call at headquarters—let me see—at ten tomorrow morning."

Agatha thanked him and replaced the receiver. "We're to go to Mircester in the morning," she told Charles. "He'll see what he can do."

"So you're beginning to hope again that James is alive?"

"Yes, damn him," said Agatha. "If only I knew one way or the other."

• • •

In the morning, as they travelled to Mircester, Agatha was half-dreading seeing James's diary, that is, if she was allowed to see it. What if it contained awful things about her? At last, as they were approaching the town, she voiced her worries to Charles.

"I should not think dear James has one deeply personal thought in the whole of that diary," said Charles. "Probably observations he made on his travels."

They waited in an interviewing room at police headquarters for what seemed, to Agatha, like ages, but was in fact only half an hour. At last Bill appeared carrying a small, thick, leather-bound book. "I can't let you take it away with you," he said, "but you can have a look at it and call me when you're ready to leave."

Agatha and Charles sat side by side at a plain wooden table, the top scarred with cigarette burns and coffee-cup rings. Agatha opened to the first page, feeling a pain at her heart as she recognized James's small, crabbed handwriting. "Oh, it's an *old* diary," she said. She flipped to the last entry. "And it finishes five years before I even met him."

"You should be relieved there's nothing about you in there," said Charles heartlessly. "Let's start reading. Maybe there's somewhere he liked more than anywhere else. Patiently they read descriptions of Nepal, of Cyprus, of Saudi Arabia, even a long description of a trip to China. Prices were marked down, lodging houses and hotels. Then he had taken a walking tour of France. Agatha stifled a yawn as her eyes skittered over descriptions of chateaux and vineyards. She was about to turn the page, when Charles put a restraining hand on hers. "Back to that page," he said. "At the bottom."

> *I was tired and thirsty* [Agatha read]. *I had been walking from early morning. I saw a monastery in front of me. I knocked at the gate and pleaded for somewhere to rest and for some water. A monk told me it was a Benedictine closed*

order, Saint Anselm, but he let me in and said I could sit in the shade of the cloisters for a little and he brought me a jug of spring water. I don't suppose I've ever had a very strong faith in God, but while I sat there, I could almost feel a spiritual presence. After resting for an hour, I went on my way and . . .

She turned the page and then looked at Charles impatiently. "What?"

"James was interested in this business of mind over matter. Miracles do happen to cancer victims. He might have gone back there," said Charles. "He was in the valley of the shadow of death. A closed order. That might explain why nobody can find him."

But Agatha did not want to believe it. Somehow a James closer to God seemed to her to mean a James farther away from one Agatha Raisin. "Read on," she said. "There must be something else." But the diary finally finished with a description of a tour of Turkey which ended in mid-sentence.

"Nothing there," said Agatha, closing the book with a sigh.

"I can't help thinking about that monastery," said Charles. "Want to check it out?"

"He doesn't say where it is."

"Here. Give me that diary again."

Charles flipped back through the pages. "Here we are. I had just left Agde and had decided to head south towards the Spanish frontier."

"Where's Agde?"

"South of France, on the Provence side."

"Too long a shot," said Agatha. "Besides, we've got this meeting on Saturday."

Charles looked at her curiously. "Don't you want to find James?"

"Of course I do." But Agatha did not want to think for a moment that he was in a monastery. "Maybe after the meeting," she said. "But don't tell Bill about your idea. A bunch of British flatfeet descending on the south of France might alert him."

"They'd just send the French police to check the place out."

"Leave it at the moment, Charles. I'll think about it after Saturday."

Charles went home for a couple of nights, leaving Agatha alone with her thoughts. She made notes about everyone they had interviewed, and found she could not build up a clear picture of the murderer. She found she was pinning her hopes on Saturday's meeting too much and tried to depress them. What if the end result was pages and pages of things like, "Didn't see anything. Watched telly. Went to bed." And always at the back of her mind, Charles's suggestion that James just might be at that monastery nagged at the back of her mind. James in a monastery would be as lost to her as if he were dead. On the other hand, were he there, he could surely tell them who had attacked him. She decided it was time to take her appearance in hand while she waited and had her hair cut and styled at the hairdresser's and had a facial at the beautician's and a leg wax. Then she took a trip into Oxford and bought some new clothes. It was a sunny day and shopping was enjoyable.

She found herself wishing the case were solved. She was beginning to think that a life without James might be quite pleasant. She could begin to feel good about herself, be her own woman again.

By the time Charles arrived early on Saturday morning, Agatha was beginning to feel she had enjoyed a short holiday.

As she walked to the village hall with Charles, she noticed a crowd of people streaming in the same direction. "There's going to be masses of odd reports," warned Charles. "A lot of people might start imagining things. Or daft things like, 'My mother's picture fell off the wall, so I knew something bad had happened,' that kind of thing."

"Let's hope there's some nugget among the lot," said Agatha, "because if there isn't, I can't think where we would try next."

There was an air of excitement in the hall as Agatha and Charles mounted to the stage. Agatha noticed the local press were there.

She checked the microphone and then began to speak. "This unsolved murder is affecting the tranquillity of our village," she said. "Now, you will have found on each chair a sheet of paper. I want you all to think back to the night Melissa Sheppard was murdered and to the day James Lacey was attacked. I want you to write down anything out of the way you might have seen. You may have not told the police because at the time it seemed silly or insignificant. I will now move to that table by the door. When you have finished, give me what you have written. Please, do try very hard. I find it strange that no one saw anything at all."

Agatha and Charles descended from the platform. "Did you supply them with pens?" asked Charles. "Or time will be taken up as everyone tries to borrow a pen from everyone else."

"Rats! I forgot," said Agatha.

"I'll nip along to the village store and get some."

Charles was soon back with boxes of biros, which he began to pass around. Some people were writing busily, some were chewing the ends of their pens and staring at the ceiling, and some were casting covert glances at their neighbours' papers, like children at an exam.

At last, one by one, they began to leave, placing their papers in front of Agatha. With a sinking heart, she noticed most of the first ones had simply been scrawled with, "Didn't see anything."

Agatha stood up and shouted to the remainder, "Even if you *heard* anything."

At last, after an hour, everyone had left. Agatha and Charles and Mrs. Bloxby stacked away the chairs. "Better get this lot home," said Agatha, "and pray there's something."

• • •

When they reached Agatha's cottage, Charles said, "Let's have a drink and something to eat. It's going to be a long day."

Agatha made a fry-up of sausage, eggs, bacon and chips, Charles's favourite food.

"Now," she said impatiently, "let's get to work."

They moved through to the sitting-room. Agatha divided the papers into two piles.

They began to read. "Here's an unsigned one," said Charles. "It says, 'You murdering bitch, you did it yourself.'"

"Put it to one side," said Agatha. "I wonder who could have written that? There were a few strange faces there."

"And children. Might have been a nasty child."

Agatha ploughed through some quite long descriptions of what people had been doing on the night of Melissa's death. They seemed to think they had to furnish an alibi. "Listen to this one," said Agatha. "It's from Mrs. Perry, who lives out on the Ancombe Road. 'I made ham and chips for me and Dad at six o'clock and then we went to the Red Lion for a drink. Dad had half a pint and I had a shandy. Then we walked home. I let the cat out. We switched on the telly. Rotten film where people took their clothes off and did you-know-what. Me and Dad could hardly bear to watch. Then we went to bed after I had got our hot-water bottles ready. Hoping this finds you as it leaves me. Amy Perry.' What good's all that supposed to do?"

"Plough on," murmured Charles. "So far all I've got apart from the bitch letter are alibis and superstitious warnings. 'The house grew suddenly cold,' that sort of thing. 'The fur on my cat's back rose.'"

"Here's another irritating one," remarked Agatha. "It's from Mrs. Pamela Green. Widow. Tall, rangy, acidulous. Look at the italic handwriting! Pure eighteenth-century. 'I could not sleep on the Night of Mrs. Sheppard's Unfortunate death. It is one of the great Disadvantages of age. As is my wont, I put the leash on Queenie'—that's her dog, nasty, vicious little bunch of hair—'and went out. The roads were deserted, except for a Child. I said to her, Why aren't you home in bed? And she said cheekily I ought to mind my own Business. I had let Queenie off the leash and she had disappeared into one of the gardens. I went to Fetch her, and when I returned, the Child had gone. I would like to say to you, Mrs. Raisin, that at your age, it would become You better to confine yourself to Charitable Pursuits and leave Police Matters to the police.' Horrible cow."

"I wonder who the child was," said Charles. "Are there any children in this village of the geriatric and retired?"

"A lot down at the council houses. Press on."

After some hours, Agatha groaned, "Well, what a waste of time."

"Let's swap," said Charles. "You take my bundle. I'll take yours. We may see something the other has missed."

They both began to read again.

At last Agatha said wearily, "What a waste of space!"

"We've got that child to look for. Maybe we should call on Mrs. Green tomorrow and get a description."

"Did I tell you she wears glasses like the end of milk bottles?" said Agatha. "No? Well, she does. We'll never get anywhere."

"Let's go over them all again in the morning," said Charles, stifling a yawn.

After a late meal, Agatha went up to bed and Charles went off to the spare bedroom.

Agatha found sleep would not come. Jumbled thoughts about the murder and all the people they had questioned drifted in and out of her brain. At last she fell asleep and plunged down into a dream where she was dressed in white, on her wedding day, and standing at the altar of Carsely Church. She could not make out the features of the man she was marrying. Beside her stood Mrs. Bloxby as maid of honour. "You shouldn't be doing this," she whispered in Agatha's dream. "You were unhappy with James and now you'll be unhappy with him. Remember what happened to poor Mrs. Allan. People who have escaped from one unhappy marriage go out and do the same thing again, choose the same type."

"Shut up," mumbled Agatha in her sleep. "No one's going to stop me getting married. I don't want to be alone." She was conscious of her husband-to-be turning and walking away from her down the aisle. She tried to turn and call to him, to stop him, but she could not form the words. She must try to call to him. She must call him back. She must get married.

She awoke to find Charles shaking her. "What's up?" she cried.

"You were having one hell of a nightmare, groaning and crying."

"Oh, that," said Agatha, blinking in the light. "Such a silly dream. I dreamt I was getting married and Mrs. Bloxby was warning me it would all turn out like my marriage to James. She said, like Mrs. Allan, people always went and married the same type of person when they married again."

Charles sat down on the bed. "Wait a minute. Let's think about this."

"It was only a stupid dream."

"But Mrs. Bloxby said that in the case of Mrs. Allan, she had married the same type of person, and that people do."

Agatha stared at him. "Do you mean that in some way Megan Sheppard might be like Melissa?"

"Could be. Remember James was trying to find out about *another* psychopath."

"Pass me my dressing-gown," said Agatha, swinging her legs out of bed. "Those papers downstairs."

"What about them?"

"Mrs. Green said she met a child. A child! With Megan's

girlish appearance and Mrs. Green's bad eyesight, she could have met Megan!"

"Bit far-fetched, but I'm game to try anything."

They went downstairs and began to look through the papers again. "Here's Mrs. Green's paper. Is there anything else about a child?"

They settled down to go through the papers again. "Nothing," said Charles at last.

"Let's see Mrs. Green in the morning."

TEN

†

BUT in the morning, both Agatha and Charles were beginning to think that they had leaped at the idea of the child's being Megan, of somehow Melissa and Megan having the same personalities.

"Might as well have a go anyway," said Charles. "We're at a dead end otherwise and all that church-hall business will have been a waste of time."

Agatha and Charles walked out to Mrs. Green's cottage, which lay up the hill on the road leading out of the village. It was a mellow day with misty golden sunlight flooding the countryside. "If we don't get anything out of this," said Agatha suddenly, "I'm going to forget about the whole thing." She waved an arm to encompass the sunny village. "Ever since James left, I've been wandering around in darkness. I want to start living again."

"Without James?"

"Yes, without James. Even if by some miracle I found him, even if he wanted to come back to me, it wouldn't work. I kept expecting him to change and he kept expecting me to change, and neither of us could."

"You haven't been smoking. That's a start."

"But how long does it take for the craving to go away?"

"You could stop carrying cigarettes in your handbag."

"Works for me. As long as I've got them with me, I feel the strength to keep on resisting them."

"If you say so," said Charles. "This the cottage?"

"Yes. Here goes."

Mrs. Green answered the door and looked on Agatha Raisin with disfavour. "Oh, it's you."

"I found what you wrote in your report very interesting," said Agatha, giving her that crocodile smile one gives people one doesn't like. "May we come in?"

"No."

"You said on the night Melissa was murdered you saw a child," said Charles. "Can you describe this child?"

Mrs. Green was a snob and her face softened at the sound of Charles's upper-class voice. "It was dark, Sir Charles, and . . . Won't you come in?"

"Thank you." Charles stepped past her into the cottage and she promptly shut the door in Agatha's face.

Face flaming, Agatha opened the door and followed them into the cottage parlour, which was a dark room in which framed photographs covered every surface. The darkness of the room was caused by the leaves of a large wisteria growing outside the window and by the leaves of a large cheese plant just inside the window. Mrs. Green's autocratic face swam in the gloom.

"I would say she was in her early teens," she said. "She was chewing gum, a disgusting habit, and had one of those little rucksacks on her back that young people affect these days instead of carrying a handbag."

"Colour of hair?" asked Charles.

"I couldn't really tell."

"What was she wearing?" asked Agatha.

"Shorts with a bib top and these ugly boots they all wear these days."

"Did you tell the police?" asked Charles.

"Of course not. They are looking for a murderer, not a child. And if I may say so, you would be better off leaving the whole thing to the police. What do we pay taxes for? I suppose such nosiness is understandable in the case of a person like Mrs. Raisin, but you, Sir Charles, should know better."

"You forget," said Agatha icily, "that my husband is missing."

"Poor Mr. Lacey. I am not surprised. According to the people of this village, you led him a dog's life."

Agatha, who had taken a seat on a sofa, rose to her feet. "You are a nasty, acidulous old bat and I hope you rot in hell." She stormed out.

Charles rose as well. "Just one thing," he said to Mrs. Green, who was gasping and goggling. "What was this child's hair like? I mean, long, short, pigtails?"

She looked up at him through her thick glasses. "It was in little clumps at either side and tied with ribbons. Now, I must say, Sir Charles, I do not know what you see in that woman. I don't—"

Charles simply walked out. Agatha was standing outside, lighting a cigarette. He plucked it out of her hand and threw it into Mrs. Green's garden and then waltzed her down the road. "What's up with you?" cried Agatha, disengaging herself when she could.

"The child wore its hair in bunches, or clumps, as she called them, and tied with ribbons. Now, who do we know wears her hair like that?"

"Megan," breathed Agatha.

"What do we do now? Go to the police?"

"No, I want to go and see her and confront her."

"Might not be safe."

"You'll be with me."

"I'm not much protection against a psychopath wielding a hammer. But she won't be on her own. Sheppard'll be there. And how did she get from Oxford to Carsely and back without her husband knowing about it?"

"Taxi?" said Agatha.

"I'm sure the police will have checked that. And buses."

"Unless Sheppard was in on it. If only we could make sure he's not at home when we call."

"I think that could be arranged," said Charles. "Let's get home and I'll phone him and say there's been a break-in at his shop."

"What if she goes with him?"

"We'll chance that. If not, we'll need to wait until Monday morning, when he goes to work."

They hurried back to Lilac Lane. Charles looked up the Sheppards's number in the phone book. "Don't listen," he said to Agatha. "I'm going to disguise my voice and I can't do it with you listening. I've got to pretend to be a copper."

Agatha went into the kitchen. She took out her packet of cigarettes and then put them away again.

She heard the murmur of Charles's voice and then he came into the kitchen. "That's it," he said. "Let's go."

Charles drove quickly to Blockley, hoping he did not meet Luke Sheppard driving out of the village. He parked in front of the Sheppards's cottage and took a deep breath. "Here we go, Aggie," he said.

Megan answered the door. "You again," she said. "What now?"

"May we come in?" asked Charles, smiling at her. "We have some news for you."

"I suppose. Luke isn't here. There's been a break-in at his shop."

They followed Megan as they had done before, out into the garden. "So what have you got to tell me?"

Charles opened his mouth to start with a diplomatic way of approaching the subject, but Agatha said brutally, "You murdered Melissa. You were seen in the village at the time of her death. We have a witness."

Megan sat very still, the pupils of her eyes seeming huge. Then she laughed. "Nice try. I was in Oxford all night. How was I supposed to get from Oxford to Carsely?"

"I don't know," said Agatha. "But we have this witness. It places you at the scene of the murder."

"And what do the police have to say to that?"

"We haven't told them yet," said Agatha.

"Why not?"

"We wanted to know what you had to say for yourself."

"Aren't we all supposed to be in the manor-house library?" jeered Megan. "While the great detective accuses and the guilty one breaks down? Why don't you both take your fairy-tales and run along, or I will call the police and charge you with harassment."

"It was you James found out about," said Agatha doggedly. "You were sectioned at the same time as Melissa."

"I'm going to count to ten, and if you're not out of here by the time I have finished, I am going to call the police. One . . ."

"Come on, Aggie," said Charles.

"Two . . ."

Agatha rose reluctantly to her feet.

"Three . . ."

Charles urged Agatha through the cottage. "Four . . ." Megan's voice chanted.

Outside, Charles said. "That's it. We're going to see Bill Wong."

"What can he do that we can't?" demanded Agatha.

"We've got a suspect, we've got a witness. We've got to show Bill where to look."

Mrs. Wong looked outraged when they asked to speak to Bill. "It's Sunday," she protested, "and we're about to have Sunday dinner."

"Bill!" shouted Agatha.

Bill appeared behind his mother, who was blocking them off on the doorstep. "What is it, Agatha?" he asked.

"We've found the murderer."

"You'd better come in. Do stand aside, Ma."

Mrs. Wong backed off, mumbling under her breath. Bill led them out into the garden. "Sit down," he said. "Tell me about it."

Agatha took a deep breath and began to explain about how Mrs. Green thought she had seen a child on the night of the murder, about how the description of the "child" fitted with the description of Megan Sheppard.

"But why?" asked Bill.

"Wait a minute," said Agatha, screwing up her face in concentration. "Something's coming. What about this? James was inquiring if there was a possibility of one psychopath befriending another. What if Melissa and Megan met in that psychiatric unit years ago, when Megan was sectioned. What if they did become friends, and then maybe lost touch. What if . . ." She screwed up her face even harder. "What if there was an earlier will? What if Melissa had originally left her money to Megan? What if Melissa thought that Megan was dangerous? By coincidence or by plot, Megan marries her ex. Damn, we should have asked her lawyer if she had made a previous will. Anyway, somehow Megan finds out that Melissa has changed her will and blames James's influence and attacks him. Then she goes on to murder Melissa."

Bill put his head in his hands. "Agatha, Agatha. A lot of

police work and time went in checking out the Sheppards' alibi. Their car was in the hotel garage all night."

"Oh. Wait a bit. What sort of car?"

"A Range Rover."

"You could get a motorbike in the back of one of those."

"Agatha, all vehicles that went out of the hotel garage that night were checked."

"But they wouldn't need to leave a motorbike in the car. They could leave it at the station or in Saint Giles. Oh, Bill, if they had a motorbike, or a scooter, it might be registered to one of them. Please, Bill, do try."

"I'll see what I can do. Wait here."

"The more we discuss it, the thinner it gets," mourned Charles.

Bill came back. "They'll get back to me. We have to wait."

"You see," said Agatha earnestly, "she could have slipped out of the hotel when no one was looking. I know Mrs. Green's got bad eyesight, but she could pass for a child and no one would think of reporting seeing a young teenager."

"Dinner's ready," called Mrs. Wong.

"You'll need to put mine in the oven," Bill called back. "Important police business."

Mrs. Wong appeared in the garden, holding a ladle like a weapon. "It's a disgrace, that's what it is, bothering people on a Sunday."

His mother retreated. "You can check the records at the hospital," said Agatha. "If she was there at the same time as Melissa, it's something to go on."

"It still won't make her a murderess."

Agatha sighed. And then the phone rang. Bill ran into the house, calling out, "I'll get that."

"If Mrs. Wong answers the phone first and that's the police, she'll give them a long harangue about Sunday dinner," said Agatha gloomily.

"It just might not have anything to do with Megan at all," said Charles quietly. "Don't build up your hopes."

Bill came back and his eyes were gleaming. "What?" asked Agatha eagerly.

"You're a witch! There's a motorbike registered to Megan Sheppard. I wonder if they still have it."

"The shed," said Charles. "They have a shed at the bottom of the garden."

"I'll need to go into the office," said Bill. "I hope they haven't got rid of that motorbike. I wish you had come straight to me in the first place. She may have fled. Go home and wait. Yes, Agatha. It's out of your hands now."

So Agatha and Charles waited. The long afternoon dragged on into evening and Agatha's phone remained silent.

They ate a silent meal, waiting, always waiting. Then, just before nine o'clock, the doorbell rang.

"At last!" cried Agatha, leaping to her feet.

She rushed and opened the door. Megan Sheppard stood there, the outside light over the door gleaming on a small but efficient pistol she was holding in her hand. "Back into the house slowly," she said.

Numb with shock, Agatha did as she was told. Charles came out of the kitchen and stood staring at the pair of them.

Megan waved the gun in the direction of the sitting-room. "In there," she snapped.

When they were inside, she ordered, "Sit down."

Agatha and Charles sank down side by side on the sofa.

"So it was you," said Agatha, through dry lips.

"And I would have got away with it," said Megan, "if you hadn't come blundering around."

"Why?" asked Charles. "Was it the money?"

"She said she would leave it all to me. We were friends, she thought. Actually, I never liked her. But I kept in touch with her over the years. I didn't take Luke Sheppard away from her. He got sick of her and asked for a divorce. That was when I moved in. She didn't mind, she said."

"But no one knew you had been seeing Melissa," said Agatha. "Didn't you call at each other's houses?"

"No, she didn't want to see Luke again, or so she said. Then Luke came back one evening and said Melissa had sent for him."

"That was when she told him," said Agatha, thinking, I must keep her talking. Where is Bill?

"No, that was his story. She actually told him that she had a friend in the village, James Lacey. He had advised her to change her will and leave the money to Julia, her sister."

"I phoned her up to protest, to say she hated Julia and that we'd always been friends, but she said that Lacey was right. Sorry, and all that. The worst of it was she really got a kick out of telling me.

"I was red with rage. I found out where Lacey lived and went round and attacked him. He got away. I thought he would go to the police and I couldn't believe my luck when he just disappeared. I realized I had to silence Melissa, and silence her fast. She would guess it had been me who attacked James. I told Luke. He was as anxious to get his hands on the money as me. That shop of his is hardly selling anything and he had just re-mortgaged the house. So we planned to put the motorbike in the car and stay at the Randolph in Oxford. We left the motorbike in Saint Giles. I slipped past the desk. The porter was on the phone and I crawled past under the desk."

"What did you kill her with?" asked Agatha.

"An ordinary hammer. Now I am going to shoot you both and get out of here."

Charles rose from the sofa and walked towards her. "No, you're not."

"Charles!" cried Agatha in an agony of fear. Megan aimed the pistol at his face and tried to pull the trigger. Nothing happened. Charles seized her wrist and twisted it until the gun fell on the floor. He clutched the struggling Megan tightly, yelling to Agatha, "Get the gun. The safety catch is on."

Megan was kicking out wildly and screaming and trying to twist around and claw Charles's face. Agatha grabbed the gun. "Get rope or something," shouted Charles.

Agatha stood blindly. Rope, rope, where on earth is rope? She ran into the kitchen. Nothing. She seized a large roll of cellophane and ran back with it. Megan's screams were awful, mad, unearthly.

"Oh, for heaven's sake," panted Charles.

And then there came the wail of police sirens. Charles succeeded in throwing Megan onto the floor and sat astride her, holding her hands above her head.

Agatha rushed and opened the door and waved frantically to the arriving police cars.

Villagers were gathering at the end of the street. They *would* turn up now, thought Agatha.

Bill was in the first car. "She's here?" he cried when he got out.

"Inside. Hurry," said Agatha.

Megan was handcuffed and taken off. Charles and Agatha followed in another police car to Mircester to make their statements. Agatha felt quite limp and also disgusted with herself. She had been so frightened when Megan pointed the pistol at her that she had wet herself. Why hadn't she just told the police that, and begged to be allowed to change?

She had no sense of triumph, no gladness in being proved right. She felt old and messy.

Inspector Wilkes sent Bill to take their statements. As he went to switch on the recording machine, Agatha said, "Where's Sheppard?"

"We took him in for questioning. We got him just as he was

returning from Mircester. We found the motorbike, and in one of the saddlebags we found the vacuum cleaner. It was one of those small ones people use for cleaning cars. I hope it hadn't been emptied. That's the trouble with dealing with mad amateurs. If James had not disappeared, we would have been able to arrest her and Melissa might still be alive. Megan had the most amazing luck."

"I wonder if Melissa ever intended to leave her any money," said Agatha. "I wonder if James found out about Melissa and dumped her because she was dangerous. I wonder if she told Megan that in the hope that Megan would make life a misery for James."

"Unless we find James Lacey, we'll never know," said Bill. "Now, let's begin."

They both made statements and Bill disappeared with them, leaving them alone. "I can't bear this," said Agatha to Charles. "When she pointed that pistol at me, I wet myself."

"If they keep us here much longer," said Charles, "you'll soon be dry."

"Doesn't it disgust you?"

"No, ordinary human functions do not disgust me. Stick it out now. Can't be much longer."

But Bill returned with Wilkes, who said he would like to go over their statements again. Agatha was too weary to do other than repeat everything she had told Bill, but Charles was sure that Wilkes really wanted to know how they had managed to figure out it was Megan when the police had not.

It all seemed like a dream, thought Agatha, as she and Charles went through their investigations once more, step by step. At last the statements were approved. They signed and were told they were free to go.

Agatha regained some of her usual spirit. As they were leaving the room, she turned and said to Wilkes, "You might at least say thank you."

"For what?" said Wilkes, shuffling the statement papers.

"For solving your case for you."

"We would have got there sooner or later," began Wilkes pompously.

"Pah," said Agatha Raisin and slammed the door behind her.

Oh, the luxury of a warm soapy bath and dirty clothes spinning in the washing machine. Wrapped in their dressing-gowns, Agatha and Charles met in the sitting-room for a nightcap.

"That's over at last," sighed Agatha.

"Except for James," said Charles. "Fancy a trip to France?"

"I feel too weary to even think about it," said Agatha. "How could James behave so irresponsibly?"

"He didn't know Melissa had been murdered."

"He must have done. It was in the newspapers, along with his photograph."

"He may not have looked at the newspapers. Say you find him, Aggie? What then?"

"I want to hear his side of the story," said Agatha, but the fact was she wanted to give him a piece of her mind. The oh-so-perfect James, who had always been picking on her, had made one big major mistake for which he ought to be deeply ashamed for the rest of his life.

"I suppose we'll have to hang around for a few days," said Charles. "In case they want to speak to us again."

"I suppose," echoed Agatha sleepily. "I'm off to bed."

"Alone?"

"Alone. I don't care now if I never have sex again. I don't want any more casual sex."

"Who said it was casual?" remarked Charles, but Agatha had already left the room and did not hear him.

Mrs. Bloxby was their first visitor the next morning. "It was Mrs. Allan who really put me on the track," said Agatha, "and that remark you once made about women marrying the same sort over again. I thought, why shouldn't a man marry the same kind as well?" She told her all about Mrs. Green's having seen a child on the night Melissa had been killed. "Megan must have parked the motorbike outside the village," said Agatha, "put the vacuum and the hammer in that rucksack and headed for Melissa's."

She went on and told her everything and how Megan had threatened to shoot them. "She must have known as little about guns as I do," said Agatha. "I wouldn't have noticed whether the safety catch on a gun was on or off. I wonder where she got it."

"Well, now you can leave all those details to the police," said Mrs. Bloxby. "Any news of James?"

Agatha shook her head. She flashed a warning look at Charles to stay quiet. She had a superstitious feeling that if she told Mrs. Bloxby about the possibility of James's being in the monastery that he would turn out not to be there at all. It was such a slim chance.

After Mrs. Bloxby had gone, Charles said he would return home and join her again when she planned to set off for France. "Leave it a week," said Agatha. "Everything will be properly wrapped up by then. I'm surprised the press haven't been hammering at the door."

"Oh, Wilkes will just have said a woman is helping them with their inquiries," said Charles. "He'll want to keep us out of it. Make it look like all his own work. Do you think we're psychic, Agatha?"

"You called me Agatha. You're improving. No. Why?"

"You must admit it was an amazing leap of deduction on the part of both of us."

"I think it was because, for my part, I'd been thinking about nothing else for weeks. It's a bit like a crossword. You stare at some clue and then decide you'll never get the answer, and the next day you pick up the paper and glance at it and the answer snaps into your brain."

"Could be. I'm off then. See you in a week."

"You really think there's a chance of him being at that monastery?"

"A slim one, but yes, I do think it's worth a try."

When Charles had gone, Agatha sat down, cradling a cup of coffee in her hands and thinking it was rather pleasant to be alone again, particularly now that she had nothing to be frightened of. Perhaps a lot of her discontent and frustration was because she would not accept middle age or the prospect of heading to old age. A life without men meant she could dress the way she wanted, be herself. No need to let herself go, exactly. She had a sudden sharp longing for a cigarette and tried to fight it down.

Then she could feel the comfort draining away. How quiet her cottage seemed! She had the cats, of course. She did not really need to do anything. After what she had been through, no one should be expected to do anything. But she rose and began to do some housework and then went out into the garden to pull up weeds. She was bending over a flower-bed when a sudden sharp longing for James engulfed her.

Faintly, she could hear her front doorbell ringing.

With relief, she went to answer it. It was Bill Wong.

"Do come in," cried Agatha. "Has she confessed? How did it go?"

Bill followed her into the kitchen. "They both ratted on each other. Sheppard said it was all her idea, and he had not known she was going to do it. He only thought she was going to threaten Melissa. Of course, when she heard that, she said he had gone along with her every step of the way. It turns out she told him about the will. He was amazed Melissa had that amount of money. Then Megan got rattled when she learned James was romancing Melissa. She phoned her and asked her if Melissa had changed her will. Melissa said not yet, but that James had persuaded her that it would be a good idea to leave it in the family. Megan decided to act before the will was changed. There was the motive."

"It's amazing, with all that money, she chose to live in a small cottage in a village," said Agatha.

"She was evidently always tight with money, preferred to spend other people's. Not all that strange a situation. You get millionaires living in council houses. There was a man won four million on the lottery. Never told anyone. Lived in a council flat, worked at a jam factory, had a pint with his mates, just as always. Relatives found out the extent of his wealth when he died. In his will, he said he had realized the money would mean he would have to give up his mates and his job."

"Is Wilkes giving me any credit for solving his case?"

Bill looked awkward. "He's going around saying I solved it."

"Oh, well," said Agatha. "That way it keeps it in the family, so to speak. I tell you this, Bill. Never again. If a body with a knife in its back falls in front of me, I'll simply step over it and forget about it."

"Ever thought of starting a detective agency?"

"You know, I did at one time, but then I thought it would probably be nasty divorces and missing pets."

"I told Ma she had been a bit abrupt with you and Charles and so she's invited you both to dinner next Sunday."

Agatha repressed a shudder. "We can't. We're going on holiday."

He raised his eyebrows. "You mean, you and Charles?"

"Yes."

"Am I looking at the next Lady Fraith?"

"No, nothing like that. He's about ten years younger than me. We're just friends."

"Where are you going on holiday?"

"Prague," said Agatha, having a sudden fear that if she said the south of France, Bill might check on her movements to see if she was trying to contact James.

"Prague, eh? Why Prague?"

"Sentimental journey. I spent part of my honeymoon there."

"Have a good time. I see you haven't given up smoking."

Agatha looked at the smouldering cigarette between her fingers in dismay. "I thought I had. I didn't even know I had started again."

"If you hear anything at all from James Lacey, remember it's your duty to contact me."

"Will he be charged with anything? Leaving the scene of the crime?"

"No, I shouldn't think so. Not now we've got the guilty parties. Megan had no end of luck. What if a chap at the night desk at the Randolph had seen her leave or return? What if Mrs. Green had had better eyesight? What if Dewey had not been so weird and distracted our investigations? And Melissa's sister must be relieved it's all over. Wilkes became convinced she was the guilty party and those students who lodged with her have been grilled over and over again. Aren't you going to put that cigarette out—that is, if you really want to stop smoking?"

"Tomorrow," said Agatha. "I'll stop tomorrow."

"That's addict-speak. If you really wanted to stop, you'd stop now."

"Will Megan be brought to court?"

"We'll try, but last heard she was putting on a very good mad act. If she gets a sharp lawyer, she may be considered unfit. Oh, the vacuum cleaner. The stuff inside matches the fibres from Melissa's carpet. She got rid of the weapon but forgot to empty the vacuum cleaner. Lucky, that."

"Where on earth did she get a gun? And if she had one, why didn't she use it on Melissa? I wouldn't even know where to start buying a gun."

"Sheppard said she was nervous about your investigations.

She probably bought in just before she ransacked your house, he says. She probably would have shot you if you'd arrived home while she was there. And where would she get it? Alas, Birmingham, probably. It's easy enough if you know where to go. We catch most of the gun dealers, but as soon as we get one, another sets up shop somewhere else."

"Would you like a coffee or something?" asked Agatha.

"No, I've got to be on my way. But don't forget. Ma will expect you for Sunday dinner when you get back."

"Won't forget," said Agatha, planning to think up any lie she could to make sure she never went.

ELEVEN

†

AGATHA did not speak French. Agatha did not speak any language other than English. And she did like to be in control at all times, but realized she would need to rely on Charles to make all the arrangements once they had crossed the Channel.

Also, she was nervous about driving on the wrong side of the road, whereas Charles was used to it, so he was doing the driving.

Then Charles insisted on making a detour to Paris first to visit an old friend and Agatha did not feel as if she had any right to object, because it was Charles's car that was taking the wear and tear of the mileage.

Besides, not being in charge of things made her feel inadequate. She decided to take French lessons as soon as she got back. Yes, that would be something to do. Forget detective work; never again.

Getting off the ferry, they queued behind a long line of cars full of families going on holiday. Would they enjoy themselves? wondered Agatha, looking at the rear window of the car in front, where three children appeared to be having an all-out fight. Or would the husband, who was driving, be marking off the days in his mind until he could get back to the peace of his office?

Agatha, who had travelled quite a lot, reflected it would be wonderful to speak languages, to be able to put down sniggering waiters and insolent hotel staff, who always retreated behind a wall of incomprehension when she shouted at them in English. She had heard jokes about the British abroad who shouted at foreigners as if they were deaf, but somehow she herself could not stop doing it.

"This friend of yours," she asked after they had cleared customs, "does he know we are coming?"

"It's a she. And no, I wanted it to be a surprise. I haven't seen Yvonne in years."

"Girl-friend?"

"Ex."

"Maybe you would like to see her on your own?"

"I say, do you think you could amuse yourself for an hour? Want me to drop you off at the Eiffel Tower?"

"I've seen the Eiffel Tower. Where does she live?"

"Montmartre. Avenue Junot."

"I'll leave you when we get there and go for a walk."

"All right," said Charles, "if you keep on walking up the hill after you leave me, you'll come to the Sacre Coeur. Get a super view of Paris from there."

Agatha was glad it was Charles driving and not herself as he threw the car into the maelstrom of traffic which hurtled around Paris.

When he had parked, she said good-bye to him and headed up the Avenue Junot. Up by the Sacre Coeur, there was a square where artists drew tourists. She stood for a while and watched them before going up and into the great church.

As she stood and looked about her, she began to wonder about what she always thought about the God bit. God, for Agatha, stood for Grand Old-fashioned Disapproval. How could anyone reach out their mind with such pure belief as to cure illness?

At last, Agatha walked out on the steps in the sunshine and looked over Paris. Tourists moved up the steps and down the steps in a colourful, almost hypnotic, stream. She sat down and lit a cigarette. If I find James, then I'll quit again, she told herself. I quit before. I can quit again.

She then rose and went to a café and ordered coffee and a sandwich, realizing she was hungry. She looked at her watch when she had finished. The hour was more than up.

Agatha walked back to the Avenue Junot to find Charles emerging from a block of flats. He looked smug, and when he got into the car he smelt of fresh soap, as if he had just taken a shower. Had he had sex with the mysterious Yvonne? And if he had, why should the very idea upset her and make her feel old and lonely?

"How was Yvonne?" she forced herself to ask.

"Same as ever. Except she got four—four!—noisy brats and one of them puked over me, so a pleasant time was wasted while she and her husband sponged my clothes and I took a shower."

Agatha's spirits lifted. Paris spread before them as they sped downwards through the ever-thickening traffic. Perhaps she should try to put ideas of finding James out of her mind and just enjoy a holiday.

Charles suggested they should break their journey in Arles and carry on to Agde on the following morning, and Agatha, anxious now to delay what she was sure was going to be a disappointment, readily agreed.

• • •

When they started out from Arles the following morning, it had begun to rain, cold, drizzling, chilly rain. The weather seemed like a bad omen. The windscreen wipers clicked backwards and forwards like a metronome.

Then Charles said, "There's a little bit of blue sky just ahead. In my youth, Father William, they used to say that if you saw a bit of blue sky, enough to patch a sailor's trousers, then it was going to get sunny."

"Huh," grunted Agatha, who was beginning to feel depressed again.

But Charles was right. As they headed ever south, the rain stopped, the clouds parted and a warm Provençal sun shone down on red-tiled roofs, vineyards and fields. They stopped in Agde for a meal, and Charles in his impeccable, if English-accented French, asked for directions to the monastery of St. Anselm.

"South a bit from here, towards the Pyrenees," he said cheerfully.

"I don't know if I said so, but this is very good of you," said Agatha awkwardly. "I mean, it is a bit of a wild-goose chase."

"Worth a try," said Charles amiably. "You'll need to start trying to drive on the other side of the road, Agatha. Delicious sea food and no wine to go with it. Only water for me."

"I've only had water as well. I didn't want to arrive at the monastery smelling of booze."

"Those monks probably smell of booze the whole time. Right, let's go."

Charles, under instructions from the restaurant owner, had drawn a map. After they had been following the coast road for some miles, he turned off onto a narrower road and the car began to climb up a steep gradient.

"That must be it at the top," said Charles after a while. "It looks more like a medieval fortress."

He parked outside the main door of the monastery. There was one of those old bell-pulls at the side. Charles gave it a tug.

"Charles," said Agatha urgently, "maybe it's not such a good idea, you being with me. I mean, if James is here, it might upset him."

"If James is here, I'll make myself scarce."

A panel in the door opened and a monk looked out at them through the grille.

In French, Charles asked if they had a Mr. James Lacey in the monastery.

"I do not recall anyone of that name," said the monk courteously, replying in English.

Agatha pushed forwards. "I am Agatha Raisin," she said eagerly. "And he has been missing, and we knew he came here before and we wondered . . ." Her voice faltered and died. She suddenly felt silly. What on earth was she doing outside a monastery in the south of France?

The monk bowed his head. "I will make inquiries."

They waited. A cloud passed over the sun and the cicadas set off a droning chorus.

They seemed to have been waiting for quite a long time when the monk came back. "I am sorry," he said. "I cannot help you."

They walked slowly back to the car.

"That's that," said Agatha gloomily. "All this way for nothing."

Charles stood frowning. "He was away a long time, and when he came back, he did not say, 'We have no one of that name here.' He said, 'I cannot help you.' "

"Forget about the whole thing," sighed Agatha.

"I could do with a bit of a holiday after all we've been through," said Charles. "We passed through a village before we turned off to climb up here. I saw a little auberge. Let's book in. Do no harm to ask a few questions before we call it quits. I saw monks working in the fields. They have to sell their produce. Maybe someone's heard of an Englishman at the monastery."

He swung the car round, and as they drove down, Agatha saw the monks working in the fields. But she did not think James could be one of them. James was probably lying dead in a ditch somewhere in England.

The landlord of the auberge said that, yes, he had one double room vacant. His wife was an excellent cook. Would they want dinner?

Charles said cheerfully, yes, they would. The landlord replied that as they were such a small inn, the guests ate en famille. Would they mind? Charles, with a grin, said, "Of course not," although wondering what Agatha would make of a dinner during which she would not be able to understand a single word.

The room was clean and dominated by a double bed. "You on your side and I on mine," said Agatha firmly.

"The bathroom's along the corridor. No en-suite bathrooms here, Aggie."

Agatha felt better after a soak in a deep and ancient tub. She had carried her clean clothes to the bathroom, so she dressed there and made her face up in an old greenish mirror.

The landlord, his wife, and two sons and one daughter were at the dinner table when they entered. Charles rattled on in French while Agatha ate a delicious fish soup followed by roast guinea fowl.

As the wine passed round, Charles, taking a chance, began to talk about the reason for their visit. The family listened electrified to the story of murder and lost husband. Then, when he had finished, the landlord began to talk. Charles listened carefully and then at last turned to Agatha.

"The landlord says he buys vegetables from the monastery from an old boy called Pierre Duval. Duval comes at six in the morning. He says if I'm up and about by then, I can question him. I gather that Duval doesn't talk much, but our host is hinting that for a little bit of money, he might tell all he knows."

"I don't know how you can keep on hoping that James is there when I've given up hope," said Agatha.

"Just a hunch."

The meal ended with an apricot tart with lashings of cream. How on earth did they manage to produce such first-class food in such a tiny place? wondered Agatha.

She had been sleepy after the long drive and all she had eaten and drunk, and when the alarm went off at five-thirty she would have gone back to sleep had not Charles shaken her awake again.

"May as well do our investigations thoroughly," he said, stripping off his pyjamas and searching in his suitcase for underwear. It must be great to be able to be so unselfconscious in one's nakedness, thought Agatha, as she retreated to the bathroom. Or maybe men didn't bother. Maybe it was only women who worried about love handles and unshaven legs.

When she emerged, it was to find Charles had already gone downstairs. She walked down, following the sound of voices, and found Charles at the kitchen door talking to a wizened old man while the landlord listened intently. Correctly assuming the old man to be Pierre Duval, Agatha saw him repeatedly shaking his head.

Then Charles took his wallet out of his back pocket. He opened it and slowly began counting out notes. Some deal seemed to have been struck. The old man took the money and counted it with maddening slowness, and then he began to speak.

Agatha waited impatiently. He must be telling Charles something. Charles would never have paid up unless he was sure of getting some hard information.

At last the old man shuffled off.

"Well?" demanded Agatha.

"It seems as if there is an Englishman at the monastery," said Charles. "Sounds a bit like James. He should be working in the vegetable garden at ten this morning."

"But how do we get near him?"

"There's a little lane leads up to the back of the monastery. If we go up there, there's only a low wall at the back. We climb over that and we're in the vegetable garden."

Agatha clasped her hands. "Do you really think it might be him?"

"I wouldn't get your hopes up too high. Duval says there are all sorts of nationalities amongst the monks. We'll try anyway. Plenty of time for breakfast."

As they ate buttery croissants and drank bowls of milky coffee, Charles told their landlord of what he had learned.

Then the landlord fetched a piece of writing paper and began to draw a sketch map.

"He suggests we leave the car at the foot of the side road and walk," said Charles. "The back of the monastery sprawls down the hillside and it would be easy to miss the lane if we were driving. It's a bit overgrown."

They set out at nine o'clock. Charles parked the car at the side of the road and locked it. Agatha found her heart was beating so hard that she was beginning to pant as they made their way up the steep side road, looking for the lane. She forced herself to be calm. James was probably not there. They would be ticked off if any other monk found them trespassing, and that would be that.

"There it is," said Charles. "Hasn't been used for anything in ages. Those bushes in front of the lane have practically grown across it."

They climbed on up. The lane was rutted and grassy and at times almost seemed to disappear. The sun was hot. Stunted pines growing out of the rocky outcrop on either side afforded some shade at the start of their climb, but now they were out in an unshaded bit.

After what seemed an age, the monastery towered up before them and they plodded on.

"Is that what you call a low wall?" asked Agatha in dismay

as the lane ended against the stonework of an eight-foot-high wall. There were newer stones set into the ancient ones where the lane came up against the wall, as if there had once been an entrance and it had been sealed off.

Charles cupped his hands. "I'll give you a leg up. When you get to the top, tell me what you can see."

Agatha struggled to the top and heaved herself up until she was straddling the top. "There isn't a garden here," she said. "That old man tricked us. Nothing but a weedy field."

"Go over anyway," said Charles, "and I'll join you. The gardens might be on the other side of the field."

Agatha tried to climb down, missed her footing and fell heavily. As nimbly as a cat, Charles climbed over and dropped easily to the ground beside her. "Haven't you got any sensible shoes?" he complained.

"I'm wearing flats," said Agatha, struggling to her feet and brushing herself down.

"Thin sandals with thin straps are hardly suitable for a walk in the country. Okay, look over there at the end of the field. There's another wall with a gate. That could be the vegetable gardens. I gather they're pretty extensive."

They walked across the field, trying to keep clear of thistles and nasty jagged bits of dried plants. Agatha felt her tights rip on a particularly evil thorny plant. Why on earth had she decided to go on this hike wearing designer sandals and ten-denier tights? Madness. But it had been cool in the darkness of the inn and she had envisaged nothing more arduous than a gentle stroll.

They came up to a wrought-iron gate set into the wall. "Locked," said Charles. "Sorry, Aggie, it's another wall and a higher one. But it's so broken in places with bits of stones sticking out, we should find an easy way of getting over."

"Why are you whispering?" demanded Agatha.

"It's very quiet and sound carries a long way here."

"If it carries a long way, then everyone in that monastery is dead. No chanting, no prayers, and worse, no sounds of digging coming from anywhere."

"Here's what looks like an easy bit," said Charles. "The wall has broken away at the top and it makes it lower and it's bulged here with age and bits of stone are sticking out. Should be like walking up a ladder."

James Lacey had retreated to the quiet calm of the herb garden to rest and contemplate. He had not yet told Brother Michael the truth about his marriage. He had told him everything else, about the attack on him, about his shame and fear of death. He would shortly be taking leave from the monastery. He said he had to return to put his affairs in order, to sell his cottage. He was afraid Agatha would not agree to a divorce. If she did not, then he would simply return and carry on as a single man. The monastery was where he had been cured and he did not want anything to stand in his way of joining the order.

He tried to conjure up a picture of Agatha, but could not quite remember what she looked like.

And then there was a great thump from the bed of orange thyme behind the stone bench on which he was sitting. He leaped up in alarm and turned round.

Agatha Raisin was lying among the crushed plants. She straightened up, her face flushed and hot.

She looked at the robed figure of the monk standing in front of her and said in a faint voice, "James?"

Charles, who had reached the top of the wall, saw the scene below him and quietly backed down again. Let Agatha get on with it. But what a strange pair they made. What a tableau! Agatha, hot and dusty, struggling to her feet. James, thin and robed, his eyes very bright blue in his tanned face. Charles sat down and prepared to wait. Agatha's cigarettes and lighter had fallen out of her pocket when she was climbing the wall. He leaned his back against the warm stone and lit a cigarette. He hoped for Agatha's sake that this was the end to her romance.

"You are not supposed to be here," James was saying sharply. "There are official visiting days twice a year, and this is not one of them."

"Is that all you have to say?" demanded Agatha, her hands on her hips. "Melissa gets herself murdered, there's a police hunt for you, I think for ages you're probably dead, and all you can come up with is that it's not a visiting day!"

James sat down suddenly on the bench and put his head in his hands. Agatha sat down beside him, suddenly weary.

"Tell me about it," he said.

So Agatha told him all about Melissa's murder and how she had finally discovered that Megan was the culprit. "If you had not run away," she said waspishly, "then Megan would have been arrested for assault and Melissa would still be alive."

James looked at her. Under his tan, his face had gone quite white.

"So why did you run away?" asked Agatha.

"I was a mess," he said. "I thought you were having an affair with Charles."

"Don't judge other people by yourself," snapped Agatha.

"I started spending some time with Melissa. But she began to frighten me. I couldn't quite put my finger on it. I had been consulting a psychiatrist in Mircester and he let slip that he had all the files from the psychiatric unit. I had begun to think Melissa was a classic example of a psychopath. . . ."

"Didn't stop you shagging her," put in Agatha.

"Please." He held up his hand. "I looked in the files and found she had indeed been sectioned at one time and diagnosed as such. She had got quite drunk over dinner one night and had told me she had a lot of money and was going to leave it to her old friend Megan, who, by coincidence, had married her ex-

217

husband. She said Megan was the only friend she'd got. They'd been through some hard times together. Then, one day when I got home, I went out into the back garden. At first I thought it was a teenager and called to her sharply. She introduced herself as Megan Sheppard. I asked how she had got in. She said, 'Over the fence.' She said she had come to warn me to leave Melissa alone. She said Melissa was her friend.

"I got rid of her quickly. But something made me wonder if Megan was another psychopath, and if such, could be dangerous; if such, could only be interested in Melissa for the money."

He sighed. "I couldn't leave well enough alone. I simply had to go back to the psychiatrist and check the files. Yes, Megan had been in the psychiatric unit at the same time as Melissa. I felt I had not long to live. Our marriage was a disaster. I thought I could at least help Melissa." Agatha winced. "There are different levels of psychopathy. I thought Melissa probably had a personality disorder, whereas the little I had seen of Megan pointed to a stone-hard psychopath.

"So I called on Melissa and told her about Megan's visit. I said that Melissa would be better off leaving her money to her sister, and telling Megan that. Melissa's eyes lit up at the prospect and I realized with a sinking heart that she was actually looking forward to the experience and that she was as incapable of affection and friendship as Megan.

"She must have told Megan it was I who had counselled her to change her will. Megan walked in on me and started berating me. She then swung a hammer at my head. I staggered off. I got in the car and drove until I realized I was too ill to drive any more. I got out. I wanted to get away from the whole mess. I hitched a lift and told the truck driver I had suffered a fall. He said he would drop me at the John Radcliffe hospital in Oxford. I did not go in. I waited in the meadows until dawn and sponged the blood from my head.

"I got out on the A-40 and another truck driver took me as

far as London. I got a bus from Victoria coach station to the coast. You see, in all my distress and shame, all I could think of was this monastery."

"The police were looking everywhere for you," said Agatha. "They must have missed the coach station. How did you get over to France?"

"Friends, with a yacht. I worked my way south until I got to here. I never thought for a moment Melissa was in danger. I thought someone would have seen Megan leaving my cottage, have heard the noise. I thought that by now Melissa would have realized that when I told her Megan was dangerous, she would now know it to be true."

"So where do we go from here?" asked Agatha, searching his face for some sign of that old affection, but James's face was set and bleak.

"I would like to join this order. I found a faith here, Agatha, and that faith cured me." He smiled wryly. "I've always missed army life, and this is very like it, the order and discipline."

"What about us?"

James looked at her sadly. "I hope you will give me a divorce, Agatha."

Agatha shrugged. "Sure," she said. Another woman she could have battled against, *would* have battled against, but how on earth did you fight God?

"I planned to return in a week's time to clear things up. I shall see you then." He stood up. "I must go. Someone will soon come looking for me and you should not be here."

Agatha stood up as well. She held out her hand. James gave it a firm handshake. "See you next week."

Then he smiled sweetly at her and raised his hand in benediction. Agatha suddenly found she was so angry, she was shaking.

"Get stuffed, James," she said evenly.

He gave her a sorrowful look, and putting his cowl over his head, walked away through the garden.

Agatha felt old and weary and the sustaining anger drained out of her. She hoisted herself up the wall and rested for a moment, lying across the top. "Want me to come up and help you?" came Charles's voice.

"No, I'll manage." Agatha fumbled her way down the other side.

"That was James," said Charles, "and what did he have to say for himself?"

As they walked across the field to the other wall, Agatha told him. Charles made an odd sound. She stopped and stared at him. "You're laughing?"

"I can't help it," chuckled Charles. "My husband, the mad monk."

Overwrought, Agatha slapped him across the face. Charles promptly slapped her back, hard, and then fell onto the ground, rolling over and over, holding his sides and roaring with laughter.

Agatha stared down at him, holding her cheek where he had slapped her, the anger ebbing out of her.

And then she began to laugh helplessly as well.

"That's better," said Charles, getting up and putting an arm around her shoulders. "So does he want a divorce? You didn't say anything about that."

"Yes, and he's welcome to one. He'll be back next week to wrap things up."

"How's his tumour?"

"He says he's cured."

"I can see where he's at," said Charles. "If I'd had a brain tumour and a bunch of monks cured me with their religious belief, I'd be joining a monastery as well."

"Not if you loved your wife, you wouldn't."

"So do you think you'll be able to live with it?"

"Yes," said Agatha. And with increasing surprise: "Yes, I think I can. It really is all over now."

EPILOGUE

✝

"AND is he definitely coming back?" asked Bill Wong. "Or do we have to send out men to bring him back?"

"Oh, he'll be back any day now. To wrap things up."

"I don't see that we can really charge him with anything," said Bill. "A good lawyer would get him off like a shot. Attacked and injured, not himself, thought he was dying, didn't look at newspapers. How did he get over to France?"

"Friends with a yacht."

"I can understand James not knowing about the hunt for him, but his friends surely would. He'd better come and see us when he gets back and make a statement. I haven't asked you: How did you know where to find him?"

"It was that diary of his."

"But we went over it. Nothing there."

"There was a bit about the monastery and the spiritual peace.

221

Charles said it was a long shot, but James had been interested in miracle cures and he said it was worth a try."

"Amazing how you pair discover things. Where is Charles, by the way?"

"He felt like staying on in France, and he'd done so much for me that I got him to drive me to Marseilles and got a plane from there." Agatha laughed.

"What's funny?"

"I thought Charles had turned all generous, but before I left, he asked for my share of the petrol money, and then he'd bribed some old fellow, and he asked for the money he'd given him because it was to find James. But it was good of him to urge me on to going to that monastery."

"Megan is not going to trial."

"Oh, why?"

"Unfit to stand. We've had every sort of psychiatrist to try to prove she's faking it, but she does seem to be really mad."

"I'm relieved I won't have to go to court."

"You still will have to. Luke Sheppard is being charged with conspiracy to murder. I'll let you know the date of the trial. My bosses would have been really angry to find you were out of the country. They'd have expected you to be available for further statements. So I suppose I'd better put in a report about James."

"Can't you leave it? He'll be here. The man of God has promised. And he does want that divorce."

"All right. I'll give it another week, and if he isn't at police headquarters by then, I'll send the gendarmes to get him."

"But you said he wasn't going to be charged with anything?"

"That's true. But to wrap things up, he'll need to make a statement about his long disappearance, and Wilkes will no doubt give him a dressing down about wasting valuable police time. But then, he didn't murder Melissa, knew nothing about it, so he can hardly be blamed for anything. And if someone hits you on the head with a hammer and you don't report a crime—well, that's that."

"James said he thought Melissa was just someone with a personality disorder, not a dyed-in-the-wool psychopath."

"Then he's probably right. But if she hadn't been so manipulative, holding out the offer of riches after her death to Megan, she'd still be alive. I wouldn't blame James. I think even if he had reported her, she would have bided her time until the fuss died down, and then she would have killed Melissa anyway. I can't see that one waiting years to see if Melissa died without helping her on her way. Oh, there's one other thing."

"What's that?"

"As far as we can gather, Melissa had not made a previous will. She had lied to Megan."

"Why?"

"I think it might have amused her to think that if she died first, Megan was going to be one very disappointed woman."

"And James got involved with someone like that?"

"He was thrown by his illness. Most of the people we interviewed seemed to find her very friendly and charming. What will you do now?"

"I'll wait for James and we'll go to a lawyer and start proceedings for a divorce. After that, I don't know."

"You'll find something. Let's hope it's not another murder."

"I don't care if a body drops at my feet," said Agatha. "Never again."

"We'll see. Now what about you and Charles coming for Sunday dinner?"

"Charles is in France and I can't really think of anything other than getting things straight with James," said Agatha. "I'll let you fix a date when this is all over."

"All right. I'll hold you to it. What does Mrs. Bloxby have to say about all this?"

"I haven't told her yet. I only got back last night. I'll drop along and see her this afternoon. How's your love life?"

"Dead. Nothing happening. Didn't work out. We're quite a pair."

"You'll find someone," said Agatha, although she privately thought if Bill would stop taking them home, he'd find someone. "It's different for you," she went on. "You're young. Lots of girls around. At my age, if the man isn't married, then there's something up with him, and nice widowers don't pop up all over the place."

"You could join one of those dating agencies," said Bill. "You know, one of the good ones, where they try to match up people."

"Thanks, Bill. But right now I feel like steering clear of involvements."

After Bill had left, Agatha fed her cats and was about to go along to the vicarage when the doorbell rang.

When she answered it, she stepped back a little and tried to wipe the look of dismay off her face. Jimmy Jessop and his wife, Gladwyn, stood on the doorstep. "We were touring the Cotswolds," said Jimmy, "and I found I still had your home address. So I said to Gladwyn, 'Agatha will be thrilled to see us.'"

Gladwyn gave Agatha a small, thin smile.

"Come in," said Agatha reluctantly. "Can I offer you lunch?"

"No, we had some in a pub."

"We only have a few minutes," said Gladwyn. "What a quaint little cottage you do have. Me, I like modern. Still, it takes all sorts."

"Where is your baby?" asked Agatha.

"My mum's looking after him."

"I heard they got someone for that murder," said Jimmy. "You didn't have anything to do with finding out who did it, did you?"

"I did indeed," said Agatha, glad of an opportunity to show

off. She outlined how she had discovered that Megan was the culprit while Gladwyn fidgeted and yawned.

"That's fascinating," said Jimmy when she had finished. "But what about your husband?"

"Oh, he turned up," said Agatha airily.

"Everything all right?"

"Marvellous," said Agatha. "We're a very happy couple."

"So where is he?" asked Gladwyn, her eyes boring into Agatha's.

"Over in France on business. He'll be back soon."

"Mrs. Raisin?" called Mrs. Bloxby's voice. She came into the kitchen. "You left the front door open, so I just walked in. I met Bill Wong and heard the news."

Agatha shot her a warning look, but Mrs. Bloxby was smiling at Jimmy and Gladwyn. "I'm so glad James is alive and well. But going to be a monk! And you're getting a divorce."

Gladwyn was smiling now.

"This is Mr. and Mrs. Jessop," said Agatha hurriedly. "Gladwyn, Jimmy, Mrs. Bloxby. They're just leaving."

"Oh, no," said Gladwyn, settling back in her chair. "I want to hear all about how you can have a marvellous marriage with a monk."

But Jimmy saw the look on Agatha's face and stood up and helped a reluctant Gladwyn out of her chair. "I won't take up any more of your time, Agatha. No. We can see our way out."

Agatha sat down and put her head in her hands. She heard the outside door slam and then a high cackle of laughter from Gladwyn out on the road.

"Oh, I am sorry," said Mrs. Bloxby. "I just blurted it out without thinking. Was that your police inspector?"

"Yes, and I told his dreadful wife that me and James were happily married and that he was away on business in France. Never mind."

"So tell me all about it."

Agatha felt she had told the story so many times that her voice was beginning to echo in her ears. When she had finished, Mrs. Bloxby said, "How dreadful for you."

"You mean, Melissa trying to shoot me?"

"No, James being a monk."

"I thought you would approve. 'Nearer my God to thee,' and all that."

"I'm glad he is well and alive. But finding that he plans to enter the monastery must have come as a great shock to you."

"I think I've gone through every emotion from grief to anger, but it's all over now. Perhaps it would have been easier for me if he had died."

"Oh, I don't think so. Before you came to live here, there was a woman in the village who adored her husband. He was actually a rather nasty man. When he died, she elevated him to sainthood and wasted lots of money on mediums trying to get in touch with him. Now if he had lived—they had not been married long—then she would have found out what sort of man he was. You see, when one of the nearest and dearest dies, the one left behind feels irrationally guilty and remembers all the nice things about the dead person and blames themselves for not having been nicer, better, kinder. And you say James is coming back? Good. That will give you some much-needed time to accustom yourself to the idea of divorce."

"I wouldn't have thought a divorced man could become a monk," said Agatha.

"You weren't married in the Catholic Church, so possibly it doesn't count."

"Maybe. Maybe he won't tell them. I'm going to start planning my life, figure out what I'm going to do in the weeks and months ahead."

"Oh, I wouldn't even bother. You're the sort of person that things happen to. Are you sure you are going to be all right?"

"Yes, I've come to terms with it all."

• • •

But during the following days, Agatha found herself going to the beautician twice and the hairdresser twice. She walked and cycled, she cleaned her cottage herself, although Doris Simpson had already cleaned it, and then went next door and cleaned and dusted James's cottage.

Every time she cycled, walked or drove back and came into Lilac Lane, her eyes always flew to James's house. She was so used to seeing it standing there, closed and silent, that a week had passed and she was driving back from the market at Moreton-in-Marsh when she saw the door to James's cottage standing open.

She cruised to a halt and got out of her car. Would he be wearing his robes? She rang the bell. James came to the door. He was wearing a coarse white cotton shirt and faded jeans.

"Agatha!" he said with genuine pleasure. "Come in. I was just about to call on you. Coffee?"

Agatha followed him in.

"Yes, please," said Agatha, sitting down on the sofa.

"Only instant," he called from the kitchen.

"Fine."

James came back with two mugs and settled down in an armchair opposite and stretched out his long legs. His eyes in his deeply tanned face looked bluer than ever.

"What are you going to do with all your stuff?" asked Agatha.

"I'm hiring a van and taking the lot over to my sister. She's got lots of space in her cellar. She says she'll hang on to it all until she is sure that I really want to enter the order."

"And you are really sure?"

"Oh, yes. We've a lot to organize. I'll phone my lawyer and we'll go along and start proceedings for a divorce. Then I think I'll see an agent and rent this cottage. That'll save me moving out all the furniture as well."

"Why Melissa?" asked Agatha suddenly. "Why someone like that?"

"She could be very warm and understanding. As I told you, I thought you were having an affair. I was thrown by the idea that I was dying, that something was eating into my brain. I then began to notice it was all an act. I began to notice that she was very cunning and manipulative. You know I'm like you. I have to ferret. Can't leave things alone. It was actually a doctor friend at Mircester Hospital—Melissa came with me on one visit—who tipped me off about her, and then I checked the psychiatrist's files. I can't tell the police about the doctor friend, because by rights, he shouldn't have told me. When Megan attacked, and I stumbled off, I don't think you can understand the deep shame I felt at betraying you, and with such a woman. I knew if I went to the police and charged Megan, then my affair with Melissa would be out in the open, and you would find I had lied to you. I remembered the monastery. It was a beacon, a sanctuary, leading me on. I would say I'm sorry for the way I have treated you, Agatha, but 'I'm sorry' seems so inadequate. The faults in the marriage were all mine. Old bachelors like me, set in their ways, should not marry at all."

"It's all right," said Agatha. "It's all over now. Do you want me to help you pack?"

"No, I'll be all right. What I would really like right now is to walk along to the Red Lion for a pint. Like to come?"

"Of course. I'll just unpack my groceries and I'll join you."

As Agatha sat opposite him in the Red Lion, she examined her feelings rather in the way that someone who has sustained a bad fall examines herself for broken bones. She found she was feeling only relaxed and content. James told her stories about the monastery and how, when he had finally visited the local hospital for an X-ray, it was to find the tumour had gone.

"I thought the police were checking hospitals everywhere," said Agatha.

"I think I was simply entered in the record books as Brother James."

"Oh, that explains it."

"I phoned the lawyer and he is free this afternoon," said James.

"May as well get it started."

The weeks James spent in Carsely passed like a dream of good company and sunny days for Agatha. They had meals together, they walked and talked. The new thatch on James's cottage was completed. He had asked the estate agent to consult Agatha before letting his cottage so that she could choose pleasant neighbours for herself.

Charles phoned several times, but Agatha told him to stay away until James had gone.

And then, just when it seemed as if this happy, dreamlike existence would go on forever, the day of James's departure was upon them.

He packed a few things into his car, which he had reclaimed from the police station. He gave Agatha a warm hug and climbed into the car. "Don't forget visiting days," he called.

He drove off along Lilac Lane, turned the corner, and was gone.

Agatha walked briskly back to her cottage. She felt happy and well. She picked up the phone and dialled.

"Charles. Is that you? Remember you promised me dinner at the Lygon?"

KEEP READING FOR AN EXCERPT
FROM M. C. BEATON'S NEXT
AGATHA RAISIN MYSTERY

AGATHA RAISIN AND THE
DAY THE FLOODS CAME

NOW AVAILABLE FROM
ST. MARTIN'S/MINOTAUR PAPERBACKS!

IT was one of those grey days where misty rain blurs the windscreen and the bare branches of the winter trees mournfully drip water into puddles on the road as if weeping for summer past.

Agatha Raisin turned on the switch to demist the windscreen of her car. She felt that inside her was a black hole to complement the dreariness of the day. She was heading for the travel agent in Evesham, one thought drumming in her head. Get away . . . get away . . . get away.

For miserable Agatha felt rejected by the world. She had lost her husband, not to another woman, but to God. James Lacey was training to take holy orders at a monastery in France. Sir Charles Fraith, always her friend and supporter when James went missing, had just got married, in Paris, and without even inviting Agatha to the wedding. She had learned about it by reading a small item in *Hello* magazine. And there had been a photograph of Charles with his new bride, a Frenchwoman called Anne-Marie Duchenne, small, petite, *young*. Grimly, middle-aged Agatha sped down Fish Hill in the direction of Evesham. She would escape from it all—winter, the Cotswolds where she lived in the village of Carsely, a broken heart and a feeling of rejection. Although, she reflected, hearts did not break. It was one's insides that got twisted up with pain.

• • •

Sue Quinn, the owner of Go Places, looked up as Agatha Raisin walked in and wondered what had happened to her usually brisk and confident customer. Agatha's hair was showing grey at the roots, her bearlike eyes were sad, and her mouth was turned down at the corners. Agatha sank down into a chair opposite Sue. "I want to get away," she said, looking vaguely round at the posters on the wall, the brightly coloured ranks of travel brochures, and then back at the world map behind Sue's head.

"Well, let's see." said Sue. "Somewhere sunny?"

"Maybe. I don't know. An island. Somewhere remote."

"You upset about something?" asked Sue. In her long experience, unhappy people often headed for islands, unhappy people or drunks. Islands drew them like a magnet.

"No," snapped Agatha. So deep was her misery, she did not want to confide in anyone and, in a sick way, she felt her misery still somehow tied her to James Lacey.

"All right," said Sue. "Let me see. You look as if you could do with a bit of sun. I know; what about Robinson Crusoe Island?"

"Where's that? I don't want one of those Club Med places."

"It's in the Juan Fernández Archipelago." Sue swung her chair and pointed to the map. "Just off the coast of Chile. It's where Alexander Selkirk was marooned."

"Who's he?"

"He was a Scottish seaman who was marooned there and Daniel Defoe learned about him and wrote *Robinson Crusoe* based on his adventures."

Agatha scowled in thought. She had read *Robinson Crusoe* in school. She couldn't remember much about it except it conjured up a vision of remoteness, of coral beaches and palm trees. She would walk along the beach and feel the sun on her head and get her life together.

She gave a weary shrug. "Sounds okay. Fix it up."

• • •

Three weeks later, Agatha stood in the hot sunshine at Tobalaba Airport in Santiago and stared at the small Lassa Airlines plane which was to carry her to Robinson Crusoe. There were only two other passengers: a thin, bearded man, and a young pretty girl. The pilot appeared and told them to climb on board. The girl sat in the co-pilot's seat and Agatha and the bearded man on one side of the plane. The other side was laden with a cargo of toilet rolls and bread rolls. Agatha's luggage, as per instructions, was limited to one travel bag. But the temperature in Santiago had been a hundred degrees Fahrenheit, so she had only packed underwear and light clothes. Her lunch was in a paper bag: one can of Coke, one sandwich and a packet of potato chips.

The plane took off. Agatha gazed down at the vast sprawl of Chile's capital city and then at the arid peaks of the Andes. Then, as they headed out over the Pacific, her eyelids began to droop and she fell asleep. She awoke an hour later. She knew it was no use trying to talk to her fellow passengers because she didn't speak Spanish and they didn't speak English. There was nothing to see but miles and miles of ocean. She shifted miserably in her seat and wished she had brought a book to read. The pilot had a newspaper spread over the controls. She hoped he knew where he was going.

And then, suddenly, after another two hours of flying over the seemingly endless ocean and just when Agatha was beginning to think they would never arrive, there was Robinson Crusoe Island. Boo! It seemed to rear up out of the sea in front of them, black and jagged, as if the Pacific had just thrown it up. The small plane chugged towards a cliff, closer and closer. What's happening? thought Agatha as the plane appeared to start heaving its way up the cliff face. He's not going to make it. But with a sudden roar the plane lifted up and over the cliff top and came to land on an airfield. No airport buildings, no control tower, just a flat cliff top of dusty red earth.

It turned out the pilot had some English. Agatha gathered

they were to walk down to a boat and the luggage and cargo would be taken down separately. She could feel goose-flesh rising on her arms. It was cool though sunny. Like a good Scottish summer's day in the Highlands. Agatha did not grasp she had moved into a subtropical zone. She only knew that she should have packed a sweater. The pretty girl who had been one of her fellow passengers indicated the road they were to take, and, with the bearded man, they walked across the airfield of dry red earth where locusts flittered in front of them like so many pieces of blown tissue paper.

The road curved down and down. The Jeep with the cargo and luggage roared past them. "Bastards," muttered Agatha, who was a strictly five-star-hotel traveller. "They might have given us a lift."

Just when her legs were beginning to ache with all the walking, she saw the sea below, a cove and a launch bobbing at anchor. Seals floated on their backs in the green-and-blue water. Hundreds of seals. There were already people waiting on the jetty, all young men carrying backpacks. Agatha, when she was miserable, liked to be fussed over and cosseted. When the luggage was stowed and they climbed on board and were given life jackets and told to sit on the hatches, Agatha suddenly wished she had stayed at home.

"You English?" asked a tall hiker type.

"Yes," said Agatha, grateful to be able to speak after such an enforced silence. "How long until we get there?"

"About an hour and a half. You could have gone by road, but it's pretty rough."

"Everything seems pretty rough," remarked Agatha. Above her, black mountains and sheer cliffs soared up to the blue sky. No beaches. Nothing but barren rock. A great setting for a horror movie or a movie about aliens. Amazing, thought Agatha, how, because of satellite television, one forgot that the world was really still a large place.

234

"I thought it would be tropical," she said.

"That's because Daniel Defoe set *Robinson Crusoe* in the Caribbean."

"Oh," said Agatha and relapsed into gloomy silence.

She brightened only when the launch cruised into Cumberland Bay and she saw a small township and trees and flowers. She turned to the hiker. "Where is my hotel? The Panglas?"

"Over there. That red roof."

"But how do I get there? It seems miles."

"Walk," he said, and he and his companions laughed heartily.

They disembarked at a quayside. The pretty little girl tugged Agatha's sleeve and led her towards a Jeep. "We get a lift," said Agatha with relief. But the relief was short-lived.

The Jeep set off up a mountainous dry river bed of a road, lurching and bumping, swinging round to hang off the edge of a cliff, and then plunging down a steep gradient and roaring up the other side almost at the perpendicular. I'll kill Sue when I get back, thought Agatha, and then realized with a little shock that from the airfield to this scary journey to the hotel, she had not thought of James once.

To Agatha's relief, the hotel was beautiful. There was a huge lounge with picture windows looking out over the bay. Her room was very small, but the bed was comfortable. Outside the lounge was a deck with easy chairs. She searched through her luggage and put on a T-shirt with a long-sleeved blouse over it.

She went out onto the deck and ordered a glass of wine from an attentive waiter. It was warm in the sun and the air was like champagne. An odd feeling of well-being began to permeate her body. What a strange place, she thought. She could almost feel the darkness lifting out of her.

Her spirits rose even further at dinner, when as a starter she was served with one of the biggest lobsters she had ever seen. She tackled it with gusto and then looked round at her dinner companions. The pretty girl was there, but not the bearded man. The central table was dominated by a large family, speaking in Spanish. They were made up of an obviously married couple, thin and athletic, with three children—beautiful little girls—a middle-aged woman, and a young man. To Agatha's right, a husband and wife sat eating lobster in silence. Some of Agatha's old misery crept back. She did not know any Spanish. She was marooned on Robinson Crusoe island and condemned to silence for the rest of her stay.

The middle-aged woman, who had been casting covert glances at her, suddenly rose and came over to Agatha's table. "I hear from the staff you are English," she said. She had a plump, motherly face and little twinkling eyes. "I am Marie Hernandez and I am here with my daughter and her husband and my son, Carlos. The hotel does not hold many guests. Perhaps we should all sit together?"

Agatha happily agreed. She joined the Hernandez family, as did the pretty girl, but the silent couple in the corner merely shook their heads and stayed where they were. All the Hernandez family, from Santiago, spoke English, apart from the small children, and they translated for the young girl, who said her name was Dolores. They all said, like Agatha, that they had expected a tropical island. Marie said she had a spare sweater in her luggage and would lend it to Agatha.

Marie told Agatha that the island was a national park. Her son, Carlos, proceeded to give Agatha a lecture on the history of Alexander Selkirk. He had been a seaman aboard the *Cinque Ports*, a privateer, and he had complained all the way around Cape Horn about the accommodation and the food on board. When the ship reached Juan Fernández to take on fresh water, he had demanded to be set ashore with a musket, powder, and a Bible. But when he saw the captain was actually going to go ahead with it, Selkirk said he'd changed his mind, but the captain had had enough of the grumbling seaman and so he was left. Most castaways would have shot themselves or starved, but Selkirk was saved by goats, introduced by the Spanish, which he hunted down, using their skins for clothes and their meat for food. He survived for four years, until 1709, when his saviour arrived: Commander Woodes Rogers of the privateers, *Duke* and *Duchess*, with famed privateer William Dampier. When Selkirk returned to London, he was a celebrity.

Agatha, not used to making friends easily, found at the end of the meal that she felt as if she had known this family for a long time. Dolores seemed to be picking up words of English with amazing rapidity.

When Agatha finally made her way to bed, she glanced curiously at the couple who had not joined them. The woman was blonde, dyed blonde, but very attractive in a baby-doll way, and the man, dark and Spanish-looking. They were sitting side by side on one of the sofas in the lounge. The woman was whispering to him urgently and he patted her hand.

Agatha felt there was something wrong there. Perhaps the journey had made her tired enough to give her odd fancies. She went to bed and plunged down into the first dreamless sleep she had experienced for a long time.

At breakfast the next day, Marie said they planned to walk up to Alexander Selkirk's lookout. She indicated the silent couple. "I'll ask them if they would like to go." She approached their table and plunged into rapid Spanish. But it appeared the couple did not want to go.

They all went down the cliff steps from the hotel after breakfast, where one of the staff relayed two lots of them in a rubber dinghy over to San Juan Bautista, the only settlement on the island. *"High Noon,"* said Dolores who, it transpired, had an English vocabulary confined mostly to film titles. She looked down the wide and dusty deserted main street and they all laughed as she drew and twirled an imaginary pistol. They began to climb, first up shallow steps leading up from the township, then onto an earthen track. The stream below them was surrounded by various varieties of wild flowers. Then they entered the silence of a pine forest. Agatha's legs began to ache, but she felt she could not give up while plump Marie soldiered on and even the little girls showed no signs of flagging. On and up they went until Agatha stopped and exclaimed at a flash of red. "What was that?"

"Hummingbirds," said Carlos. They waited and watched. Green-and-red hummingbirds whirred about. There was something about the beauty of them that caught at Agatha's throat and she suddenly sat down on a rock and began to cry. They gathered around her, hugging her and kissing her while Agatha poured out the whole story of her divorce. When she had finished, Marie said, "So you begin a new chapter, here on Robinson Crusoe Island. A great place for beginnings, no?"

Agatha gave her a watery smile. "Sorry about that, but I feel miles better."

"We'll have our packed lunches now," said Marie comfortably, "and take a rest. Before you arrived at breakfast, I was wondering about the couple that would not come with us. They are Concita and Pablo Ramon, also from Santiago. They are on honeymoon."

"Something odd there," said Agatha, unwrapping a sandwich. "They don't look like a honeymoon couple."

"No. She is very much in love with him, I think. But he looks at her as if he's waiting for something."

"Perhaps he feels he has made a mistake," volunteered Carlos.

They finished their lunch and though no mention was made of Agatha's outburst, she felt enfolded in a warm blanket of friendship and sympathy.

To get to the lookout involved a final climb up sheer rock. Agatha and Marie said they would wait below with the children while the more athletic ones made the ascent. "Are you Catholic?" asked Marie.

"No," said Agatha. "Not anything, really. I go to the village church—that's Church of England—because the vicar's wife is a friend of mine."

"And your husband? Was he Catholic?"

"Before? No."

"But I do not understand. How can he become a monk if he was divorced and not even Catholic?"

"He didn't tell them when he first went there."

"But they surely know now."

"Maybe because I am not a Catholic, they do not consider it to have been a real marriage. Let's talk about something else," said Agatha quickly.

Marie's attention was taken up then with the children. Agatha looked out at the vast stretch of the Pacific and was hit by a sudden thought. What if James had not really planned to take holy orders? What if he simply wanted to be rid of her and had found the monastery a convenient excuse? They had gone through an amicable divorce. They had talked about safe things—village gossip, James's plans to sell his house, but not once had he discussed his newfound faith.

Like the rest of the guests, Agatha had only booked into the Panglas for a week. The following few days took on a dreamlike quality of fresh air and exercise. They went to Robinson Crusoe's cave, they tramped the hills, returning at night, happy and exhausted. There was something about the remoteness and strange beauty of the island that seemed to heal the past and restore courage.

In the evenings, Agatha found her eyes drifting over to the honeymoon couple. On the last evening, the new bride was flushed and animated and talking in rapid Spanish. Her husband leaned back in his chair, listening, his face expressionless, but with that odd waiting feeling about him.

The farewells were affectionate and tearful. Agatha and Dolores were going on a later plane than the family. They exchanged addresses and promised to keep in touch. "Sad," said Dolores.

"Yes, sad," agreed Agatha, "but I'll be back."

Agatha broke her journey home with a few days in Rio at a luxury hotel. But she found she did not enjoy her visit. The heat was immense and the humidity high. She took a trip up Sugar Loaf Mountain and then decided to explore no further. Among the tourist brochures in the hotel was one advertising a tour to see where and how the poor of Rio lived. What kind of people, wondered Agatha, would go on such a tour—to gawp at the unfortunate? It was with a relief that she finally boarded a British Airways flight for London. She had booked economy. She was at the back of the plane. There was only one screen at the end of the cabin and so she could not see any of the movies, and during the night she shivered in the blast of freezing air-conditioning. She complained to a female attendant, who shrugged and said, "Okay," and walked on. Nothing happened. People struggled into sweaters, huddled into blankets, and no one but Agatha showed any desire to complain. Bloody British, thought Agatha, finally collaring a male steward. He glared at her and nodded. The plane finally warmed up.

In future years, Agatha thought, they will have models of this hell-plane in a museum and people will marvel that humans actually travelled in such circumstances, rather in the way that they wonder at the cramped accommodations in old sailing-ships.

At Gatwick, there was no gate available for the plane and so they waited an agonizing time before they were herded onto buses on the Tarmac. Agatha then began the long walk to collect her luggage. She began to feel that the plane had landed in Devon and they were all walking to Gatwick.

By the time she collected her luggage, she was in a blazing temper. But her temper dissipated as soon as she had located her car and had started to head home. She began to worry about her two cats, Hodge and Boswell. She had left them in the care of her cleaner, Doris Simpson, who came in every day to look after them. James was gone; Charles, too. Only her cats remained a permanence in her life.

It had been a night flight and she had been unable to sleep because of the freezing conditions. By the time she turned down the road in the Cotswolds which led to her home village of Carsely, her eyes were weary with fatigue. Her thatched cottage crouched in Lilac Lane under a winter sky. Agatha parked and let herself in. Her cats came to meet her, stretching and yawning and rubbing against her legs. She crouched down and patted them and then caught sight of herself in the long hall mirror that she had put up so that she could check her appearance before going out. She straightened up slowly and stared.

She noticed the grey roots in her hair, the dull skin and the lumpy figure and drew her breath in. How she had let herself go! And all over two useless men who weren't worth bothering about. She phoned her beauticians, Butterflies, in Evesham, to make an appointment for the following day. "Rosemary is having a Pilates class," said the receptionist, "so she can't do you in the morning. It'll need to be the afternoon."

"What on earth is Pilates?"

"It's a system of exercises for posture and breathing and it exercises every muscle in your body."

"I'm interested."

"She has a space in her workshop tomorrow morning. It's an introductory class."

"Put me down. When is it?"

"Starts at ten and goes on until one."

"That long! Oh well, put me down."

Agatha rang off. She fed the cats and let them out into the

garden and then carried her luggage up to the bedroom. Too weary
to unpack or undress, she fell on the bed and plunged down into
sleep.

In the morning, as she drove to Evesham, she began to regret
booking in for the Pilates class. Agatha was the type who booked
an expensive course at a gym, went twice, and then chickened out
and so lost her money. Still, she had to do something.

"Upstairs," said the receptionist. "They're about to start."

Agatha climbed up the stairs. Four women were struggling
into leggings and T-shirts.

"Agatha!" said Rosemary, the beautician. "Welcome back."

"Home again," said Agatha with a grin. Rosemary was a
very reassuring figure with her creamy skin and glossy hair. There
was something motherly about her that made women feel unas-
hamed of their lumpy figures and bad skin. Something reassuring
that seemed to say, "Everything can be made better."

The class began. After relaxation, the exercises seemed gentle enough but required fierce concentration. The exercises had to
be combined with breathing and strengthening the stomach and
pelvic muscles.

They finally took a break for coffee and biscuits. Rosemary
began to tell the small group that Joseph Pilates had been interned
in World War I and that was when he had developed the system
of exercises and after the war had gone to America, where he had
set up classes next to the New York Ballet School. She broke off
and took Agatha aside. "I know you must be dying for a cigarette.
You can nip downstairs and go through to the room at the very
back."

Agatha longed to be able to say she wouldn't bother, but the
craving for nicotine was strong. She stood in the back room feeling guilty, but nonetheless lighting up a cigarette. Sarah, Rosemary's assistant, was working on someone in the next room.

A girl's voice said, "I didn't want to do this. But Zak wants me to get a bikini wax before I'm married." This was followed by a giggle.

"Don't marry him!" Agatha wanted to scream. She had a feeling of feminist rebellion. It was all very well to keep oneself as fit and beautiful as possible, but all this total removal of hair, so that one looked like a Barbie doll, Agatha felt was going too far. And what sort of fellow ordered his girl-friend to have a bikini wax? "Thanks, Sarah," she heard the girl say. "I'd better go. Zak'll be waiting for me. He wants to make sure I've got it done."

Agatha heard her leave. She had a sudden urge to see this Zak. She stubbed out her cigarette and went through to reception.

A young man was standing there, hugging a pretty blond girl. "You ready, Kylie?" he said. With his dark good looks and the girl's blond prettiness, Agatha was reminded of the couple on Robinson Crusoe Island. She was snuggling up to him, but he had the same waiting feel about him as the man on the island.

She shrugged and went upstairs just as the class was resuming. When it was over, Agatha cheerfully signed on for ten lessons. She felt relaxed and comfortable and the exercises appealed to her common sense. Time to fight against old age. Strengthen the kneecaps and avoid kneecap replacements; strengthen the pelvic muscles and avoid the indignity of incontinence. She told Rosemary she would go for lunch and come back to get her face done. She took out her mobile phone and called the hairdresser and booked herself in for a late appointment to get her hair tinted.

By the end of the day, when she returned home with her hair once more glossy and brown and her face massaged and treated, she began to feel like her old self, her old pre-James self. The "For Sale" sign had gone from outside his cottage. She wondered what the new neighbour would be like.

The next morning, Mrs. Bloxby, the vicar's wife, called. "You look great, Mrs. Raisin," she said. "The holiday must have done you good."

Agatha began to tell her about the family on Robinson Cru-soe Island and how much she had enjoyed their company. As she talked, she realized that she had not once bragged to them about her skill as a detective.

"Have you heard from James?" asked Mrs. Bloxby.

"James who?" asked Agatha curtly.

Mrs. Bloxby looked at Agatha curiously. Agatha, before she had left, had refused to talk any more about James.

But Agatha suddenly remembered Marie saying that James could not surely take holy orders as he had been married. The thought that James might just have said that to get off the hook was something she did not even want to contemplate.

"So what's been happening?" asked Agatha lightly. "No crime?"

"No murders for you," said the vicar's wife. "Very quiet."

"Who's bought the cottage next door?"

"We don't know. There's a newcomer to our ladies' society, a Mrs. Anstruther-Jones. She's just moved into the village. She wanted the cottage but someone else got it first, so she bought Pear Tree Cottage . . . you know the one, behind the village stores."

"What's she like?"

"You can judge for yourself. There's a meeting tonight."

"Meaning you don't like her."

"Now, I never said that."

"If you don't have a good word to say for anyone, you don't say anything. How's Miss Simms?"

Miss Simms was secretary of the ladies' society, an unmar-ried mother.

"Miss Simms has a new gentleman friend. He's in sofas."

"Married, I suppose."

"I think so. Listen to that. The rain is on again. It's been raining since you left."

The doorbell rang. "I'm off," said Mrs. Bloxby.

Agatha opened the door and found Detective Sergeant Bill Wong on the doorstep. "Hullo," said Mrs. Bloxby. "See you tonight, Mrs. Raisin."

"I thought you women would be on first-name terms by now," said Bill, following Agatha through to the kitchen.

"It's tradition in the ladies' society that we use second names, and in this over-familiar touchy-feely world, I rather like it," said Agatha. "Coffee?"

"Yes. I see you haven't given up smoking."

"Did I even say I would try?" demanded Agatha with all the truculence of the heavily addicted.

"Thought you might."

"Never mind that. Here's your coffee. How's crime?"

"Nothing dramatic. Nothing but the usual cut-backs. Village police stations are closing down all round. Did you know they had closed Carsely police station?"

"Never!"

"Yes, and the one at Chipping Campden and the one in Blockley. So we spend most of our time on the road. Someone called nine-nine-nine last night and howled it was an emergency. Got there and found it was her cat stuck up a tree."

"And how's your love life?"

"On hold."

Agatha looked at him sympathetically. Bill had a Chinese father and an English mother, the combination of which had given him attractive almond-shaped eyes in a round face and a pleasant Gloucestershire accent. "How's yours?" asked Bill.

"Non-existent."

Agatha saw Bill was about to ask about James, so she began to describe her odd feeling about the couple on Robinson Crusoe Island.

"It sounds to me as if you were bored and looking for a bit of action, Agatha."

"On the contrary, I wasn't bored at all. I met some super

people. Still . . . there was something odd there. And I saw a couple in Evesham yesterday who reminded me of them."

"You'd better find some work quickly or you'll be seeing crime everywhere. Thinking of doing any public relations work?"

"I might." Agatha had once run a highly successful public relations company but had sold up to take early retirement and move to the country. Since then, she had often taken on freelance work. "Public relations is a different world now," she said. "It used to be you were neither fish nor fowl. Despised by the journalists and the advertising people as if you weren't doing a real job. Now the public relations people are often celebrities themselves."

"I hear Charles is married."

"So what?"

"Oh, well," said Bill hurriedly. "I'd better get on. Let me know if you stumble across any dead bodies. I could do with a change."

After he had left, Agatha switched on her computer to see if she had any e-mail. There was one from Roy Silver, a young man who used to work for her, asking where she was; and one from Dolores, the pretty young Chilean girl. To Agatha's dismay, it was all in Spanish, but she noticed the names Concita and Pablo Ramon. She printed it off and then drove to the Falconry Restaurant in Evesham, where the owner, Juan, was Spanish, and asked him for a translation.

"She says," said Juan, " 'Dear Agatha, Such excitement. Do you remember the couple, Pablo and Concita Ramon? Well, Pablo has just been arrested. It is in all the newspapers. Concita was drowned on Robinson Crusoe Island and Pablo said she fell out of the boat. But a hiker up on the hills saw him push her. He knew she could not swim. He had her heavily insured and her family are very wealthy. How are you? Let me know. Love, Dolores.' "

So that's why he seemed to be waiting, thought Agatha. He was just waiting for the right opportunity. She wished now she had said something, let him know she was on to him. But she hadn't really noticed anything significant at all.

Agatha sat at the ladies' society meeting that night as Miss Simms, the secretary, in her usual unsuitable dress of tiny skirt, bare midriff, pierced navel and stiletto heels went through the minutes of the last meeting. The teacups clattered, plates of cake were passed round, and outside the rain drummed down on the vicarage garden. Mrs. Anstruther-Jones turned out to be one of those well-upholstered pushy women with a loud braying voice. Agatha detested her on sight. She could feel some of her old misery creeping back again and tried the breathing exercises she had been taught and, to her amazement, felt herself beginning to relax. She would phone Roy and see if he had any work for her. James was gone and Charles was gone and Agatha Raisin was grimly determined to move on.